WRITERS FOR TOMORROW

SECOND SERIES

a collection of fiction by writers of

tomorrow for readers of today =

Edited by Baxter Hathaway and John A. Sessions

CORNELL UNIVERSITY PRESS

ITHACA, NEW YORK

Foreword

AS TIMES change, so do people. There was a time, not long ago, when it would have been natural to assume that a book of short stories coming from a university environment would be grossly immature, imitative, too uncertain in its probings to have any validity for a wise though turbulent world that had its being, miraculously, everywhere outside the confines of the university. The presupposition was, during that time of not so long ago, that a writer might do important work almost immediately after he departed from the ivied halls, or that he could be expected to mature early if he decided never to darken the doors of a college. One needed experience as a longshoreman, as a bank clerk, or as a dishwasher before he could be expected to make sound inquiry into the motivations of human action. And of course one would have to spend some time learning his craft before he became an accomplished writer.

The assumption that underlies this book and many books like it is that times have changed. During the nineteenth century and the early years of our own century, it was probably true that the writer in a college milieu was grossly immature, imitative, and uncertain. The kind of education he endured, even if he did not positively seek it, encouraged him, forced him, to be immature, imitative, and uncertain. The vestiges of the classical tradition surely discouraged writer and thinker from reacting primarily to the life around him, but even more important probably in the repression was German literary scientism which could subject a work of art to cold analysis only when it was thoroughly dead. Mentors assumed that out of the maelstrom of the vast unreason which was the contemporary world would come more works of art, to be fingered over in turn at an appropriate time and distance. But the function of a university was to impart knowledge and create a gentleman, not to descend into the arena of purposeful action and responsibility for a now existing world.

The changes that time has wrought do not apply to the campus only. Shifts have taken place because of partial failures and lapses in our culture at large. In his introduction to the O. Henry Awards volume of short stories of 1948, Mr. Herschel Brickell noted the extent to which the interesting new writing of the country is coming from college communities, either from writers who are still technically students by virtue of paying tuition fees, or from writers who are technically professors by virtue of being paid for their activities. In either case, the distinction is that these good writers are to be found in or around college campuses, notably concentrated there, rather than scattered throughout the country, isolated in separate communities, or collected in bohemian metropolitan centers. The implications in this shift are, of course, significant. It may well represent the turning of the artist toward his own kind because he repudiates his community or is repudiated by it, and the shift would then be a bad one, particularly if the colleges were to remain unconcerned with the pestering problems that face our society as a whole, here and now. But it must be remembered that the shift also brings the artist in closer contact with breadth of knowledge and intellectual responsibility, and this would have bad results only if responsibility came to exist in college communities alone, while the rest of our society embarked upon a Walpurgis Night of commercial banality and mass exploitation of the sensibilities of the lowest common denominator at the expense of the penetrating insight which gives human life its peculiar validity. It should be noted in passing that the shift to the campus affects the composer of music and the painter as well as the writer, and it may be said of the arts in general that the college campus is becoming their citadel, either by providing favorable conditions in which the established artist can perform or by altering emphasis in learning so that the young artist is encouraged to do his developing there.

The college writer of the past was a dabbler. His excursions into literary creation were haphazard and random, brief forays into unknown country, quick trips into the hinterland of the art of his time, and his discoveries were the tourist's experiences rather than the native's insights. He took a fifteen weeks' course in behaving like the monkeys in the bohemian zoos, and no one should be surprised that he did not become a monkey, that his production was immature, imitative, and uncertain. And the art products of the college professors of the period show exactly the same attributes as the products of those who were technically students in their universities. The time and their predispositions determined the results, not the writer's age or his habitat.

This is all argument, patently—an attempt to break down a stereotype that came into being, not without justification, in the past, but that now gets in the way of sound critical judgment at a time when the vast multiplication of the printed word confuses and corrupts critical insights. The writer who finds himself in a university setting today is first of all encouraged to be more than a dabbler. He is invited to come to terms with himself, his art, and his society over some considerable period of time. He is no longer a mere beginner who on the basis of one or two slight attempts at expressing himself gives evidence of a talent that he may choose to develop at some future date. The writer in a college environment today may have no more native talent than his predecessor of fifty years ago, but now he is in the thick of the process of developing and exploring his talent, and he is doing it under conditions that remove some of the worst elements of the devastating trial and error method. At Cornell University, as at Iowa, Stanford, Michigan, Columbia, and many other colleges and universities, can be found a flourishing group of young writers who bear little resemblance to the college writers of fifty years ago. They know what they are doing to a greater degree than did their predecessors. They are more conscious of the relationships between art and society. And in comparison with the young writers of the not too distant past (the writers who were writers and not mere college dabblers) they have greater familiarity with literary history and tradition. Here are writers with interlocking virtues and defects of their own, and to judge by the frequency of comments like that of Mr. Herschel Brickell mentioned above, they may be doing much of the best writing of our time. At their best, at any rate. Even the less striking, more mediocre product has an honesty and sophistication (in the best sense) that makes it worthy of attention. In the main these stories, selected from stories written in connection with the Cornell Writers' Workshop, exhibit the earmarks of the work being done in general these days in university environments. This selection does, it is true, omit the work of the more seasoned of the university practitioners, the already well-established, but the earmarks are otherwise much the same.

What the writer learns especially in the process of developing his talents and mastering his art is the necessity of increasing selectivity of materials. Among other things, a work of fiction is an act of definition, and this definition is usually achieved through the story's structure—what the follower of Aristotle has always called the "action." The reader of fiction presumably always asks, "What am I looking at here?" "What is going on here?" With the author's help he soon discovers what traits of behavior are being subjected to scrutiny, and he forms his first significant hypothesis about the story when he discovers "why" these traits are being scrutinized. Of course, if the story follows a pat formula, like the love story in the popular magazine, the "why" of the story—its act of definition—is implicit in the formula and the whole logic is pretty much evident to the reader as soon as he discovers the nature of the story he is reading—so evident in fact as to be absorbed almost unconsciously, and the primary function of the story is to reassure the reader, with variations, that his traditional value structures have not changed overnight.

After the reader has determined what object is being held up for his scrutiny and why, the writer is in a position to arrange his action and make the pertinent differentiations, expressed in terms of the potentialities that the varying forces in the story represent. The real task that faces the writer of short fiction is to invent and deploy forces that will make possible sharp insight and accurate and significant definition.

There has been much talk in the last twenty-five years of the need for concretion—for particularity—in literature. We wish to propose that the important kind of particularity in a work of fiction is the particularity of its question. Here is where go astray the "mucker-posers" who try to reduce actions like those of *Macbeth* or *Hamlet* to mere murder stories comparable to what one finds in the comic strips. The question in *Macbeth*, whatever it is (and in a writer's terms it is sharply defined), is something infinitely more particularized than "Does crime pay?" or "Will he get away with all this?" And the writer's task is to handle his situation so that the reader does not end up with only the vague and insufficiently examined question. And it is in this sense that the writer's answer to his questions cannot reasonably be found in any simple moral maxim that can be applied like a rubber stamp indiscriminately to each and every practical moral problem, for its universality is one of depth and not of breadth like that of the scientist or generalizer. A story can be significant in ways that a case history cannot be, for it must present its own kind of question and must not be subservient to a question that is external to it, which the action exemplifies only and does not define. And the best way to make discriminations among kinds of fiction is not to look at style, however important that is in itself, or at exactness of characterization, but to inquire into the importance and the particularity of the question that the story poses and solves. The question cannot be properly defined unless the writer uses his action to present the differentiations that make the question precise. The ironies that are now fashionable are efficient devices for achieving this precision. The task of the writer of fiction is like that of the debater to the extent that both must find the issues, define them, and order them. But there the similarity stops, since the ordering done by the writer of fiction is of a different kind from that of the persuader and the issues he defines are quite different.

The young writer who is only beginning to establish the

foundations of his own value structures is, left to himself, likely to be less definitive than an older writer, for he has to define his general attitudes before he can refine them. But a university writers' workshop is useful to him in this respect, for it provides the environment that forces the more exact definitions, over a considerable period of time. And in these circumstances, even while he gains increased control over his narrative questions, he can retain the freshness of his own experiences and the plasticity of his own reactions in a world where most people have become, in comparison, unable to break away from the old questions that have become stale or have lost their pertinence.

This selection should provide an adequate cross section of what young writers are doing these days. One of the notable features that may either please or disturb some readers is the increased interest in abstractionism—in the kind of story that is not a realistic replica of some facet of geography or history, but is a mirror of an action that takes place in the land of the mind. But social realism, though it less imperiously intrudes upon the consciousness of the young writer, is still practiced. We have, in selecting stories, deliberately tried to include examples of several kinds and have not tried to determine *a priori* any conditions that all stories must meet.

J. A. S. AND B. H.

Contents

CONTENTS

ACKNOWLEDGMENTS

Acknowledgment for permission to reprint copyrighted works is hereby made to the following periodicals for stories in this book that have previously appeared in print:

Commentary for Edgar Rosenberg's "The Happy One."

Epoch for Bernard Harper Friedman's "As I Am, You Will Be," Stanley Sultan's "And Jacob Called," Faye Riter's "A Sense of Destination," and H. D. Rossiter's "Black Bile."

The Cornell Review for Monika Basch's "Second Act," Lin Gatty's "Did He Touch You?" David Kaula's "The Huntress," and H. D. Rossiter's "Allan Franklin" and "How Dear to My Heart."

The Cornell Widow for Finley Hunt, Jr.'s "An Egg from the Sky."

How Dear to My Heart

H. D. ROSSITER

WE COULD see the river from where I lived. On summer mornings the sun would rise over it, crossing the narrow slit between the tall white-bricked buildings of the hospital, throwing long shadows over the tenements. In the evenings it would set in the west, dipping behind the warehouse, a great red circle of fire.

We lived on the ground floor in a house a few blocks from the river—a red brick house with small courtyards on both sides of the stoop, concrete squares trimmed with iron spikes. There was a hall door that squeaked. Mrs. Marek, the janitress, clutching her blue kimono would yell from the window in Czech and we would answer in Italian. Not that we understood the Italian but it made her mad. And it was fun to see her pock-marked face turn purple and red. Sometimes she even called the cops. That was the best fun of all. We would hide like fugitives in the coal barges by the docks or spend the whole day in Central Park. It was exciting—the danger, the forever hunted. Running through the streets, our lungs hurting. We knew people were watching, wondering what great evil we were fleeing from, and so we ran harder and faster. And in the evenings, sneaking around street corners, going home the long way to make the danger last, we would finally split up, swearing never to squeal though offered the cruelest tortures. And each to his home, with beating heart, to await the morrow. The hunt, the chase; another hunt, another chase.

But in winter it was different. There was school all week and clean clothes and church and no fun on Sundays. After school we played ringolerio or nations or skated in the streets. But supper was always near, and we could not go far. And after supper, homework and then bed. There were too many people for real fun and too little time.

On Saturdays we worked. Coal was too expensive to buy, and all winter, every Saturday, getting coal was our job. While Mom went out to work, my brother and I would go to the river and pick up coal. "That's your job," she would say in her resigned voice. Her voice was always resigned, as long as I can remember.

And one Saturday in particular, I remember—the mid-winter morning we found the lamp. Memory writes of the past in shorthand; it writes of single events and puts them in its wallet which is not large, and in the jarring of onrushing time the unimportant spills away into forgetfulness. And the heavy essential remains to haunt us. But let me tell you about this day.

Mom woke us at seven. She made sure we were up and dressed. We had often gone back to sleep after she left for work, but this day we were up. She left our breakfast on the stove, and we ate it sleepily. By eight we were on the street with our wagon of two-by-fours, apple cases, and baby carriage wheels, rolling down the hill toward the river.

Rob, sitting up front with his feet on the front axle, steered. He held the clothes line high and firm, straight in front of him like the hackmen on Fifth Avenue behind their shiny black cabs and tasseled horses. I had to push because I was younger. Rob was nearly twelve and I was ten.

"Faster, faster," he snapped at me. And time and again I stuck one foot to the gray blur passing beneath me and gave a great push. The wind was cold and whipped our hair. Rushing toward the river.

When we came to the hospital though, we had to slow down. For the pavement was no longer smooth. Rectangular red stones receded in zigzagging patterns in all directions. I liked to count the number of patterns. There were hundreds, I think.

The nurses in starched white uniforms and blue caps watched us. We vibrated down the street, slowly, toward the river. Sometimes we let our lower jaws dangle loosely, the teeth tingling nicely against each other like the drills of a thousand playful dentists.

[2]

But the ride lasted only a short time. The wind turned damp and we could smell the coal dust and breathe the oily flat vapors of the steam engines as the wind carried them toward us. At the bottom of the hill I again stuck my foot to the ground. This time I let it drag and we soon came to a stop.

Robby pulled the wagon the rest of the way, across the driveway, crunching the frosting of gray dust and fine black coal. We knew the fun was over and the tiresome work would begin.

Some boys were there already, crawling over the coal heaps of a waiting barge. They would work in pairs. One threw the coal from the boat, the other picked it up on the shore. The boat job was the hardest because the loaded barges were deep in the water, and at low tide, six feet below the top timbers of the dock.

You could jump down easily, but getting up again was more difficult. Sometimes the current moved the barge two or three feet from the dock. And then you were stuck. The year before, a boy saw a barge captain coming and tried to jump it. He fell and was crushed between the boat and the stone wall of the dock.

It was all right. We got nearly a half a bushel before we were chased. To a bargeman anyone who steals coal is illegitimate. But we enjoyed his curses more than he imagined and we ran away laughing. We stuck our tongues out at him.

"You'd think he owned the coal," Rob said. And then he cursed in Italian, enunciating the words very slowly, and twisted his clenched fist from the elbow—the powerful rhetoric of the streets. We both laughed.

Some of the boys had lit a fire in an old rusty oil barrel. It looked warm, so we made for it.

We always had a break like this. We stood by the fire, saying little, just looking at the fire. The flames puffed in and out of the holes gashed in the rolled steel. Little darts and spits of orange flame, lighting a second or two.

Some of them smoked cigarettes and they preached to us half seriously against the habit. They had pride in their debauchery, their personal evil.

"Don't ever get the habit, kid," one of them said. "You'll be sorry. Why, look at me! My lungs shot to hell. Coffin nails!" As he went into a mock fit of coughing, someone went up to support him. And then everyone laughed.

A barge was not the only place to get coal. Sometimes the coal derricks would miss the funnel openings of the black bins, dripping tons of coal over the iron roofs, and to the ground. If we could get there while the shovelers weren't watching, we could get all the coal we wanted.

"There's no one at Stokers," someone cried. "Look! There's no one there!"

We turned—looked—ran. Twenty of us ran toward the bin, dragging wagons, our breath quick and chilled white in the air.

Rob and I got another half bushel before we were chased by a great black-eyed Negro who came running at us with his shovel.

We went back to the fire. Ashes had choked the air holes and the fire was dying. Trucks were backing under the bins and scores of men, some with shovels, some with bills of white tissue paper, milled around the yards. There were too many people. We knew when the odds were against us.

"Let's go home," said Robby after awhile. "No use now. We can't get any more."

I nodded.

We did not go up the street by the hospital: the guard would chase us, and besides it was too steep to pull the wagon easily. Instead we took the street past Cushman's bakery, the garages, and the power plant. We stopped many times on the way. We were tired.

The bakery was a nice place, and we looked in as we passed. A white-enameled machine squeezed three lumps of sticky white dough on a moving belt. The ceiling and floor and walls were incrusted with greasy flour dust. Men in white aprons and rolled-up sleeves twisted long rolls of dough into neat little patterns. A man with a brush painted grease on enormous black pans. And from everything, above everything, the smell—the smell of freshly baked bread and crispy rolls, sugar-coated buns, and cake. It was all in the air. It was wonderful just to stand in the doorway and breathe.

We were passing the warehouse with its long rows of ash cans and steel-shod rolling doors when I noticed something on the top of one of the cans. It was black and shaped like a tiny vase.

"Look what I found," I cried to Robby. "A lamp, an old oil lamp."

"And what good is that?" he said. "It's all dirty. Come on, let's go home."

I put the lamp on the top of the bag of coal and looked at it as I pushed the wagon. It might be brass. I can shine it up and sell it, I thought. Joe might give me something for it.

At home we emptied the coal in the box beside the coal stove, and Rob put the wagon in the cellar. I got out a cloth and some cleaning fluid my mother used. And then I started polishing. Sitting by the kitchen table, I worked on the lamp for over an hour. Robby was in the front room reading a funny book.

I used a knife to clean out the depressions, black with ashes and grit. It really was brass. I scraped and shined and polished, rubbing as hard as I could. When the work was finished, I was warm and triumphant.

I called Robby.

"How's that!" I said in a hushed voice. "Have you ever seen anything like that?"

It stood in the dim light—a short, shining lamp of brassy gold, a beautiful hope—against the checkered oilcloth table.

"It's all right. Now what'ya going to do with it?"

"Wish! We're going to light the lamp and wish. And everything we wish will come true—everything." I was excited and pleading.

"How do you know?" Rob was always the sceptic.

"Aw, you remember. Aladdin's lamp. We'll play Aladdin's lamp—like the story in the book."

"Has it got oil?"

The lamp was empty. I had forgotten about that. And it seemed important that there be a light.

"No," I said, "but maybe we can find something."

We did. I filled the lamp from a bottle of furniture polish. Some of the orange liquid spilled on the floor. We waited a minute for the dry wick to draw the oil, and then we lit it. A smokey black flame reached up—long, triangular, and smooth. I pulled down the shade and closed the door to the bedroom. Now we were ready. My heart beat strangely. The muscles of my neck were tight and I swallowed as I looked at the lamp. The beauty of it—the darkness, the flame of a golden lamp in the darkness. Aladdin's wish, and all mine.

But Rob sensed it too. I could see the flame was for him too. He was looking straight at the lamp. His cheeks were in his hands.

"What should we wish?" I spoke jerkily but could not help it. "You start."

"Well," he said, taking a big breath, and narrowing his eyes, "I wish for a baseball and a pitcher's glove and a good hockey stick and a car and . . . and . . . and all the money in the world."

"Now, rub the lamp."

Rob stroked the lamp with his right hand, holding it with his left so it could not tip.

We waited.

"Aw. Nothing happened," Rob said after a few minutes. "It's no good."

"It doesn't have to happen right away. This afternoon or tonight maybe."

"Well, maybe," he said a little doubtfully. "Now, you try."

I held the warm lamp in my two hands and spoke slowly.

"I would like to know everything in the world . . . and . . . see all the countries . . . and . . . know all the people . . . and . . . read all the books."

I rubbed the lamp and shut my eyes. Oh, how I wished. . . .

. . . A bearded man on a throne of books. Pilgrims from afar. From the East, wise men in golden robes with gifts—incense, myrrh, the costliest ivory of Africa, the greenest jade of China, pearls from Persia. Alabaster. Knowledge. Power. Any question, any answer. . . .

When I opened my eyes the lamp was flickering. A sign, I thought. It will come true. The lamp will make it come true. It will.

A key turned in the lock. I looked around for an escape, but it was too late. I looked at my mother and she seemed far away. There was a black mist between us, and suddenly I knew why. The room was black with the smoke of the lamp. It poured out of the doorway, billowing black clouds against the dim hall light.

My mother's resignation was broken.

"What are you doing?" Her voice was high with fright, almost a scream of fear. "Do you want to put the house on fire! Robby, *you*, I thought you had more sense! *An oil lamp!*" The flame had gone out leaving a dull red glow and a charred wick. *"An oil lamp!"*

She hit us until we cried. I crouched against the runged back of a chair, my eyes closed, one hand behind my head.

"We were only playing, Mom," I said between tears. "Only playing."

"Playing with a lamp, will you?" The tightness of her lips was in her voice. "I'll teach you—teach you—teach you!" My hand was no use.

And she hit us some more.

When we stopped crying she told us to get rid of the lamp. She never wanted to see it again. And if we ever tried anything like that again, she would teach us.

I took the lamp and went out. I stood awhile on the stoop looking at the lamp. The wick had stopped glowing and the orange oil was seeping out, covering the shining sides with a sticky film. Smudges—my fingerprints—were all over the lamp. It was dirty and cheap in the winter sun, yellowish-cheap in the light of day. Brass that I could sell. And that was all.

I ran across the street to the junk shop. Joe said nothing to me, and I said nothing to him. He threw the lamp in the corner on top of a pile of scrap brass.

He gave me fifteen cents for it.

A Sense of Destination

FAYE RITER

GRANDMA Westerman surrendered to circumstances after she broke her leg in a fall on the short flight of steps leading down to the kitchen. She began the descent with the righteous irritation of one prepared to reprimand the housekeeper for filching secretly from pantry stores. And, one foot catching in the hem of her long black skirt, she had fallen with all the gracelessness of her age. A leg had twisted beneath her so that brittle bones cracked and splintered.

And she lay there almost the whole morning, for the housekeeper, having heard her approach, had snatched bonnet and shawl and hurried out of the basement door to do the morning marketing. Then she had met an intimate friend, quite by chance, of course, in the fresh, meaty atmosphere of the butcher shop and had been invited to step over to the coffee shop, where the remainder of the morning had vanished.

The housekeeper had screamed at finding her mistress lying as in death upon the floor. "Lord, help me," she babbled, trying to decide whether it was best to inform first the doctor so that he could attend the old lady, or to call the eldest son, who could at once take over the responsibility of the injured woman.

"There," she soothed distractedly, standing over the quiet figure.

At that moment Grandma Westerman opened accusing eyes. "Robber," she pronounced with finality, and closed them again.

"It is good, maybe, that you fell," the doctor told her later, scratching his neck reflectively. "For once you are pinned down, and one can look at you and see that you need attention for other things."

She snorted indignantly at that.

"You were dizzy, perhaps, when you fell?" he suggested.

"What an idea! I was in absolute health."

"Just like my mother," he commented, writing out prescriptions, "never ready to admit an ailment. Why do you have such pride?"

It was at this period, more shamed by the disease of her body than by the breaking of bones, that Grandma Westerman announced to her son, Albert, the eldest although the last of them to marry, that he might now move into the family home.

"It will come to you, anyhow," she said heavily from the brass bed. "I will not be in your way."

"We shall come to look after it," he agreed at once, stiffening his shoulders, "and you, too," he added in haste. "It will not do for you to be here alone now."

Afterward she declared that if nothing else good came from the disaster, at least she had got rid of a corrupt housekeeper and gained the devoted Clara.

Meanwhile, Albert and Leonie and the three children moved in, and Clara, whose duties were restricted to the dim bedroom and pocket-handkerchief of a sitting room and to the care of the grandmother, faithfully reported the changes that the household was seeing. Since she herself was elderly, and at once in sympathy with Grandma Westerman, Clara regarded the alterations with certain suspicions and even with jealousy.

"You will not know the ground floor when next you see it. They are throwing paint upon the walls with abandon—unpractical, foolish colors that will show every touch. And the fine heavy draperies have been taken down and packed away. There will be only glass curtains of silk, and the sun will shine in to fade the flowers on the carpet. It is too much to expect that they will close the shutters on the sunny side."

In the beginning Grandma Westerman did not feel much interest in the mysterious proceedings below. The shock of exchanging a vigorous life for a bedridden one was all she could handle for a time.

"The young do not have the solid, conservative ideas that I was brought up on," she told Clara gloomily. "Let them do what they will."

After a time, when she had reconciled herself to pain and to lying abed, she hunted ponderously in her mind for means of passing the hours when her hands were tired with the weight of the lace she was knitting, or her fingers stiffened after working with an embroidery needle and thimble on the cut-work of a bureau scarf. She would sigh and call out to Clara, "Did they leave the painting of fruit over the sideboard?"

"That was carried off long ago," Clara would respond with relish. "And in the bay that looks out on the garden She has green things growing. Likely they will die soon."

"I suppose my good tablecloths are used for everyday," the old lady would go on. "Finally they will fall to pieces in the wash-water."

"No-o-o-o," Clara would shake her head. "Mats She uses for everyday. With children, too. They are more practical, She says. But it keeps her girl polishing."

"I came here the same way," Grandma Westerman said abruptly one day. "I made my changes, too, though not with such speed. It is not easy to go into the household of another without seeing what might be done."

"You have good understanding," Clara approved. "They have taken out the hall trees, and your heavy carved table. They had things of their own, too, She said."

By the time they were finished with the renovation, Grandma Westerman thought, by the time the painters and carpenters were gone and every pin was in place, then they would come to sit with her longer. As it was, Leonie must answer every summons of the workmen and of Christine, the hired girl, to whom the big house was confusing. The children were at school, and Albert was gone all day. Save for the clumsy movements of the workmen, the house was quiet; it was not quite as she had visualized, living with three careless children.

Leonie, thin, sallow, sharp-eyed, her face softened only by abundant, wavy hair, came in every day, naturally. She would sit down a moment, but her eyes would wander restlessly away from the bed as though contemplating brisk activity. "Do you not want these blinds opened? I myself would become spiritless in so dark a room." She might arise to straighten the bureau top that was disorderly with medicine bottles, fancy work and newspapers. "At the pharmacist's I saw Belle Speas; she asked for you and sent word her mother would come soon. She is suffering from kidney stones—old Mrs. Bartel." And then, with a sigh, "I must hurry down and make the noodle; that Christine cannot make one fit for a pig, and Albert insists on the kind you taught me when first we were married."

In the evening, Albert would come in for a short while, expansive after a heavy supper despite his thin, slightly-stooped figure, smelling of cigar smoke and faintly of the cologne applied that morning after shaving.

"Well, Mama," he would say without expecting an answer, "have you had a good day? Business is something to make your eyes pop, believe me. It was not like this in Papa's day. All the forms and permits to be got!" He would shake his head and cluck his tongue, sitting down then to talk about the business for a time. "You will fall asleep if I speak longer of business, eh, Mama?" He would chuckle paternally at his own jokes.

Once she heard him reminding the children that they were to stop in every day to speak to their grandmother. "Every day, mind you," he repeated.

"I do, Papa!" Elizabeth, the oldest, cried indignantly, so that her father hushed her. "I do nearly every day, anyhow. Maria is the one who sneaks out of it, and I am quite sure Theodore doesn't go in more than once a week."

Curiously the old lady listened to the objecting young voices, and that of her son, leading them, then, like the concertmaster setting the pace and the tone, so that the three fell into the murmur habitual upon this floor of the house when one of the parents was near.

When spring bloomed into summer and she found herself promoted to a yellow wheel chair shiny with varnish, she asked Clara to push her into the carpeted hall, and it seemed that she entered another house upon leaving her own room. It was not merely the new brightness of the walls, nor the glimpse of the lower hall with its table and heavy mirror in place of the hall trees; it was that she had been gone from most of the house so long that it was unfamiliar and no longer hers. She was a stranger, looking at the home of another.

Surprisingly it was less painful than Grandma Westerman had anticipated; she was ready to admit that the house belonged now to Leonie, whom she did not know intimately and never would, and to Albert, who lacked the vigor of his parents. And it belonged, too, to the children. A tennis racket rested carelessly in a corner, and in the upper hall a doll carriage, its hood primly up to shield the occupant, stood against the wall as though possessing perfect right to its position.

With Clara she schemed clumsily to get the children, one at a time, into her room. It was like snaring animals that were neither timid nor sly; they were all absorbed in inconsequential activities more important to them than the turning of the earth.

Elizabeth, the eldest, was first. Fidgeting in the small rocker, she frowned at fleeting thoughts as though at ease and yet forgetful of her surroundings.

"You are old enough to begin a marriage chest," Grandma Westerman suggested. "Do you embroider well? Can you knit lace?"

"That's old-fashioned, Grandma," Elizabeth explained, rocking lightly and playing with the gold locket she wore. "I can hemstitch very well; Mama says I take smaller stitches than she can."

"Maybe you would like to learn to knit fine lace yokes for your nightgowns," the old lady ventured.

"That is no longer the fashion," the girl said with pity, and smiled as though her grandparent were a child still learning the ways of the world.

Grandma Westerman would not stoop to luring any of them with gifts or promises. No bribes, no candy bowl, no coins. Gifts were strictly associated with occasions—birthdays and Christmas, Confirmation, graduation.

Theodore did not know what to do with himself when he was in her room. He studied the floor, described circles on the carpet with his shoes, played tricks with one hand upon the other, and labored with a frown to think of subjects for dutiful conversation.

"I know a boy that collects birds' eggs," he said with sudden inspiration. "He let me blow one out. A swallow's egg with speckles. First you punch a needle in each end, and then you blow. You barely blow at all, or the egg breaks."

"Your grandfather collected stamps," Grandma Westerman told him. "Do you like stamps? Some day they may come to you."

"I might collect wild animals," he confided, "some day." Then the look of faraway dreaming left his eyes, and he hurried away with complicated but vague explanation regarding a ball game.

Of a cool summer morning Maria could be heard lurking in the upper hallway, passing her grandmother's door without apparent reason other than curiosity or perhaps some half-murmured and mysterious game she played with invisible companions.

If Grandma Westerman called out to her, the little girl appeared shyly in wordless question, cradling a doll with battered face or carrying scraps of paper, bits of cotton material, a fancy box, or some other subject worthless in the eyes of an adult.

"Will you let me see your leg?" Maria asked hopefully in an undertone at one of the first intimate encounters.

Grandma Westerman lifted the light cover, revealing the plump cast upon her old leg. And when Maria reached out exploring fingers to tap the cast, Grandma Westerman chuckled aloud.

"You find that interesting," she stated, watching the child's soft face, feeling a faint flush of pleasure as Maria stared long with respect and admiration.

"What do you do, now that there is no school?" the grandmother asked when the leg was modestly covered again.

"Oh—things," Maria answered vaguely, her eyes turning away and dreaming momentarily upon vacancies. "Lots of things." A secret look of pleasure entered her eyes.

"All day you play," Grandma Westerman said wonderingly. "From morning till nighttime."

Maria nodded slowly in pleased agreement. "Sometimes I work, though," she spoke virtuously in afterthought.

[13]

"What work do you do?" the old woman asked indulgently.

Maria frowned in recollection. "One day I made a penwiper for Papa's desk."

"Very good," Grandma Westerman praised.

Maria shook her head in distaste. "It was ugly. Ugly, ugly, ugly. Mama would let me use only old dark cloth—so the ink would not show."

"That was sensible."

"I don't like to be sensible," Maria demurred. She rocked so hard that the chair moved over the faded carpet.

"Everyone must learn to be sensible. The earlier, the better." Grandma Westerman fell into an unexpected doze, and by the time she opened her eyes again Maria had slipped away.

It was the elusiveness of the household that caused Grandma Westerman to brood for slow, stuffy hours. She was outside the magic circle they occupied, and there was no way to step over the boundary. She was outside in time and in space, in person, even. There was no way to enter but with the assistance of a spiritual hand from one within, and that hand was not offered. They saw her, but they looked with shallow, absent eyes—those people within this one small magic circle. They saw the plump, old-fashioned little woman, lips disciplined, standing soberly outside, watching, ready to speak phrases of another world, another time, phrases that were dull and stiff and hopelessly outmoded. They felt sorry for her, sorry for the detached position of her years and her physical being, but they did not feel compassion; their mental eyes could not penetrate that far.

They did not know, she would tell herself mournfully, that they were all moving with unsuspected speed toward the very position she held. The parents surmised it, perhaps, at shadowy moments in the night's midst when they lay in uneasy wakefulness, but they would never speak aloud of it. As for the children, they had not one idea in the world that they would ever proceed past a wonderful age of fresh adulthood where the universe would open like a sorcerer's ball to offer dazzling beauties.

"If they could but know—," she would speak to herself in alarm. "If they could but know—." And she might utter a faint sound of consternation that would rouse Clara if she were in the room, and then Grandma Westerman would have to mumble that she had merely cleared her throat.

When Albert's birthday arrived, a celebration was planned; it was as though, in taking over the family house, he had come of age or attained a position of increased prestige, at least. Grandma Westerman's other sons and their families came from their homes in nearby towns to celebrate the occasion. When the gala day arrived, two of them carried her from her rooms, down the steep flight of carpeted steps, through the rear hall and the tiny conservatory, where a long table was set under the chestnut trees. Her wheel chair was there, awaiting her, and Clara fussed over her, shaking out a light shawl to cover her legs, rearranging the lace collar on her black silk dress.

It was a drowsy summer afternoon; the languid wind played with the corners of the white tablecloth without intent, and the bees droned monotonously in the arbor. The families made a fine showing, ten children and the half-dozen adults, the sister of one of the daughters-in-law, and then herself, apart from the others, eating from a tray upon which Clara high-handedly placed some of the choicest morsels—the livers of chicken, the most perfectly-shaped little dumplings, the tiniest of the new potatoes dripping with black butter.

Grandma Westerman's mind journeyed back to the times that she herself had been the one to plan such occasions. She it was who arose early to cook and bake, to turn out the richly-seasoned dishes, to give orders to the housekeeper, choose the cloth to be used, cut the garden flowers and lay the silver on the table. Now it was another; now it was Leonie. She had arisen when the dew still drenched the grass. The precisely-decorated cake that stood before Albert now, bearing his name and birth date, was of her baking.

Albert cut it with a long silver knife, light-heartedly pretending for the children's sake to make a wish as the blade disappeared beneath the snowy icing.

"The first piece is yours," the smaller children repeated solemnly. "The first piece is yours, because this is your birthday."

He set to one side the plate holding the first slice, and when he cut a second, Clara, hovering over him, whispered in his ear.

[15]

As he was about to hand her the second plate he put it aside and impulsively reached for the first. With a courtly bow in his mother's direction, he announced, "To Grandma I present the first slice with the birthday wish."

As Clara with a proud smile bore the plate to her, the children all clapped loudly in approval, and the women joined in for an indulgent moment. Their clapping was flat and hollow in the sleepy summer air. It was as though for a moment they were expressing all the half-spoken excitement of the day in the wild movements of their palms meeting, parting, meeting vigorously again. It was not Albert's act or the honor accorded the grandmother they were applauding; it was the summer day, the good heavy dinner, and the expectations and secret dreams of their age.

They toasted the day with sweet pale wine. The old woman became drowsy for a time; Albert's voice, as he arose to make a solemn speech, drew farther and farther away from her, and she awoke only when the air was quiet again.

With lazy whoops, then, the boys arose and went to assemble at the far side of the garden, and the girls followed them hopefully. Christine and Clara had cleared the table of all but the coffee cups and the wine glasses and the remains of the cake, and the parents received news of the past months, relating what mutual acquaintances had died, what families had been blessed with births, describing illnesses and other misfortunes that had overtaken some. They spoke of old Mrs. Bartel dying suddenly, of the division of property, the quarrel between two of the children over certain land.

"She had nothing left," Grandma Westerman said unexpectedly.

From their positions at the table they all turned to stare at her, sitting aside in the varnished wheel chair.

"I myself am ready to go," Grandma Westerman continued calmly. "I am ready to die."

In abrupt shame and alarm the faces turned away from her again, all but those of the two older granddaughters, who, lips parted, watched her frightenedly.

"Now, Mama," one of the sons murmured uncomfortably.

"It is not right to talk so," another reprimanded gently.

All were silent for moments. Then one of the women spoke hurriedly, asking Leonie about the burnt-sugar birthday cake, of which now only a thin wedge remained.

After a while Grandma Westerman fell into a light, restful doze. And she dreamed that the sons and sons' wives had drawn into a clandestine group at the end of the table to speak of her in deep whispers.

"Grandma is failing so fast; I could not believe it when I came yesterday. . . . She is becoming a different woman—fleshy still, but quiet and watchful, with little to say. . . . She is slipping—slipping slowly away. Leonie says she sleeps more and more—little naps here and there. . . . And what she said a while ago. 'I am ready to die,' she said; I thought my heart would turn over. . . ."

Afterward she did not know if they had really spoken such words or not. Perhaps she had not even slept, but had withdrawn into a cocoon apart from consciousness but not remote enough for unconsciousness.

The thought fretted at her brain. If she were going to die, she wanted the quitting to be abrupt, not lingering. She wanted to move rapidly from one world to another without having time to think about it, to be fearful of the moment and to conjecture as to what internal strength she might have.

Above all, she desired to be heard before departing. How could she tell them what occupied her thoughts? They did not have time to listen. They were, in addition, deaf and blind to what was to be heard and seen.

Her own mother had died without speaking of what lay within her heart, but she had been unwarned of death. One hour she had gone about household duties; the next hour she had been carried to her bed to draw final breath. Yet there had been her paternal grandmother, who lived with them for the long years of her widowhood. She had calmly bade them draw about her bedside. Grandma Westerman had huddled there with her brothers and sisters, terrified into wordlessness, yet bound by a terrible curiosity for the labored breathing, the ashen face, and the determined voice speaking solemnly, almost wistfully, but still commanding them so that the hour remained in her mind all this time.

"Honor thy father and mother . . ." the old woman had said hoarsely to the frightened children. And to the parents, "Above all, live prudently. . . ."

But it was not enough, Grandma Westerman told herself. It was as though her grandparents were bidding a stern farewell before making a visit elsewhere, or merely giving reprimand for some misdeed. The young should learn what lay before them; knowledge of that kind would give purpose to their lives, contemplative wisdom to their youthfulness. How could they live prudently when the reason for prudent living was unknown to them?

And how could she tell them except at such a moment as death, when they would gather round with respect upon their faces and respect within their beings, respect for death first, and then for the one about to close her eyes forever to the world? It was too plain that she could not command from the weak position she held now. To them all she was but an ailing old woman with a crippled leg upon which she would never walk again, a sick old grandmother who was classified nearer the children than the adults.

She had lost the independent vigor of being that had been a foremost quality. It had begun slipping unnoticed from her long before she fell upon the stairs. And now she had ceased expecting its return, ceased caring, even. Yet it was better that way; if she had known it was dwindling into nothing, she would have been angry and frightened. Now it was gone, and she was ready to accept the loss just as she had accepted whatever came.

Yet there remained this one desire, this yearning to reveal to her children and her grandchildren the direction in which they walked.

She began dwelling upon what she would speak to them. Beneath the sky, she must tell them, the earth turns slowly. No one feels the motion of its turning, but there it is. The seasons follow one another; the years tread softly on each other's heels; the generations are born and given maturity, and the move-

ment is the same. The universe operates by cycle; every ele-
ment depends upon a cycle.

"As I move away," she said in the darkness of quiet night
hours, "you move up. We walk slowly, all of us, away from the
sun, that gives life." There was another thought that caused her
to digress then. Did they walk away from the sun, or did they
move toward this representation of God? She could not tell.
But whatever the focus, they walked blindly. They had little
sense of destination until all of a sudden it appeared before
them, ready to swallow them whole, to add them impersonally
to all who had gone before into the vast, solemn brilliance of
the unknown world after.

That was not all. There lay, in the invisible air, the un-
spoken bidding to serve the world in some manner, to extend
the eye and the hand beyond the fairy circle of family and
friends, to touch what seemed near untouchable. It was more
than duty: it was a spiritual bidding of a universe in which
all souls were equal in need. All were frail and open to pity; all
must, despite weak and transparent qualities, give of themselves. She herself had not become aware of this until age had
crept quietly, stiffly upon her.

She lay thinking upon all this, repeating until the thoughts
wore grooves of their own upon her mind and crowded out the
tiresome details of the physical world. The season changed, but
she hardly noticed. She was on her way; despite the old limbs
quiet in the bed, she was taking the last, dragging steps. Sharply
she attended to that one activity; when she could step not once
more she must take a stand and speak.

The sons came regularly, one by one, to sit near her, but she
scarcely noted their presence. Only Clara was left of reality,
Clara whose bent shoulders and slow, steady steps appeared
without being summoned. Grandma Westerman would look at
her with fondness, at the patient eyes and wrinkled, minister-
ing hands.

Sometimes in the heavy night hours, when Clara would pour
her a drink of water or let medicine trickle into a silver spoon,
they would speak in spare phrases with an intimacy that comforted her.

[19]

"You will have a home here," Grandma Westerman murmured. "I have spoken to Albert."

"It is wicked to imply—," Clara reprimanded as to a child. "You will be better one day soon. The medicine is slow when one is heavy with years."

"I see the truth," the old lady said stubbornly. "At my hour nothing obscures the eyes."

"One must always hope," reminded Clara. "There is nothing in the world if not hope."

"When the time comes," Grandma Westerman spoke, "you must call them in—Albert and Leonie, and the children."

"Yes, yes," soothed Clara. "You have told me a dozen times. I have promised."

"There is something I wish to say to them," the old woman said dreamily, "something they must know."

Day by day a great eagerness for the hour came over her. Sometimes she feared to fall asleep, thinking it might come unbeknownst, and be lost to her. "If you see sometime," she instructed Clara, "that the time has come, rouse me. Do not hesitate."

But in her awaiting, in the alert core of her mind, she watched stealthily. The triumph of recognition was almost overwhelming. Such eagerness flowed through her that she lost awareness. In the dazzling, blinding swirl of unconsciousness she forced her way determinedly back, and held a position divided only by a dimness of physical perception.

There was confusion in the doorway; she endured it with patience, holding proudly to her command of the hour; such strength seemed to resurge, she thought herself able to wait for long. Anticipation brought exquisite pleasure so that she trembled violently and Clara held to her while still crying to the family, "Hurry now!"

It was Elizabeth who was responsible for the commotion. Hysterically she tried to pull away from her father. "Don't make me," she wept.

"She is too sensitive for this," Leonie defended her daughter. "And at the delicate age, too."

"Nevertheless she must enter," Albert pronounced. "This is Grandma's last wish. Slap her cheeks and bring her to her senses."

When the old lady opened her eyes again, the room was quiet but for Elizabeth's muffled sobbing as she stood pressed within the circle of her mother's arm. She could see the two small children standing beside Leonie, and she frowned at the absence of Albert.

"My stomach aches," Theodore whispered, and Maria looked at him as though he were a stranger.

At last Grandma Westerman discovered that one hand was being fondled, and that at her side was Albert, his eyes pink, his face damp. Finding his nearness distasteful, she looked at the children again. It appeared that two large tears stood on Maria's cheeks, that they had come unbidden from the round, wondering eyes to roll gently only a little way. She wished Maria were beside her rather than Albert; the child would be less disturbing than the man, but there was not time to request the change.

Clara she could not see at all, but sensed that the elderly woman was close to her. Sighing, prolonging the moment a bit, Grandma Westerman wet her lips with unwieldy tongue, and spoke.

"The universe turns slyly, and unseen," she said. In a little the church bells would be tolling ponderously for her; she and her brother had run swiftly down the street to the church when their grandmother departed.

"She is out of her head," Leonie murmured. "She does not know what words she speaks."

"As I move away," the old woman went on softly and deliberately, as if repeating a lesson, "you move up into my place . . ."

Blinking her eyelids, she looked at them long. What she had already said was beginning to penetrate; she could tell by the increasing mistiness of the faces as though the spirits had arisen to the very surface.

Exultation flowered as she bid the next phrases come to her

[21]

lips and tongue, and she could not speak at all for a moment. But she had only begun. Her triumph must carry her through to the end of the precise revelation.

"We are all walking faster and faster," she wanted to say, "to our destination . . ."

But with a rude rush it all receded from her—the words, the faces, the brilliance, the universe. And she was alone.

The Teletype Machine

NORMAND R. POIRIER

IT WAS a very hot summer night and the few sounds of the city were muffled by the heat. The young man sat on the wide window sill, looking down the long, empty street. The only lights were the street lights. Trash cans lined the curbstones. A dog appeared from out of the shadows, sniffed a pole, then disappeared again. A car approached, its headlights dissolving the dark patches, its engine spoiling the quiet, then passed by, leaving the city quieter. But there was a tension in the air. An occasional flash of heat lightning blued the sky. The young man flicked his lighted butt out the window. He watched it fall, arcing its way over the sidewalk into the street. He tapped with his fingers on the wood and blew on the shade-cord so that it pendulumed. He spat. Then, a ringing shattered the stillness.

He sat up with a start, walked the few steps to the other side of the small, crude office, and flicked on the machine. First, there was only a quiet hum. Then the carriage snapped automatically back to the left of the yellow paper. Then the keys slapped against the roll—poppop pop pop poppop—as the young man's fingers typed out in even purple letters

THIS RIDGEVILLE

There was a pause. The young man waited. He cracked his

knuckles. Then the keys rose and fell, without rhythm, tiredly.
THIS IS FATJFXXXXX FATHER ROBUXX ROBINSON
CALLING HIS FLOCK
 —sure i'm good, good enough for the county but not good
enough for the city, Robinson said
 —the paper has to have at least one good man in the county.
Otherwise the whole network would fall apart, the young man
answered
 —if you insist on following that stupid line of sympathy, I'll
quit talking to you. I know where I am all the time. I always
know the situation
 They went on drinking their beers, looking up occasionally at
the people who entered the bar. It was a quiet room.
 —maybe you should get out of the business, the young man
said
 —and do what? No, this is it. You can say that because you're
young. But I've just about reached my day of reckoning. I had
my chances and I missed them, I suppose. I graduated a chem-
ist, Phi Bete, and then found out that I hated chemistry. I
worked as a librarian so I could read. And I read. God, how I
read. I searched and searched. And at the end of everything
I found myself
 —I don't understand that, the young man said
 —I don't think you ever will. You've got it, or at least you
have the potential. But to find yourself at the end of every-
thing, that's the hurt. The ugliness of self. Like a growth that
can't be removed. Removal would be fatal. It has to be lived
with. I'm me, and I can't stand it.
 The young man began to type again
 YES FATHER ROBINSON WHAT SAYEST THOU TONITE
AM IN JOHNSTOWN OFFICE
 HAVEN'T HEARD IN DAYS THOUGHT U WERE DEAD
 BIG ELECTION COMING UP HERE THTEXXX THREE
SELECTMEN CITY THOUGGT IT WOIXXXWOULD B
WORTH MY XPERT /HA HA HA/ COVERAGE. SENT ME
HERE FROM GARDNER.
 IS IT GOOD TOWN
 STINKS POPULATION ABUT 2200 EXCKFXXXX EXCLUD-
ING THREE WHORES WHO FOLLOWED ME HERE   ONLY

THREE BARS IN TOWN   LIMITED SUPPLY OF LIQUOR
  R U DRUNK
  CAN T U TELL FROM TYPING REMINDS ME OF LAST
NEW YEAR S EVE WHEN I WORKED VERY ICY SLIPPERY
NUGCXXX NIGHT NOTHING DOIN BUT THERE WERE
ABOUT 12 MINOR COLLISIONS LONG STORY WITH
LOTSA NAMES I STARTED SENDIN TO DESK AT 11/m
XXXX 11.30 P.M. AND AT QUARTER TO ONE DESK CUT IN
ABD SAID NEVER MIND ROBINSON NICE TRY THOUGH
JUST WENT TO PRESS
  I M SOBER   TOO HOT
  AM DRUNK ENUFF FOR BOTH OF US   HAVING HEELL-
OFATIME WITH KEYS
  AM GLAD U CALLED WAS GOING TO BED VERY BOR-
ING THIS
  EVERYBODY IN THIS TOWN IS ASLEEP   I AM THE
ONLY ONE AWAKE IF I WEREN T AWAKE THE TOWN
WOULDN ·T EXIST   IF I PUDXXX PUT OUT MY LIGHT
THE WHOLE TOWN WOULD BE DATCCXXXX DARK
THAT MAKES ME BIG MAN SO I STAY AND DRINK HERE
  HERE HOT AND SLEEPY TOO
  THIS BAD JOB FOR YOUNG MAN BECAUSE OF ALONE-
NESS ALWAYS NEW TOWNS NEW FACES NEW BARS IN
NEWNESS ONLY LONELINESS LONELINESS GXX GIVES
HOLD ON A MINUTE FONE RINGING
  OK
The young man sat back and waited. He picked up a maga-
zine from the desk and looked at the cover. He put it back,
then slipped down into the chair, and placed his hands behind
his head. . . .

He and Robinson had driven the few miles to the lake shore
on their dinner hour after the paper had gone to press. It had
been a year before when they were both working the day trick.
They bought sandwiches of sliced meat and beer, and leaning
against the guardrail, they looked down into the water. The
reflection showed them themselves clearly, even to the brace
on Robinson's leg. Robinson could not eat his second sandwich, so he slipped the butter-splotched meat from between the
bread, broke off a length of it, and tossed it into the water.
Immediately, a school of little fish darted towards it. He tore

the rest of the meat into strips and threw them into the water. Though there were enough pieces for each fish, five or six would chase after the fish who held a piece in his mouth. The rest of the meat sank beneath the soft mud.

—look at the idiots, Robinson said.

—just like humans, the young man said.

—are they? I wouldn't know. I can't see those things. I lack the ability to see. I'm thirty-nine and I'm blind. Never be average. If you find some day, but then you won't. You have the necessary stuff.

R U STILL HERE

The young man sat up quickly as the machine started its pop pop pop.

YES WHO WAS IT

COPS   NOTHING IMPORTANT   JUST WANTED TO TALK TO ME   COPS GET LONELY TOO   THEY AREN T BAD FELLAHS AGRXXXX AFTER SKCCXXXX ALL U NO

HOW LONG WILL U B IN JOHNSTOWN

TWO DAYS   THEN TO EASTBRIDGE   GOOD TOWN EASTBRIDGE   MANY BARS   WILL HAVE HELL OF TIME

MIGHT DRIVE DOWN TO C U

DON T   U STAY THERE AND WORK

The young man placed his fingers on the keys again but he didn't send anything. The machine whirred quietly. Then it started printing again

SAY SOMETHING

I WAS TRYING TO THINK OF SOMETHING

LET ME SAY THINGS THEN   WOULD LIKE IT BRYXXXX BRTXXXX BETTER IF U WERE DRUNK TOO   BUT I M DRUNK ENUFF FOR BOTH   ME LIKES TO TALK TO THIS MACHINE   ONLY ONE I CAN TALK TOOXXX TO /PARDON THE MISTAKE PROF/   THIS MACHINE LIKE CONFESSIONAL   U TALK INTO BLACKNESS THE PRIEST TURNS BLIND EAR HERE U JUST SIT AND TALK WITH UR HANDS   MACHINE DON T TALK BACK   I WOULD LIKE TO GO TO CONFESSION MAYBEEEEEXXXX WOULD LIKE TO GET RID OF BAD IN ME   I TRY EVERY TIME I HIT NEW TOWN   I SAY NOW HERE NOBODY KNOWS ME STARTING WITH CLEAN SLATE   NOBODY HATES ME   I CAN B GOOD FELLAH I·CAN WRITE JUST GOOD THING

ON SLATE   BUT EACH TIME ME COMES OUT GET DRUNK
IN BAR   INSULT PEOPLE OR THROW UP OR BRAG OR
LIE   LIES THAT BECOME THEN TRUTH FOR PEOPLE
OF TOWN   LIES THEN I MUST LIVE AND I M ME AGAIN
BORN ALL OVER AGSXXX AGAIN   NOW NO MORE TOWNS
NO MORE BIRTHS   I M ALL BORN EVERY TOWN AND
CITY IN COUNTY I WORKED AT LEAST ONCE   WAIT PLS
GODDAM FONE RINGS AGAIN. . . .

It was the summer before when Robinson and the young
man worked the same city together. It was a hot night. The
young man had been out by himself all evening. The city was
lazy. People had gone to the beaches. He had seen the movie.
The office was open but he wanted to stay away because there
was nothing to do there. The police station was open but he
had heard all it had to say. He walked the streets, the back
streets and the side streets he had rarely seen, and observed the
tenants sprawled on unpainted back porches trying to catch a
cool breeze, seated on front steps, smoking, staring blankly,
drinking beer from cans, reading newspapers in the evening
light. He drank beer in a bar he had never seen before and
listened as the bartender discussed the recent Red Sox slump
with his three male patrons. The bartender was short and his
pot belly strained at his aprong strings. He drank eight glasses
before he left and walked towards the center of the city, towards his room. He bought three quarts of beer and walked up
the three flights. The door to Robinson's room was closed, he
noticed as he passed it, and no light shone under it. He entered
his room, poured himself a glass of beer and sat down on the
bed. The room was hot. The iron bed creaked. There was a
smell of sweat. He drank two of the three quarts. Then he
knocked on Robinson's door.

"I thought you'd like some beer," he said into the darkness.

Robinson turned on the lamp beside the bed and smiled up
at the young man.

"Sure, I'll have a glass. What you been doing all night?"

"Nothing much."

"You don't sound too happy."

"Had a little too much beer, I guess."

"You want to watch out. Beer and loneliness together are a strong combination. You find as time goes along that you get a happiness out of melancholia. You sit at a bar and drink beer alone, and alone, and maybe there's a song playing in the juke box that brings back memories, and you get a little drunker, and you get a little sadder. You look into the bottom of your glass, deeper and deeper, and you get sadder and sadder and drunker and drunker, until those memories are alive almost. They make you feel happy-sad, you know what I mean? So happy-sad that you can cry and smile at the same time. It's that feeling you have to watch out for. It's a tremendously pleasant sensation. So when you're constantly alone you look for that little joy and you find yourself sitting at bars every night, waiting for it. Eventually, the real stuff in life becomes unreal. Your dreams, memories, hopes become the reality. Your job, people, your physical life become unreal. And you wake up one day and find that you missed the train while you were reading the time table."

"Yes. What are your memories?"

"Oh, I have many. My family—my mother and father, that is—the war, friends, and a girl. Of course, a girl. THE girl. Every man has her. The girl who was perfect in every way. Not really of course. But after a sufficient number of remembrances, she becomes perfect. We forget the potential liabilities and defects in her and explore only the seeds of perfection we remember she had, so that in time, after enough afternoons in bars and enough dates with putrid women or squabbles with our own wives or fiancées, she becomes perfection and the object of our love. I know she wasn't at all, as I think of her now. But I only think of her when I'm in no condition to be this rational about things."

HELLO R U STILL THERE

YES

BOSS WILL B MUCH MAD WHEN HE GETS TELETYPE BILL FROM THIS OFFICE   HE CANT UNDERSTAND WHY THE BILLS R ALWAYS SO HIGH WHEN I GO TO AN OFFICE I TELL HIM IT S CAUSE I M EFFICIENT

WHO WAS ON FONE

THE DESK AM TO REPORT TO STILES TOMORROW
AYEM MAN SHOT WIFE AND TWO KIDS WILL B AR-
RAIGNED IN DC AT 9 I M TO HOLD HIDXXX HIS HXX
HAMDXX HAND
SHOULD B GOOD STUFF
MIGHT B SEEMS EVERY TIME DESK CALLS I M CROCKED
TONGUE WAS VERY HEAVY OVER FONE
BY THE BY WHAT EVER HAPPENED TO THAT GAL U
SAID WAS SHE OF UR DREAMS NEVER GOT FULL STORY
The machine whirred quietly for a few minutes before it
popped out
HAD TO MIX MYSELF DRINK IN CUP WATER WARM NO
ICE WHISKEY LOW SHE DEAD NEXT QUESTION
SORRY
THASSSSSS OK AM DRUNK AM SMILING HAD FUNNY
THOUGHT TONITE WAS SITTING IN BAR DRINKING
WAS THINKING ABOUT U GOING INTO CITY STAFF
I WAS JUST GOING TO TELL U BOSS CALLED UP TO-
DAY AND TOLD ME TO REPORT MONDAY
WAS THINKING OF U WHEN I SAW PIX OF FLYING
DUTCHMAN IN BAR SAID THAT S ME THAT S WHAT I
AM THE FLYING DUTCHMAN OF HOBARD COUNTY AM
DOOMED TO TRAVEL FROM ONE TOWN TO ANOTHER
FROM ME TO ME FOR REST OF LIFE LIKE A GHOST AL-
WAYS AT NIGHT FROM NOW ON I LL ONLY MOVE AT
NIGHT ONLY I GO BY BEAT UP FORD CAR ALWAYS IN
HATED COUNTY JUST DRIVING AND DRINKING DIRTY
RAINCOAT SINGLE ROOM WITH SAGGING BED PUKE
AND SWEAT AND COPY PAPER LITTLE PEOPLE DIRTY
HATEFUL PEOPLE WHO SHOOT WIVES AND KIDS IGNO-
RANCE AND SELFISHNESS CHEAP COPS AND POLITE
UNDERTAKERS HOSPITAL CHECKS AND STATE POLICE
WHORES AND OTHER MEN S WIVES LIQUOR LIQUOR
LQIXX LIQUOR THIS IS CONFESSIONAL SIXXX SO IT AINT
FAIR TO REPEAT OUT SIDE REMEMBER NOW UR CON-
SECRATED LONELINESS AND DRUNKENNESS WITHOUT
HOPE OF A MEMORY NOT EVEN S SINGLE ILLUSION LEFT
ME IF I ONLY HAD ONE JUST ONE HOT DAMN I WENT
DOWN TO SEE THE BOXX X BOSS TODAY DIDN'T KNOW
HE ASKED U IN CITY STAFF JUST HAPPENED TO GO IN
TODAY GOT SHAVED AND ATE SEN SEN SEN SAID TO

BOSS THIS IS ISX XX IT BOSS U KNOW WHAT I CAN DO
I M BETTER THAN THREE QUARTERS OF THE DOPES U
HAVE ON THIS STAFF I CAN COVER ANYTHING PULL ME
INTO THE CITY   I WANNA BE ON THE CUTXXXX CITY
STAFF I M SICK OF THE COUNTY   SO HE SAYS TO ME
UR OLD AND U BEEN OUT OF COLLEGE A L O NG TIME
U SHOULDA STARETD IN THIS BUSINESS EARLIER   U
CAN T START AT 35 AND KEEP UP WITH THE YOUNG BOYS
THE PROFESSION IS GETTING CROWDED   WE WANT
YOUNG MEN WE CAN BRING UP IN THE RIGHT TRA-
DITION   ANYWAY THE JOB YOU RE DOING IN THE
COUNTY IS JUST AS IMPORTANT AS ANYTHING YOU
COULD DO HERE   SOMEDAY U'LL GET TO BECOUNTY
EIDOTXXXEDITOR   WHAT HE MEANT REALLY WAS
THAT I WAS JUST AN OLD RUM DE DUM DUM THAT I
GOT NO CLASS   THAT MY PANTS ARE ALWAYS BEGCXXX
BAGGY AND I AIN'T GOT OUT OF COLUMBIA OR MIS-
SOURI   ANYWAY I SAYS OK TO THE BOSS AND HE SAYS
HE S GIVING ME A FIVE BUCK RAISE   I TOOK IT
WHAT COULD I DO   I LL BE FORTY IN THREE
MONTHS   I CAN T MAKE ANOTHER MOVE   I WISH I
HAD AN ILLUSION THOUGH IT WOULD MAKE IT EASIER
IF SHE WASN T DEAD   DEAD DEAD   DEAD   IT S
SUCH A FINAL LOOKING WORD   R U LOOKING AT   I LL
LOOK INTO THE BOTTOM OF MY PAPER CUP HERE AND
C IF I CAN C ANYTHING   NOPE   NO ILLUSION   NO
MEMORIES DOWN THERE JUST THE REFLECTION OF
ME SO NOW I CAN RACE AROUND THE COUNTY AT
NIGHT PLAYING THE FLYING DUTCHMAN IN MY BEAT
UP FORD FROM ME TO ME   COMPLETELY FREE AND
SAVOIR FAIRE OR SOME OTHER FRENCH THING   INCI-
DENTALLY DID U HEAR ABOUT THE SCOTCHMAN WHO
SAW A TWENTY*FIVE CENT PIECE ON THE SIDEWALK
AND MARRIED HER HMMMMMMMM I WON T BE CALL-
ING YOU   I GUESS THE TELETYPE MACHINES IN THE
CITY ARE PRETTY BUSY   ANYWAY BOSS COMPLAINING
ABOUT HIGH BILL   GOOD LUCK YOUNG MAN

The young man immediately started typing out
WAIT A MIN PLS R U STILL THERE
He waited and the machine whirred but there was no answer.
The levers began slapping again and he hunched over the

machine as it printed in purple letters on the yellow paper:
  WHAT NUMBER R U CALLING PLS
  CANCEL THE CALL PLS
  OK   END
  END V

The Happy One

EDGAR ROSENBERG

THE nine-year-old emigrant Felix Freudenreich copied with patience and precision a half-length portrait of Henri Dunant from an otherwise useless Red Cross leaflet which he had picked up at one of the stops on his journey a week earlier. His head, as he worked, was bent low over his drawing; his nose all but touched the paper, casting a shadow over founder Dunant's proud black beard; a few strands of hair had fallen across his forehead. The tip of his tongue rolled back and forth between two rows of tiny, uneven, and slightly yellow teeth, as though to encourage his fingers to clutch the pencil more firmly, as though to embolden his thick, moist hands to guide it up and down the paper with not quite so much evident prudence, deliberation, and languor.

The artist Freudenreich worked for the better part of an hour without so much as taking his eyes from his drawing except to reach out now and then for his eraser, a softer grade of pencil, or to consult, quite mechanically and needlessly, the Dunant original which he had taped to the window before him. The window standing slightly ajar and one of the tapes having come loose, the drawing now swung aimlessly in the wind, undecided whether to endure yet longer or to allow itself to be torn finally from its place, to be blown about willy-nilly in the streets beneath, brushing on the way against the busy citizens, against some soldiers, perhaps, some high dignitaries of the Republic, and, unheeded and scorned, to take flight at last over the roofs and steeples of the city, and so to vanish over Lake Geneva.

Felix had long ago ceased to pay any but the most cursory attention to the portrait on the window, on whose guidance he no longer in the least depended. For by now the artist Freudenreich knew every line, every feature of Henri Dunant's physiognomy, having, in fact, already copied it fifteen or twenty times since his arrival. Not that there were no more interesting or useful things to draw: the chest and closets in the vestibule were filled with old magazines and quaintly illustrated romances, giving off a faintly scented odor very comforting and reassuring to the mind. It was not ambition, either, or tenacity, which had prompted the fifteen or twenty Dunants in the desk drawer; the emigrant Freudenreich cared little for excellence of draftmanship and, indeed, his fifteenth Dunant was scarcely better than his first. Ambition he had none at all, and perseverance he was more than ever inclined to regard as supremely unnecessary. Oh—he had been aspiring enough once upon a time; once he had been a proud and potent Prince, going to battle on a white horse called Barbarossa; and in those days he had also been a captain in the hussars; an acrobat; a slayer of dragons; a chimney sweep; a keeper of Chinese and blackamoors; a leader of a military band; a starving poet; a starving violinist; an Englishman; the first to climb Mount Everest; somebody's private ambassador to Sir Samuel Hoare; somebody going to the gallows to save his best friend; a builder of bridges; a maker of revolutions; a maker of moving pictures; a saver of souls; an American millionaire entertaining John D. Rockefeller on the roof of the Flatiron Building. . . .

But the events of the past year, which had robbed him in short succession of a father, a mother, an elder brother, and a very good home, had robbed him of his ambitions, too, so that when one of the many elderly ladies who daily invaded his privacy (passing themselves off as "your new great aunt" or "your new second cousin," inspecting him through long-stemmed lorgnettes, mumbling courteous lies about how tall he was and what fine French he spoke) —when one of his visitors had asked him the other day what he should like to be when he grew up, it was simply because he had to tell these people something and because his choice never failed to inspire them with vast confidence, that he replied he thought he would like to be a horse-doctor.

But he continued, day after day, to copy the drawing by the window (copied it with the same air of preoccupation, indifference almost) because Henri Dunant's proud and placid features, his small, gray eyes which neither admonished nor questioned but seemed wholly content to smile as though nothing had happened, represented, all things considered, the most comforting and cheerful sight the emigrant Freudenreich had encountered.

And there was really nothing else to occupy him. He had explored his new surroundings during the first days, had seen all the sights which, his new relatives told him, ought to be seen, but he had not found them very enjoyable. The lake, certainly, was very large and, he supposed, beautiful, but there were dozens of lakes quite as fine at home. On the second day after his arrival, his new father had treated him to a ferry ride to the bastion of Chillon, a black, ugly building, rising, gaunt and uncompromising, above a small inlet of the lake, and he asked himself why people came a long way to admire it.

It was late in August, the schools would not open for another month, and in the meantime his ignorance of the language kept him from making friends with the boys in the neighborhood. (Since his new parents were Alsatian, his own language was spoken at home.) Sometimes, indeed, watching his fellows from the window as they ran back and forth in the street, playing soccer, shouting directions at each other in their high, untroubled voices, he would have liked to assert his right to be as they were, would have liked, for example, to join them in *balle au poing* or to ask one of the older boys to let him ride his bicycle for five minutes. But he always ended up by turning away from the window, and beginning another Dunant.

Before filling in the background of the drawing (a Red Cross superimposed on a sketch of the Matterhorn dissolving into a purple mist in a fashion which made the greatest demands on his artistic fidelity), Felix briefly paused in his work and, for

want of more pressing things to attend to, gazed out of the
window a while. To keep up his spirits he whistled a few of his
favorite songs to himself; he whistled, not by pursing his lips,
but through his teeth, a trick he had picked up from someone
he had met on the road. He had met so many people on his
journey, hundreds of them, and they had all been so very much
like each other, cowering noiselessly in cold railroad stations,
plodding silently along congested highways, across bare fields
and through deserted towns, showing neither anger nor yet
fear, enduring their situation not scornfully and not indif-
ferently, but repudiating it with inflexible patience and cun-
ning. . . . So many people had crossed his path, he scarcely
remembered any of them. But somebody had come along, somebody called Victor, who had taught him—before he, too, went
his way—to whistle through his teeth.

Felix whistled very much the same melodies every day, all
of them very dear and good. There was first the staunch and
spirited marching song, *"Drei Lilien, drei Lilien, die pflanzt'
ich mir aufs Grab, tralala";* then something light and cheerful,
a waltz, perhaps, some air from the *Fledermaus* or the lovely
"Im Weissen Roessl am Wolfgang See." Then came another
war song, not so tuneful as the first, but full of sadness and
longing this time, to be whistled slowly and lingeringly: none
other than the beautiful ballad of the two French grenadiers
who, on their return from Russia, learn that their good Emperor has fallen into the hands of the enemy.

> *Was schert mich Weib, was schert mich Kind. . . .*
> *Und mein Kaiser, mein Kaiser gefangen.*

Felix whistled for the fourth time, and passed on to the next
number, something utterly grand and, indeed, world-famous,
all the more to his taste because it went with a rousing-fine
story; it, too, was to be whistled very slowly and deliberately,
with a conscious emphasis on its international renown: it was
the noble and stately march from the opera *Aida.* And finally
(and this invariably concluded his little program) he whistled:

> *Muss i' denn, muss i' denn zum Staedtele 'naus,*
> *Und du, mein Schatz, bleibst hier . . .*

He loved that song; it was the song, his father had said, that was played on the piers up north whenever any of the bigger steamers, the "Bremen," for example, or the "Europa," set out on their transatlantic journeys—the song, his mother had added, that they would play for him, too, some day, would play for all of them.

Und du, mein Schatz, bleibst hier.

How sad and beautiful that was; how beautiful and sad— with the ship passing silently out of the harbor and the people on the dock waving and crying into their handkerchiefs, shouting yet another farewell, shouting some forgotten word of encouragement to the homeless, and the band growing fainter and lovelier all the time.

Standing by the window, whistling his songs of the three lilies and the mourning grenadiers, the boy Felix Freudenreich suddenly had a very good idea. He decided to write a letter home. It did not matter particularly to whom he wrote his letter so long as it was to somebody in his old town. That, in itself, limited his choice, of course, for scarcely any of his friends and none of his relations were left in the town, some having been carried off in trucks at a day's notice like his father and mother and elder brother, and the others having been scattered over the four corners of the earth, settling in all sorts of unfamiliar countries the very names of which had hitherto conveyed no meaning to anyone unless, like his uncle Justus, he happened to collect stamps—names such as Curaçao or Mozambique or Haiti or Rio de Oro or Luzon. It was not to them that he wanted to write.

He might write to Benno Loewensohn. Benno—the Lion of Judah he was called, because with his flat nose, his thick lips and black curls he looked for all the world like the Emperor Haile Selassie of Ethiopia, a person very much in the news in those days. Not that they had ever been particularly good friends, he and Benno; indeed, the Lion of Judah had always awed and frightened him a little, was something of a rowdy with his one hundred and twenty pounds. Oh—he could be nice enough when he wanted to be, would offer him a piece of

chewing gum when no one was about, or a licorice stick. But
in front of someone else, the Lion of Judah always made it a
point to pick on him, and would call him "Butterfinger Felix"
or "The Fearful Felix" (mockingly, of course), would provoke
him by poking him in the ribs a few times; and once he had
actually given him a beating in front of the entire class in order
to impress a new student who was taller and rowdier than even
the Lion. So Felix was a good deal relieved when his father had
finally and categorically forbidden him all intercourse with
Benno—the Lion having taken it into his head one afternoon,
walking with Felix through one of the busiest sections of the
city (and only a block away from the Police Bureau, at that) to
roar at the top of his lungs, for all the world to hear:

> *Heil Moskau!*
> *Der Hitler is' a' Drecksau!*

Well, he would not hold the Lion's superior airs against him
any longer; he would forgive him for the beating, too, and all
the other mean tricks he had played on him. And Benno, he felt
certain, would be very glad to get his letter. He had no assur-
ance, of course, that the letter would ever reach him; for all he
knew, the Lion might have gone away, too, gone to Curaçao or
Mozambique. But at least Felix had no definite information on
this point as he had about the others, and it was just possible
that Benno had never got out of the country at all. He would
write him immediately so that Benno would have his letter
before the week end and could show it around. He would ask
his new mother for pen and paper and a postage stamp and get
the letter out before noon. It was a very good idea.

"Come in," his beautiful new mother called from the living
room. "Is that our Felix?" she cried, laughing, tinkling, and
she opened the door for him. She looked beautiful in a merry,
pink morning coat embroidered with a whole pastoral scene:
gilded horses and cows, little chalets, little naked fauns chasing
each other along the edge of a brook, dreaming beneath poplars
and weeping willows. . . . Beautiful, too, was the way her lips
were parted in a gay smile of welcome, the way she slipped her
soft hand into his as she led him into the room.

"Excuse me, Madame," Felix began (for he still could not bring himself to call her "maman," as she had told him to), "could I please have—" and he noticed that they had visitors.

"But of course our Felix may have it, whatever it is he wants," his new mother cried. "But first you must say hello to Madame and Monsieur Weill. Monsieur Weill owns a big brewery on Avenue General Dufour," she explained. "It pays to be on good terms with him, doesn't it, Monsieur Weill? And this," she introduced him, "is our Felix."

"Ah," said the brewer Weill. "Felix, is it?" he asked in an indulgent, velvety voice, inclining his perfectly round head to one side. " '*Felix heisst die Kanaille,*' as our Schiller says, heh heh," and he held out a fat, hairless hand. "Your very humble servant, Master Felix, heh heh," said the brewer Weill with a short, discreet cackle, pinching him awkwardly in the cheek. His nose lay a little flat on his upper lip so that in speaking he breathed slightly into his moustache. On the right wing of his nose loomed, hairy and formidable, a black mole.

"This is Madame Weill," he added, pointing to his wife, who sat rigid and self-effacing on the couch by the window, her hands folded in her lap. Madame Weill's features were as tiny and angular as her husband's were massive and spherical: her nose was long and pointed and her chin was positively triangular. She wore a black sweater, adorned only by an oval brooch which depicted, in ivory bas-relief, a profile every bit as sharp and pointed as her own; her neck was covered by a broad, black ribbon. Yet she did not seem unkind: her eyes were soft, even shy—they were also slightly crossed so that Felix could not be sure whether she was looking straight at him or straight at the glass cabinet in the corner in which his new father displayed his World War medals and ribbons. But she extended her own tiny hand, slightly inclined her tiny head in her turn, and whispered, "How do you do, Felix?" Whereupon Felix, emboldened by her kindness and willing enough to suffer the brewer Weill to utter the expected remark on his expert French, artfully clicked his heels, bowed stiffly from the waist, and said: "*Enchanté,* Madame."

"Ah," said the brewer Weill, gratified, "so we know French

already; *"mais c'est épatant, mon cher, épatant,"* he repeated, lightly breathing into his moustache. "It won't be long before you know French better than the President of Switzerland, heh heh, won't he, Prudence?" he demanded of his wife.

"I'm sure he will," whispered Madame Weill, and she said further: "How do you like Switzerland?"

"I like it very much," Felix replied.

"You must be very grateful to your new *maman* and *papa* for letting you come to such a fine home," Madame Weill whispered. While she spoke, she blushed a little and kept her soft, shy eyes modestly lowered on the black-leathered bag in her lap.

"Ah," Monsieur Weill agreed, fingering a long golden watch chain which protruded from his vest, "you must be very happy to be here. Do you know," he inquired politely, "do you know what Felix means? Do you know what your name signifies, heh heh?" he asked.

"No, monsieur," Felix answered.

"Felix," Monsieur Weill said, "means The Happy One! Are you happy, Master Happy One, heh heh?" he demanded humorously, and he patted him awkwardly on the back of his head with his enormous paw.

"But of course he is," cried his new mother, and she took his face between her hands and kissed him on the forehead. "Our Felix is the happiest boy in the world. Oh, and it took him such a dreadfully, dreadfully long time to come to us, we'd completely given him up, didn't we, Felix? You know," she said, and she became quite serious, seemed to ponder something, "Joseph and I should be quite lost without him." For a fraction of an instant it appeared to Felix as though Monsieur and Madame Weill exchanged a glance of understanding, a knowing glance. *"Na, so,"* snorted the brewer Weill, clearing his throat, fingering his watch chain, "better late than never; *'spaet kommt er, doch er kommt,'* as our Schiller says, *'der lange Umweg,'* heh heh heh, *'entschuldige Euer Saeumen,'* " Monsieur Weill recited with great affection and indulgence.

Then they all began to talk very rapidly in French while Felix pretended to busy himself with a book the very title of which meant nothing to him: it was called *The Reflections of a Non-political Man.*

They were talking about him, of course; even if Monsieur Weill had not shaken his head so sympathetically, had not gone "tsk, tsk," quite so often, even if Madame Weill had not stolen quite so many surreptitious glances at him, their conversation contained enough key words to leave no doubt what it was they stuck their heads together about. *"Les nazis . . . juif . . . le pauvre garçon . . . oui, toute la famille . . . tsk, tsk, . . . ah, espèce d'animal . . . Hitlaire . . . en Pologne . . . comme dit notre Schiller . . ."* they whispered, and every so often he caught his own name, whispered more softly and guardedly than any other word. They pronounced it "Froedongreisch."

And then the good, tiny Madame Weill took a large silk handkerchief from her black leather bag and began to rub her long pointed nose with a wonderful display of fervor and intensity, and blew her nose so blatantly and resoundingly that it was astonishing to hear it from such a little woman.

"Ah, they shall pay for it," said Monsieur Weill, relapsing into German and so bringing the conversation back to safe, fundamental topics. "They shall pay for it," he repeated, his black mole quivering with the strength of his convictions.

"I do hope they won't have a mind to come marching into Zurich one fine day," his new mother cried. "We should be quite at their mercy, you know."

"Switzerland," said Monsieur Weill with an air of confidence and mystery, "will never go to war. And do you know," he asked, lowering his voice, "why Switzerland will never go to war, Madame?"

"Oh, I'm sure I don't," cried his new mother. "I'm such a goose when it comes to politics and those things," and she pouted charmingly. "But do tell us, Monsieur Weill; I'm sure you have a very clever reason!"

Monsieur Weill gave them to understand that he had, indeed, a very clever reason: slightly tilting back his perfectly round head, his eyes half closed, archly curling his lips, archly raising his brows, wagging his fleshy forefinger with an air of mischief and conspiracy, "Madame," he said, "Switzerland will never go to war because" (and he paused a second) "because Hitler and Mussolini made a little pact, a private little *entente cordiale,* that they would neither of them invade Switzerland so that, heh heh, they would have a place to spend their vacations after the war! Believe me, Madame," he repeated emphatically, "Switzerland will never go to war!"

But now the tiny Madame Weill raised her body as straight as ever she could; rapping sharply on the buckle of her leather bag, her tiny voice quivering with excitement, she said: "It is in God's hands." Her gaze fell on each of them in turn, admonishing and threatening, while her left eye lost itself ominously in the direction of the glass cabinet in the corner.

"Excuse me, my dear Prudence," said her husband ironically, "it is in the hands of Hitler and Mussolini." And then his hostess, laughing, tinkling, asked Felix what it was he had wanted; he wanted, Felix told her, something to write a letter with.

"A letter?" inquired the brewer Weill. "Ah," he said, playfully wagging his fleshy forefinger, "ah, I'm sure there's a young lady at the back of this letter. *'Erroetend folgt er ihren Spuren,'* as our Schiller says," he added mischievously, winking at his wife, his hostess. "Might one know the name of the young lady?" he asked.

"Benno," Felix answered without batting an eyelash, and he wondered what our Schiller would be disposed to say to that.

"Benno, eh? Heh heh, *touché, mon cher, touché;* the young lady's name is Benno, heh heh," Monsieur Weill cackled indulgently. "And might one know where this Benno lives?"

"Back home," Felix answered.

There was a short silence. "You mean," his new mother asked him softly, stroking his hair, "you mean your Benno is still . . . don't you, Felix? He didn't go away . . . or . . . anything?" she asked carefully and something happened to her smile. Monsieur Weill drummed nervously on the edge of his chair; Madame Weill kept her eyes modestly lowered. "I guess so," Felix said. "He never went away, I don't think."

"And this Benno," his new mother asked him, always stroking his hair with the same gentleness and monotony, absent-mindedness almost, "was he . . . is he then a very good friend of yours?"

Felix nodded.

"Well, then, we must certainly write him a long letter," his new mother cried, once more lively and bewitching, "we must certainly write our Benno a nice long letter; we mustn't disappoint our Benno now, must we, Monsieur Weill, must we, Madame Weill?" she cried, and she took three or four pieces of stationery and an envelope from the bureau drawer.

Monsieur Weill said that they certainly mustn't.

"And now, off you go!" his new mother cried, slapping him on his behind. "Say goodbye to Madame and Monsieur Weill, and off you go to write your letter. We mustn't keep our Benno waiting; I should hope not," she cried.

"I should hope not," the brewer Weill said as he shook hands with Felix. "You must come and play with our little grand-daughter some time," whispered Madame Weill, and she blushed a little, keeping her eyes modestly lowered on her black leather bag.

Felix Freudenreich wrote to his friend Benno Loewensohn:

Dear Benno:

I hope you are in good health. I am well. It is very beautiful here.

I have not seen you over two years. I hope your father and mother are in good health and your sister Olga finally got married to Herr Lobesam even if he is a goy. I hope they have a baby soon and you will be an uncle. I will not be an uncle unfortunately. How is Lehrer Schimmelpfenning and the Stinking Fritz? Did he put any more stink bombs on Lehrer Schimmelpfenning's chair? I hope so. I do not go to school yet because of vacations and I do not understand French. The name of the town where I live is Vevey. It is much smaller than Munich, there are only 9,000 people, 70 per cent Catholics, 25 per cent Protestants and 3 per cent Israelites and 2 per cent nothing, I looked it up. I also have a new father and a new mother but no brother. My new mother is very beautiful and only thirty-two. All the women wear lipstick and paint their faces up, my new father always makes fun of her because of all the lipstick. His name is Joseph like in German only ph instead of f. He is very funny. Yesterday he got mad because the soup was cold, he poured it right back into the tureen, can you imagine that. I can do what I like and it is very nice. There is a lake here, it is called Lac Leman which mean Genfer See, it is much bigger than the Starnberger See and the Ammer See put together. It is 581 sq. km. From my window I can see the mountains, the highest is called Dent du Midi, dent means tooth and also mountain peak, and midi means twelve o'clock noon and also south, so you see it can mean anything. I lost my Kodak. How is your bicycle and the poodle Fifi? We also have a cat, she has no name, they just call her "our cat."

After the word "cat," Felix who had been writing very rapidly and without apparent effort so far, indicated by the insertion of two dashes that he had exhausted this part of his letter and, putting down his pen, wondered what else might interest Benno. For two or three minutes he gazed abstractedly at the window, at the Dunant, noticed abstractedly that a second piece of tape had come loose. And suddenly a very wonderful thought struck him. It was just possible—yes, that was it; how funny he had never thought of it before. He would certainly suggest it to Benno; he would have to choose his words very carefully, of course, would use all his powers of persuasion, and perhaps—

Dear Benno [he continued, writing slowly, deliberately, pausing between each sentence] why don't you come to Vevey? I should be glad if you come here. You can't stay in Munich anyway because you are an Israelite and if you come to Vevey it will be just as good as going to South America or Africa or Mosambik and it is a shorter trip. Munich is only 200 km. from Switzerland, I looked it up, you can take the express to Friedrichshafen and take the ship to Rorschach over the Boden Sea which is very beautiful and 539 sq. km. Switzerland is a very beautiful country, it is the most beautiful country in the world, even Lehrer Schimmelpfenning said so, remember? Your father can also have his brewery here and get rich all over again, I know a man his name is Monsieur Weill, Monsieur means Herr, he is a brewer also, and I shall be glad to ask him about it, maybe he will give your father a partnership. I could tell him your father was the richest brewer in Munich and is a very good businessman, my father always said you have to wake up early in the morning to put one over on that bounder Philip Loewensohn, but please don't tell him. I shall be glad if you come very soon. Also we have a spare room and

I will ask Madame to rent it to you. She is my new mother. Also you will learn French which is much better than what they learn you if you went to South America or Africa. Also Switzerland will never go to war and you know why? Because Hitler and Mussolini made a little pact, a little private ontont kordial that they would leave Switzerland alone and have some place to go for a vacation after the War. I hope they go to Sankt Gallen which is at the other end of Switzerland, about 150 km. from here.

Felix reread what he had written so far and found it, on the whole, very good and to the point. He made one or the other correction, inserted the word "very" in a number of places, and, convinced that his invitation now left no further room for improvement, proceeded to conclude:

Well, dear Benno, that is all I can think of. I shall be glad if you come soon, write me about it when you come so I can ask Monsieur Weill about your father. Also I will be glad to pick you up at the station.

He signed the letter, "Your friend, Felix Freudenreich." Beneath his signature he wrote in parenthesis the words "The Happy One."

He tried to think of anything else he might have forgotten. Finally he added the following postscript: "Don't feel bad about the beating you gave me in front of Berthold Blutharsch, it wasn't so much." And as a crowning afterthought he printed in heavy, bold letters across the top of the first page the sentence:

"Visit Beautiful Switzerland!"

With that Felix neatly folded his letter and was about to seal the envelope when it occurred to him that he might send along one of his fifteen or twenty Dunants. Not, of course, by way of tempting Benno, not as just one more bait (for the Lion of Judah was scarcely one to be swayed by anything so wretched and mean as a drawing, would be more likely to respond to a box of caramels, a bag of whortleberries) but as a symbol of something, a token of something between him and Benno.

He took his collection of Dunants from the drawer, carefully examined each copy in turn, held them up to the light to make sure they were free from grease stains, and, picking out the one he thought the least faulty of the lot, stepped to the window to compare it with the original. At that moment, Felix noticed that a third piece of tape had got loose from the window pane so that Henri Dunant, lopsided and insecure, sustained by the single tape which remained, fluttered more violently than ever in the steadily swelling breeze. The third tape had come loose in evidently the last five or ten minutes; Felix distinctly recalled the two tapes he had noticed as he was writing his letter. . . . Something peculiar struck him, something peculiar and a little frightening. First it merely flashed across his mind, suggested itself quite superficially, on no account to be taken seriously—and in it floated again, penetrated a little more deeply, fastened itself a little more securely—and was trapped. The next moment his whole mind was already filled with his new idea; his whole being was committed to its inviolability and inexorableness. And this was the pact he made: he would count up to one hundred; if, by the time he reached one hundred, the drawing was still hanging in place, Benno would come to him and everything would be fine; but if Dunant fell before Felix reached his mark, then—

He began to count, slowly and deliberately. To make sure he was not cheating, he glanced at the alarm clock on the dresser every so often; whenever he got ahead, he paused until the second hand had caught up with him. 32, 33, 34, he counted. . . . He could hear his heart beat with suspense and fear; he did not remember whether the count was 48 or 58, and, his vision already a little blurred so that he could no longer perceive the second hand from where he stood, he decided that it must have been 48 . . . 48, 49, 50, Felix whispered, 51, 52, 53. . . . But at the count of 92 a gust of wind, more violent than any hitherto, swept into the room; rattling against the window panes, falling, cold and chilling on the boy's cheek, grazing his letter, remorselessly brushing his fifteen or twenty Dunants from the desk, it swept into the room. . . .

The fourth tape came loose without any sound at all. For a second or two, the drawing hovered by the window as though it were very reluctant and sorry to have to relinquish its position after all, clung to the window as though in a last embrace, and then, finally, it fell—to be blown about willy-nilly in the streets below, brushing on the way against some busy citizens, against some soldiers, perhaps, some high dignitaries of the Republic, and, unheeded, and scorned, to take flight at last over the roofs and steeples of the city, and so to vanish over Lake Geneva.

For a while, Felix gazed out of the window; idly, patiently, with an air of preoccupation and a little languor. Outside the air was sultry and heavy, a storm was gathering.

Shortly it would rain; he might even stay by the window until dinner, he thought, and watch the raindrops. . . . From beneath the window came the music of a barrel organ, grinding out, tinny and monotonous, the strains of *Bella Figlia dell' Amore*.

After a while, the emigrant Felix Freudenreich sat down at his desk, but, having lost all interest in Henri Dunant, he did not pick up his pencil again but merely continued to whistle his songs of the three lilies and the mourning grenadiers.

The Cave of Warm Winds

ROBERT DOUGLAS BAMBERG

THE door to the union office opened and Miss Weir entered, returning from her lunch hour late as usual. Without a word she went to the closet, hung her purse on a hook, and began taking off her hat. Both Chick and Jimmy watched her, the silence of the office broken only by the announcer's quiet description of the baseball game. As she straightened her skirt, her thick hands running over her heavy, shapeless body, Jimmy wondered what she had looked like as a young girl. He tried to picture a young girl with heavy warts and thinning black hair and couldn't. Could that be the reason why she never married, he thought; and then he felt slightly sympathetic toward her. He wondered whether she was a virgin, whether she had ever craved male companionship or love. Then she walked toward Jimmy and stood in front of him, her body exuding the pungent odor of perfume, heavily applied.

"Jimmy, your name is mud. You've sure got a lot to learn." Her voice was whining and nasal, and she gestured extravagantly as she spoke.

"What's the matter now?" Jimmy said, feigning surprise.

"McClain's gonna chew you out," she answered. "You know better than to go around telling bosses to go to hell. It took us thirty years to build this union, and you want to tear it down in a day." She sat down next to Jimmy and lit a cigarette, her arm sweeping out wide curves as she extinguished her match. "Oh, if you only knew the work we put into this union. The sweat . . ."

"Look, Miss Weir. The boss wasn't even civil. He insulted me the minute I walked into his office . . ."

Miss Weir interrupted: "Thirty years it took us. Day in, day out. And we worked hard; don't think we didn't. Worked our knuckles to the bone. Chick! Look at Chick. How many times've you been beaten up on picket lines? Tell Jimmy."

Chick, flattered by the attention he was getting, immediately took her side, and looked scornfully at Jimmy. "Thass correct. You punk kids don' know nothin' about this stuff. So you read a book? So you think you know it all."

Jimmy, resigned to the inevitable lecture, reflected that although they were usually at each other's throats, Miss Weir and Chick became comrades in reciting past glories. Chick was rolling his sleeve up in order to display his now familiar scars.

"You see these t'ings? You don' get them reading no books." He gazed at them fondly, and then looked at Hymie for approval.

Hymie looked up from his newspaper. He had been quiet and morose all morning. "Sure. So he's lucky he don't have to get no scars." He turned to Jimmy. "You're goddam lucky, kid. You're lucky you can step into a good, secure job without getting beaned. They hit me on the noggin so much I could never think straight. You study them books all you can. The hell with gettin' beaned. You worry about rakin' in a little dough, an' getting married, and buy a home . . ." His voice trailed off, his bloodshot eyes still trying to focus on Jimmy's face.

[45]

Miss Weir's expression had been annoyed and impatient as Hymie was speaking, but now it reverted to a placid and reminiscent tranquillity. "Yes," she said. "I remember the Young Socialist League parades on Union Square . . . flags waving . . . people marching. . . ." She swung her arms and smiled slightly as she thought of the past. "Nobody stopped us on May Day. They stood on the sidewalks and cheered. Thousands of them." She turned to Jimmy and said mildly, "That's what's the matter with you kids today. You're not idealistic. If you're not idealistic now, you're gonna be a bunch of reactionaries when you're older."

Jimmy tried to return to the subject which had started all this. He was frankly afraid of McClain's wrath. "Look," he said. "This guy fired a man without notice just because he was smoking. Maybe he didn't know he wasn't supposed to smoke. He's a Puerto Rican. He hardly speaks English. Maybe he can't read signs. Anyhow, it's unfair, and when I complained, the boss started to insult me. I told the guy to come here today. . . ."

Miss Weir interrupted him again. "Look, Jimmy. It took us thirty years to build this union. Are you gonna break it down because some Puerto Rican can't read signs and a boss called you names? I've been called names. Me, a woman. But you've gotta be co-operative with the bosses. They've got their troubles with these people nowadays. Oh my! McClain's fit to be tied."

Chick continued: "Yeah, we gotta help these people, but you can't go around busting good relations like that." He snapped his fingers. "We fought wi' that guy for three years before he signed a contract. He had goons, scabs, cops. . . . Jesus Christ, what battles!" He put his hand to his head as he spoke. "You know what he was paying before we signed him? You know what? Six bucks! Six lous' bucks a week. Now, when negotiations for a new contrac' come up, he's a gonna get plen' nasty."

There was a faint knock on the outside door. Miss Weir called out, "Come in." After a long pause, she shouted, "Enter!" The door opened and a black-haired man shuffled in. He was dressed in a dirty, white linen jacket and khaki army-surplus trousers.

[46]

"That's him," whispered Jimmy. "That's the man he fired." The man stood near the door, hesitating. Chick waved him in. "Speeka de Spaneesh?" Chick inquired. The man nodded. Hymie looked up from his paper and stared at him momentarily, then he returned to his reading. "Whatsa for the matter," said Chick, glaring. "Whatsa for you smoke in shop, hah?" He pointed to Miss Weir's cigarette. The man didn't answer, but looked imploringly at Jimmy. Chick continued, "You know you shouldn't smoke in shop?" The man nodded again. "Now you know. Why didn't you know before?"

After a pause, Jimmy said softly to Chick, "Do you think you can fix it with the boss?"

Chick didn't answer. He picked up the phone receiver and dialed. "Hello, Mr. Thomson, this is Chick at the union. Lissen, Mr. Thomson, that man you fired; according to our contract he's gotta get notice. You know how it is, Mr. Thomson." He paused for a while. "Sure, Mr. Thomson, endangering lives, but you know how it is . . . Oh yeah, him. He says he knows better now. Sure, Mr. Thomson; he's new here. Lissen, I'll talk with you tomorrow, private, okay? Sure. So long." He dropped the receiver loudly and turned to the man. "Okay buddy. Back to the shop, but no smoking. Get it? NO SMOKE."

The man smiled slightly and bowed gratefully. Chick waved him out of the office. "Okay, okay. Out. Back to work. Remember, NO SMOKE." Then he looked at Jimmy and said, "Now he's goin' back and blow them all to bits when he smokes again."

Miss Weir stared at the door for a while after the man had left. Then she turned to Hymie and said, "What are you reading the *Daily News* for? Whatta rag . . . Ah, those were some days, Hymie. Remember when Conner was killed in front of Continental? He was a Wobblie before he came East. He knew 'em all . . . Debs, Haywood . . ."

Chick shushed her and turned up the radio as the announcer screamed that the Yankees had scored a run. He smiled at Jimmy and winked, and then leaned back in his chair and tried to capture the full enjoyment of a slight breeze which blew through the office.

[47]

Buried Alive

CLIFF IRVING

THERE was no public announcement to advise the world that he had died. Very few people ever heard about his death, and then only many years after the funeral. However, a good many intimate friends saw him buried, although none of them were at all sure what was happening—in fact, only a few had any idea he might be dead. The remainder of the spectators were casually oblivious to the proceedings and looked on quietly. A thin March rain fell silently on the casket being lowered into the ground. A few words were spoken by someone, not very complimentary to the deceased, then the crowd pulled their wet coat collars close to their necks and went their separate ways, one or two people shivering from the dampness of the dreary afternoon.

For a long, long time, he was only dimly aware of lying in the coffin. Thirty-six inches of hard-packed earth lay above him. Inside, the coffin was very dark, and the only sounds which penetrated his stupor were the rattle of loose pebbles or the shifting of dirt in the stratas of earth surrounding the coffin. He lay like this for perhaps ten years, insensible to his environment, unconscious of anything that took place in the vicinity of the coffin. Then his mind began to clear.

Afterwards he could not remember his immediate reaction to his awakening; it was impossible to reconstruct the sharp surge of thought that burned through his brain. All the channels in his mind that for ten years had been soggy and clogged, were for a brief instant free, and then thought after thought and memory after memory raced through the dusty corridors. He summoned all his strength, and concentrating it heavily upon his eyelids, forced them open. He blinked a few times, trying to accustom his long-unused sight to his surroundings, but the coffin was too dark—he could see nothing.

It was during the rainy season, and some of the moisture had seeped down through the earth and through the tiny chinks in the coffin, so that after a while he became uncomfortably conscious of the cold, damp feeling that tingled along his legs. He lay still, hearing nothing. An awful blanket of silence surrounded him; he made a second great effort of will and drew his fingers to his palms, pressing them tightly into the soft skin. A strange, almost inaudible scream rose in his throat and filled the coffin. The sensation of skin to skin and the grating noise, the first sound he had heard in so long, were too much. The intensity of the moment caused him to black out, and he lay that way for several months.

When he woke again, he exercised great caution and lay quite still and silent for a few days, his eyes calm, staring straight ahead of him at the wall of the coffin. During this period of utter quiet and immobility, his sight gradually became accustomed to the blackness of the narrow interior in which he was interred. He was careful not to move any part of his body before he had thoroughly explored the region of the coffin that lay within his limited vision.

But the long period of sleep had served to soothe his quivering nerves, so that the first movements of his hand were altogether pleasant and titillating to his senses. To his surprise, he found that he could move any part of his body he wished—only a few inches in any direction, of course. He was extremely careful, for his muscles were stiff and tender from their inactivity, and it seemed silly to disturb them so soon after awakening. After testing his hands, feet, and knee joints, he flexed his biceps a few times; satisfied with the result, he turned his attention to his head. The problem here was more difficult. His concentrative power was simply too weak to force loose the binding tension in his neck, and try as he did, he could not move his head. The effort was tiring, and he wisely decided that he had done enough for one attempt. He closed his eyes and lay still again, dozing on and off for at least a week. During the length of this nap, he dreamed that he had forced his head to move, and he awoke feeling refreshed and invigorated. Immediately he began to work his neck back and forth, and to his complete delight found that after a few minutes of strong effort, he was able to twist his head in any direction: forward, to either side, and backward as far as the hard wood floor of the coffin permitted. By extending his toes and straining the arch of his foot, he found that there were about four inches between his feet and the bottom wall of the coffin. A similar investigation revealed the further dimensions of the box. It was quite narrow and it was only with difficulty that he could move his body at all.

Raising his head, he peered down at his body in the semi-darkness. It was not easy to see anything clearly, yet he knew he was fully clothed, just as he had been on the day of the burial. He was wearing black shoes and black socks, a blue serge suit, a starched white shirt and striped tie. With a bitter feeling of nostalgia, he remembered the bright red shirt he had worn in his youth. Strange, in his present predicament, to think of such a thing! He felt the rough edge of his coat, and realized that now all his clothes were tattered and frayed with age. His hand moved along the floor, and came away covered with the dust that had collected there over the years. How horrible the filth was! He shuddered at the thought of lying in dirt and instinctively drew his head away from the wall, laying it once more on the floor of the coffin. He gazed up at the wood planks above him and ran his hand lightly along the cracks between the boards. Then, ever so carefully, he rapped his knuckles against the wood. At first nothing happened, and then he felt something fall softly on his chest. It was a sandy substance which he rubbed between his fingers a few times, then held up to his nostrils. The odor was definitely distinct from the musty smell that hovered inside the coffin. Puzzled, he put it to his lips, and with a start realized that what he was tasting was earth—some soil that had been shaken loose by his tapping and fallen into the coffin. He was plainly disturbed, and for the first time began to wonder how he came to be in this grave, for now he realized that he was surely buried alive.

The problem occupied his mind for the next few weeks; he

spent much time minutely examining the interior of the coffin and speculating as to its position relative to the earth's surface. It was a slow process. At first he was content to lie still and meditate on his predicament, if it was a predicament at all. After all, he decided, his hours now were spent in absolute peace and silence, with nothing to bother him. At first he sincerely doubted if he had been so happy before burial. Lying here in his coffin he was completely free from all earthly care and responsibility. There were no appointments to keep as in real life, no deadlines to meet—no question of success or failure. There were only tranquillity and security. He remembered that these had also been his thoughts at the time immediately preceding his burial; this recollection disturbed him. It had certainly been his purpose to achieve this blissful security he now possessed, but never at the expense of being buried alive! Then how and why had he endured this torture for these ten long years? This was the paradox that now preyed on his mind. He lay uncomfortable in the coffin, twisting and turning about like a mouse caught in a trap. His sleep was a disturbed sleep, and more than once he awoke with a start, conscious that he had been in the midst of a nightmare, shadows of which somehow returned in his waking moments. For the next few weeks he was restless, his mind in a turmoil, struggling with the great question he now contemplated. He found that he could no longer be at ease lying silently in the coffin, inactive. He craved movement, at first only of his limbs and joints, but afterwards, he experienced a growing desire to *think*. It was at this point, fully six months after his original awakening, that he made his decision. He would leave the coffin.

But how? He had lain there for so long that his physical and mental strength must be quite useless. It had been such a habit to rest quietly in the narrow space of the coffin, that the prospect of activity frightened him. He went through a period of rationalization, during which he debated the practicability of attempting an escape, for now he had come to think of himself as imprisoned. It was this increasing mania of considering himself a prisoner that finally moved him to action. During his probings along the roof of the coffin, he had discovered that it was possible to wedge his fingers into the crevices between the boards. He would have to pry loose a board before he could attempt to tunnel through the earth above. After considerable deliberation, he raised his arm and inserted his fingers in the crack. He had calculated wrong, however; it was to be more difficult than he had dreamed, and a painful job to force even his fingertips through the space. A sharp splinter pierced his index finger on the second try, and he withdrew his hand. It was bleeding, the strong wet blood flowed down over his hand, close to the veins. He wanted to cry out at his hurt. This was the crisis—he jammed his hand into the crack, clutching the edge of the board recklessly, pouring his strength into his fingers. The muscles in his hand tensed, and his fingers became steel digits pressing hard against the pine board. When he withdrew his hand again, the skin was scraped clean from the tips of his fingers. The nails were jagged edges, wet with blood. He gasped for breath, taking stock of his progress by gingerly feeling about with the other hand. The board felt as if it had not budged at all, but in the darkness he could not be sure. He tried to sweep the discouragement from his mind, and began the task once more with his bleeding hand.

It was an arduous job, and he relieved the painful monotony by attempting to calculate the distance from the top of the coffin to the surface and the fresh air. But that was impossible to know, and he soon turned his thoughts elsewhere. He wondered if he were buried in a cemetery, if there were other graves like his nearby in the earth. He had puzzled over this same question before he chose to be buried, and he remembered with a jolt that then he had taken great comfort in the belief that he would not be alone in the earth. Now, the idea that he lay in a graveyard, one among many coffins, was sickening to him. Such thoughts drove him on in his tedious work. His fingers pressed and tore relentlessly at the board. He would stay at his labor for a few hours, then rest his battered right hand in the cool grasp of the other hand, stroking it gently with the smooth, unscarred fingers. He wanted the left hand to understand the sacrifice his right hand was making for his body. He was in part breaking a covenant he had made just before his burial, but in the light of his new purpose of freeing himself, the act seemed to him the rectification of a serious mistake.

Finally the board began to creak and loosen—then give way. He wrenched it loose completely on one side, till it hung down as if on a hinge. A shower of earth spilled into the coffin—for a moment he became panicky, fearful lest the earth should flood the interior of the box and suffocate him, but the stream of dirt stopped in a few seconds. He was genuinely elated; in fact, it was the first pure joy he had experienced since his interment. So his efforts were not to go unrewarded! The powerful feeling of achievement that he felt was far beyond the lethargic peace he was used to knowing. He felt he must go on immediately, and he hurriedly began to dig at the firm earth, thrilling to its touch. It was a process of trial and error, but eventually he eliminated all waste motion, scratching with his right hand and at the same time piling the soil on one side of the coffin with his left hand.

He soon realized that this was a far more complicated problem than the removal of the board. For as soon as he would painstakingly claw a section of dirt away and pile it in the coffin, the earth on either side would rush in and fill the gap; thus any progress he made was minute. He began to wonder if it were possible to reach the surface of the earth, and it slowly began to dawn upon him what a terrible mistake he had made in accepting the burial. The weeks and months of his labor lengthened into years, long years of endless digging and scratching, disappointment after disappointment as the earth continually rushed into the passageway to nullify his excruciating labor. He began to occupy his mind solely with thought, and sleep less, devoting whole days on end to the work. He thought about what he would do when he reached the free air above. Memories of his former life above the earth began to trickle back into his mind. He thought of the magnificent, unruly freedom he had exchanged for this unholy interment— what dreams of fame and fortune had been his! Undisciplined, selfish dreams they were—if only he had had faith in himself and allowed them to mature! He was sure now that they would have ripened into some worth-while fruit, but he had been

[53]

afraid, and had chosen instead the grave, and given up his dreams. And what of those who had advised him to do so? How clever they had been, talking smoothly and quickly, telling him what a wonderful, secure future he would have if he listened to them and heeded their advice! He remembered being drawn to them, yet wanting to leap to his feet and tell them they were wrong, they were wrong! had he not felt the weight of centuries upon him. But in the end he had succumbed to their experience. He tried to rationalize his position and declared to himself that he had not known of the burial clause when he agreed to the covenant. But he had known, he had sensed it. He had taken the tragic step and exchanged the conflicts of freedom for the security of burial. If only it were not too late!

His life moved on, and he scratched diligently at the earth, continually probing. He progressed slowly, until after many years of toil his arm reached almost straight up through the passageway he had dug in the earth. He could extend the passage no further than the length of his arm—was all this work to count for nothing? Surely then, something! When his arm straightened at the elbow and could probe no higher, he encountered a stone. His body was tense, exhausted from his labors. His fingers tore wildly at the loose dirt surrounding the stone. Every bit of his energy was concentrated on this final effort. At last the stone dislodged itself, and he grasped it firmly between two bloody fingers and lowered it to his bosom. A gentle breeze flowed down the narrow passageway, and suddenly the atmosphere was sweet with a heady fragrance of clean air. A thin shaft of white light flashed into the dark interior of the coffin, and he was able to see his hands, which he realized with surprise were old and gnarled, and quite incapable of further excavation. In his joy he lay back quietly, anticipating his real death, knowing that he had come as close to salvation and the kingdom of heaven as was possible for him.

Christmas Is a Time for Great Things

IAN ELLIOT

ARTHUR pushed his way through the revolving door into the cold winter air. The wind was blowing east across Rockefeller Plaza. It was certainly much stronger and colder than he had expected, for the first blast left him breathless and numbed. In a few seconds, however, he hurried across the street toward the skating rink.

The bitterness of the day had left the usually crowded lanes around the skating rink bare. Today, only a few people stood watching the skaters even though the city was jammed with crowds doing their pre-Christmas shopping. He stepped close to the railing and looked down into the rink and was surprised to see that it was crowded. Elderly men and women glided smoothly and sedately around the outer edges of the ice; young children stumbled and fell with shouts of laughter; and in the center, the exhibitionists performed, pirouetting and leaping with more courage than grace. Arthur noticed that even in this freezing temperature, the young girls all wore thin sweaters and short skirts. He shuddered slightly as he watched the bare legs flash against the cold ice.

Watching the skaters made him dizzy, and with this dizziness came the realization that he was slightly drunk. He had not noticed this inside at the office Christmas party. There, he had felt only a mellowness. It was true that he had flirted with some of the stenographers and had, perhaps, been just a bit too confidential with a few of the junior employees. Yet, at the time, he had felt all of these actions to be voluntary and controlled. At any time he wished, he could have reverted to his everyday role of junior vice-president. But now, standing in the Plaza and becoming more and more dizzy as he watched the spiraling motions of the skaters, he knew that he was drunker than any man should decently be at three o'clock in the afternoon. He turned away from the rink and began to walk toward Fifth Avenue.

Unlike the Plaza, Fifth Avenue was crowded. Holiday shoppers, their arms heavy with brightly wrapped packages, pushed and bulled their way past him. Little groups of people who, in all probability, were tourists visiting the city for the Christmas week end, walked slowly down the Avenue, looking upward at the tall buildings, stopping and pointing at some landmark to their companions and occasionally holding a small child aloft for a better view. Arthur looked upon them all with benevolence. The dizziness, the first moment of drunkenness of a few minutes ago had passed and in its stead was warmth and happiness. For the first time in many months Arthur felt a sense of charity and love towards his fellow man. As he stood on the corner of 50th Street, he smiled amiably at a small child walking hand in hand with his mother. The child smiled back, and Arthur started across the Avenue.

On the other side of Fifth Avenue, Arthur heard the tinkle of a small bell rising above the traffic sounds. And although he could not remember having spent any of his Christmases in the country, the sound of the little bell seemed to remind him of all the moonlit sleigh rides and all the old-fashioned Christmases he had never seen.

He soon discovered the source of the sound. A dejected little man dressed as Santa Claus stood a few feet in front of Saks ringing a small silver bell. The little man rang the bell slowly, more as if he were tolling for a funeral than a festive occasion. The arm that held the bell was motionless at his side; only his wrist and hand moved. He was a miserable caricature of Santa Claus; the suit he wore was ill-fitting, made of cheap and flimsy material; the beard was stringy and grayish in color; and underneath that beard was a lean and miserable face with miserable eyes that were forever looking above and beyond the heads of the crowd. The face seemed totally unaware of either the people or the spirit of Christmas it was representing. Yet, to Arthur at this moment, the little man was the symbol of all that was good and joyous. He walked up to the man and dropped a dollar bill into the large cauldron that stood beside him. He did not even bother to notice what organization it was to which he was contributing. He smiled at the little man and in a hearty voice wished him a Merry Christmas. The little man did not answer—did not even look at him. The miserable eyes continued to stare at something above Fifth Avenue. Feeling a bit foolish as a result of this rebuff, Arthur turned and began to stroll up Fifth Avenue.

As he passed St. Patrick's Cathedral, he noticed a small crowd standing on the steps. Arthur joined the crowd and found himself staring at a plaque affixed to the wall. The plaque, however, contained only a number of uninteresting names, none of which was familiar to him. He was about to turn away when he heard the notes of the organ. A loudspeaker on the cathedral steps transmitted and amplified the sounds of the great organ inside. The notes were bass notes, long and deep, and from where Arthur stood they drowned out all the other sounds of the city. The notes seemed to flow out over the Avenue and cover the holiday shoppers, the brightly decorated stores with a layer of solemn mysticism. Arthur felt jubilant and, at the same time, proud as he listened to the organ. He felt as if at last his true self were coming to light, a self that for years and years had remained hidden. The feeling was a pleasant one. He stood on the steps, feeling suddenly pure, watching the many people enter into the cathedral. And then, quite impulsively, he entered the cathedral too.

Arthur had been in St. Patrick's only once before. He had gone in with a business acquaintance from another city who had professed a desire to see the inside. Arthur had not been overly impressed at the time; afterward, he had thought of it as being more garish than beautiful. But now it was all different to him—so very different. Here spread out before him in all directions, towering above him and solid beneath his feet, here was the symbol of man's love and devotion to his God. The genius of the artist, the rich man's power, the poor man's toil— all had been brought together in this monument. It was a commemoration to the goodness of the Almighty. Arthur stood in the rear of the cathedral and bowed his head in humility. He wished he could have this feeling when he was sober.

The interior was crowded. Some people were in the pews or before the side altars kneeling in prayer; others, like Arthur, gazed wide-eyed about them. He walked down the side of the cathedral, down past the altars of the saints, down past the many candles flickering in colored jars. He stood long before the altar of St. Therese watching a young man and his wife— the woman held a small child in her arms—kneel before the altar. Even the baby seemed to be affected by the surroundings, for it returned his gaze soberly, almost gravely. He walked behind and around the great altar in the front of the cathedral. He looked at the bas-reliefs illustrating the Stations of the Cross. Arthur found himself greatly moved by the relief of Christ falling beneath the cross for the second time. He saw himself, no longer a junior vice-president of an insurance firm, but now a citizen of Jerusalem on that fateful Friday. He saw himself helping Christ to His feet, attempting to shoulder the cross for his Master, and finally being beaten into submission by a number of Roman soldiers.

As he stood there, a second attack of dizziness reminded him of the many cocktails he had taken at the office party. But it was only a momentary reminder, for the dizziness passed as soon as he turned and began to walk up the aisle again.

Halfway up the aisle he saw the woman, little and gnome-like, wispy gray hair floating about her head, her face wrinkled and strange, filled with something Arthur could not understand, something he had never before seen in the face of anyone. The woman was moving down the aisle slowly and with great difficulty. Her right leg dragged as she walked and, to balance this, her left shoulder was pushed far out in advance of the other shoulder. Arthur noticed that the people around her tried to avert their gaze from the old woman's struggles.

Arthur felt sorry for this woman, sorrier, it seemed, than he had ever felt before. He admired her braveness and the fact that she had not become too bitter to pray. He felt like crying, or saying to the woman that it was all right, that there was eventual justice in life. The struggling old woman, the crowds behind her, and the cathedral itself suddenly seemed to go out of focus, for his mouth and nose became filled with alcoholic fumes.

Later, in trying to recall the ensuing incident, Arthur could remember nothing in clear detail. He remembered what he had done, but it was all in the vague, misty way of a dream. Things did not become sharp and vivid again until after the incident. He did remember, though, that as the organ began to play more loudly and in a rising harmonic scale, he had walked toward the old woman with words of consolation on his lips. It had seemed the only thing to do. He also remembered that the words were dry and useless. He gestured to the woman's twisted shoulder and then to her dragging leg. The woman stared at him, the strangeness in her face intensified. She looked into Arthur's eyes as if to ask a question and then, twisting her head around, peered at her shoulder and then her leg.

Arthur felt that the woman did not understand and spoke again to her. Here again, his memory failed him, for he could not remember exactly what he said. It was something like "Have faith" or "God be with you"—something, at any rate, completely alien to his normal self and rather inane.

Then it was done. The eyes of the old woman widened until all of the wrinkles at the corners disappeared. Arthur stood quite still, meeting her gaze with silence. The woman's lips began to tremble; she seemed about to speak for the first time. Then the emotion of the scene swept into Arthur's mind with a rush, cleansing it of all dizziness and drunkenness. Suddenly sober, he looked about him and saw that crowds of people were standing and watching him. He realized that they must be regarding him as the world's worst fool and, before the old woman could speak, he turned and hurried up the aisle to the front entrance of the cathedral. When he was about five steps from the door, he heard the old woman's voice behind him.

Arthur could not understand what the woman was saying. She laughed and cried forth with high animal-like sounds. He turned and saw with astonishment that the woman was running toward him. She did not drag her leg behind her, nor did her shoulder bend forward. It was as if the paralysis, or whatever it was the woman had been afflicted with, had never existed. Arthur looked wildly about him and noticed that an elderly Italian woman dressed in black was staring at him. Their eyes met and the Italian woman started back involuntarily. Then she dropped the rosary she was holding, hurriedly made the sign of the cross, and fell to her knees. Arthur felt a sudden panic at what he had done. For an instant he felt a complete confusion fall over him and then, seeking the safety of the streets, he rushed through the door of the cathedral.

The next day was Christmas Eve and a Saturday. He lay in bed for a long time after awakening and listened to the cleaning sounds his wife made in preparation for the cocktail party she had planned for that afternoon. He tried not to think of the incident in the cathedral, yet his thoughts continually turned back to it. Time and time again he saw the old woman running toward him, heard the clatter of the rosary as it dropped to the marble floor. Finally, he could stand it no longer. He got up, dressed, and went down to the corner for the morning newspapers.

He did not open the papers—he had bought them all—until he got back to the apartment. Then, with a cup of coffee and a cigarette, he cautiously opened the *Times*. He had to hunt for the article, but it was there tucked in on page 5; the *Herald Tribune* had not even thought it that important and had placed it on page 9. Both accounts tended to minimize the whole incident by treating the woman as a harmless crank, the victim of hysteria. The tabloids, however, found the incident far more newsworthy. Both the *News* and the *Mirror* had played it up for all it was worth; both papers had featured it on page 3 under screaming black headlines (or so they seemed to Arthur).

From what he could gather from the stories, the "miracle" (as it was referred to by the tabloids) had taken place in front of a score of witnesses. Had the woman been alone she would most likely have been brushed off as either a crank or a publicity hound. But it had all taken place in a crowded cathedral. There were witnesses who had seen the whole incident, from the entrance of the old woman to the exit of Arthur. There were even witnesses, unfortunately enough, who knew the old woman, a widow who lived alone in some West Side tenement, and who could testify that she actually was a paralytic and had been one for the past five years. The woman, it seemed, had made quite a scene after the incident, at one point becoming quite hysterical and insisting that she had been visited by Christ Himself. She, along with a few of the spectators, had managed to magnify the incident beyond all normal proportions. When interviewed, all these people had different descriptions of Arthur. He read of himself as being "a man of mystery," "a tall dark man with fiery eyes," and "a spiritual-looking man who vanished into thin air." The *News* even quoted one woman as saying she had observed a faint halo glowing around the man's head.

Arthur began to help his wife clean the apartment for the cocktail party that afternoon. He did so in the hope that he might be able to forget the questions that had been nagging him all day. For the same reason he rather looked forward to the party. Anything, so long as he did not have to think about the incident. His wife, busy with the dusting and the preparing of hors d'oeuvres, did not notice his silence, although he thought that she glanced strangely at him once or twice. Arthur did not want to tell his wife what had happened. It would involve too much discussion—discussion he was not prepared to face at the moment.

All in all, he was glad to see the first of his guests arrive at four o'clock. His duties as a host kept him on the move and restricted his conversation to only the politest of pleasantries. It was not until five o'clock that he had a chance really to join the party, and by that time he had taken enough cocktails to feel mellow again. He was standing in a corner with Myra, his wife, Sam Winthrop, a fellow executive in the insurance office, and a woman whose name he did not know, when they began to speak of the cathedral incident.

"Say," Sam said, "did you see about that thing that happened in St. Patrick's yesterday?" Sam was looking straight at Arthur.

"No," Arthur said.

Myra looked at him. "Of course you did, Art," she said. "I saw you reading about it at breakfast today."

"Oh that? I was thinking about something else. Yes, I saw it."

"What do you think about it?" Sam asked.

Arthur was feeling wary now. "I haven't been thinking about it at all. I don't know anything about it," he said. He would have liked to leave, but the three people seemed to be crowding around him.

"Sam means, dear," Myra said, "do you think that an actual miracle occurred?"

"I personally think," Sam said, "that the age of miracles is definitely past. How about that, Art?"

"I tell you I don't know anything about it," he said.

The woman whose name Arthur did not know was speaking now: "But you've got to know whether or not it was actually a miracle. I really don't see how you can have no opinion on a thing like that." Arthur saw that the woman was slightly drunk.

It was Myra who rushed to his defense. "The poor boy has been ordered around by me all day. He hasn't had a chance to think about anything much." She kept looking at Arthur as she spoke.

"Well, it's time he started thinking now," the woman said. "Don't be shy with us now. Do you really think that the woman was a paralytic?"

Arthur saw that she intended to question him until she got what she considered a suitable answer. "No," he said. "I don't. I think she was suffering from hysteria."

"Then why did the man, whoever he was, make all that hocus-pocus?" Sam asked.

"He was probably a drunk who didn't know any better."

"It sounds pretty fishy to me," Myra said. "It sounds just a bit too pat."

"Maybe it was all a publicity stunt," Sam said. "Are they showing any miracle plays in town?" He began to laugh at this.

"No," the other woman said. "I think it's the real thing, an honest-to-God miracle. I actually think it happened." She took a large gulp from her cocktail.

"Nonsense," Arthur said. "Those things don't happen."

"They do happen. They happen every day. Look at Lourdes or whatever it is."

"Don't be a fool," Arthur said angrily.

"I'm not being a fool," the woman said. Her voice was beginning to sound angry too. "I'm not being a fool. What would you know about miracles anyway? How do you know what it's like to be a saint?"

"I'll tell you what it's like," Arthur said. "You're too drunk to remember what I'm saying, but I'll tell you anyway." He heard both Myra and Sam gasp in astonishment at his words. He realized he was speaking too sharply, but it was too late to turn back now. "This is what it's like," he continued. "It means you can't figure out who you are. It means you can't live a human life. You cease being John Smith or whoever you are and become something else. You lose your identity completely. You don't exist. That's what it means. It's a mess, and you can't trust anybody." Arthur brushed past the three people who were standing dumbfounded in front of him and went into the kitchen. He poured himself a cocktail from the shaker standing on the kitchen table.

Myra came out almost immediately afterward. She was frowning, but it was a frown of worry rather than anger. She came up to him. "Art, honey," she said, "what's wrong?"

"Nothing," he said.

"Yes, there is. You've been acting differently ever since you came back from work yesterday. Has anything happened at the office?"

"No," he said.

"I didn't think so. Sam would have said something if there had. What is it then?"

"If I tell you, promise you'll keep it a secret." She nodded once. "Supposing I were to tell you that I was the man they were talking about in there? The man in the cathedral. And now I don't know. I don't know whether that woman was hysterical or whether I've done something. I'm confused about it all."

Myra looked at him and said, "Don't be silly, Art. Talk some sense. What would you be doing in St. Patrick's Cathedral?"

"I was drunk."

"You were perfectly sober when you came home yesterday afternoon. I think you're drunk now though." For a long moment she looked silently at him. "You weren't in that cathedral, were you?"

He turned his head away and stared at the half-filled cocktail glass in his hand. "No," he answered finally.

"Well then, what's wrong?" Myra said. "Why did you blow up like that in there? She was just a little high, that's all."

"I'm lonely," he said.

Myra gestured with annoyance. "Art, for God's sake talk some sense. How could you be lonely in an apartment filled with people?"

"It's a different kind of loneliness. It's in here." He patted his chest.

"Well, when you sober up a little and get rid of your loneliness"—she spoke the last word contemptuously—"I want you to come inside and apologize to Sam and that woman. I'll hold them off until you come in." She turned on her heel and swept into the crowded living room again.

Arthur finished what was left of the cocktail and then looked at the empty glass in his hand. Then he reached for the shaker and poured himself another. He would need at least one more drink before he went inside to face the woman again. Why had all this ever had to happen to him anyway?

Open Season

DAVID LYLE

"IS THAT it?" I said.

"Is that what?" Gus was pretty tired.

"White Forks."

"Sure it's White Forks, Stupid. You think we'd hit Denver already?"

"No, no, but it's pretty small though." I just felt like talking, like you get after eight hours on the road listening to an engine so loud you can't talk. We were going to lay over till morning at White Forks, before going on over Berthoud Pass to Denver for the load of septic tanks.

"What in hell did you expect? Jesus Christ!"

"I was just talkin', Gus."

"Talk to yourself if you got nothin' to say."

"All right."

"I'm tired."

"O.K., Gus."

I knew Gus would be all right after he got a beer in him. He must have been tired. He had that six-wheeler down to the floor and it sounded like we were dragging rubbish cans. Gus wouldn't have done that if he wasn't tired. He was good to an engine, but that army dump job wasn't ever meant for hauling over Berthoud or Rabbit Ears or any other pass. I was worried about it, bringing the tanks back over the pass tomorrow. You can't pile three-foot cement tanks on top of each other forever, and I didn't want to be half-way down that pass tomorrow and coming around one of those hairpins with the edge six feet away and have that load start to rock up in back of us. Not me. Gus chained a load so it never came off and once she started to rock the whole thing would go. I've seen lumber trucks that way, top-heavy on a mountain road, start rocking and then end over end down the side. You can't load for a mountain haul like you do on the flat.

"Think she'll come back over the pass tomorrow?" I said.

"She'll come all right."

"That down grade's gonna be worse than hauling up." I was worried about not having any brakes to speak of and carrying an overload too.

"She'll come all right."

"There's a lot o' cement in them tanks."

"Don't worry about it. You aren't driving."

"I know," I said. But it don't make any difference who's driving if you go over the side. "You know who's gonna put them tanks in when we get back, don't you?"

"All right, so we dig ditches for a week. It's a job, isn't it? I got you a job, didn't I?"

"Sure, Gus. I didn't mean that." I guess he was pretty tired.

"Dude's gotta take a crap, you got a job. Relax."

I saw the lights of the town coming up on both sides of us from the houses on the outskirts, low white clapboard shacks with a lot of rusty junk in the front yards—cut down truck bodies with a lot of power they use to get around in winter, a couple of half-track tanks that somebody got surplus from the army to run over the snow, and a lot of beat-up fenders and hoods off old cars stacked up and rusting.

"Well, we're here," I said.

Gus didn't answer and he had us half-way through White Forks before he ground the truck downgears fast till the engine screamed so loud you couldn't hear and he pulled off down a side street next to Hank's Nugget Bar and Restaurant. It was quiet on a Monday night.

There weren't many lights on around the town. They shut up early during the week except for a few places like the Nugget that stays open for traffic along the road. Everybody goes to bed at nine o'clock, not like the city.

We got out stretching and walked over to the Nugget. I felt dirty like I'd had bugs on me and I wanted that beer to wash them out of my mouth. I knew Gus'd be better once he had one. Inside, the place was empty except for the barkeep sitting on a wire chair down at the end of the bar reading the *Rocky Mountain News* with his feet up on an empty nail keg. He had high-heel boots and levis. All the barkeeps do out there.

"Two Coors," I said, surprised at the sound of my own voice so loud after the engine noise.

"Make 'em cold," said Gus.

The barkeep dropped his paper on the floor so it landed all spread out and messed up and went to get us the beer. "You boys come outta Laramie today?" He put wet glasses on the bar. "I seen your plates when you drove up."

"Cheyenne," I said. "We came down from Cheyenne this afternoon."

[66]

"Goin' over the pass tonight?"

"Depends on how we feel."

"Bad night for the pass. It'll rain later."

"Looks like it might later on."

I looked down into my glass so he wouldn't ask any more questions. When I heard his boots click going down to the other end of the bar, I went over to the juke box and put a quarter in it and pressed the first five keys. The place was too quiet and you could hear the barkeep chewing pretzels clear across the room in his wire chair. "Red River Valley" was the first song that came up and it made the place seem a little better, the music.

I got my beer and went back by the juke box to look out the window and see if there were any stars. I didn't want to sleep in the bed of the truck if it was going to rain. It's bad enough sleeping there in good weather with those rivets poking up and hitting you in the back like pebbles only without the sand between them. There weren't any stars.

I guess I must have stood there by the window quite a while. When I looked around Gus had two empties by his glass and he'd gone around behind the bar to get another. I hollered at him to get two and went over to put another quarter in the box. The barkeep didn't pay any attention to Gus getting the beers and just went on reading the paper.

"How'd you like to be in Denver tonight?" Gus said when I came up to the bar.

"All right," I said.

"How about one of those?"

Gus pointed to a calendar hanging back up above the whiskey bottles that had a picture of a hot little number bent over teasing-like and holding a big sombrero over the part of her that should have had a dress on. She had her head to one side and looked surprised.

"Not bad," I said.

"Like to have us a couple o' them señoritas they got down to Denver," said Gus.

"We'll get us a couple sometime."

"I got a knife I took off one of 'em still. Oh, they're hot little

[67]

bitches. Sharp as a razor that knife is, all silver plate. Has one o' them blades that pops out when you push a little button. Little bitches." Gus shook his head.

"I'll take 'em without the pig-stickers," I said.

"You'd take 'em any way once you had one."

"You'd have to prove it to me."

"Nothing like 'em once you had one. A good one."

"What do you mean, 'a good one'?"

"You know, hot tamale. Young ones, raised on pepper and tequila."

"I don't like 'em so hot they carry knives."

"Oh, they stick to you like a burr once they like you, but just don't look at her sister. Oh Jesus! Don't do that! You'll be picking splinters out of your head for a month."

"That how you got the knife?"

"That's how I got the knife."

That Gus was a good boy. He'd worked through twenty-three states when I tied up with him in Kansas City, never a bum, always had a job or a deal someplace. "Anything with an engine," he said, "I can run it." And he did. Nobody ever told that boy what to do, he was all right, and he got me a job like he said he would when we were in Kansas City. I didn't have any kick, hell no.

The front door of the bar banged open and I looked around to see who was coming in. Gus didn't turn around but I saw his eyes look up to the mirror across the bar so he could see when they walked behind him. It was two greasers that came in the door banging it open and talking loud in Mexican so I could see they were already drunk. Both of them were short, dark young guys, probably about as old as me but it's hard to tell with Mexicans. They stomped down to the other end of the bar still talking and with their shoes sounding loud on the bare floor. There were khaki pants tucked into the tops of their combat boots and one of them wore a yellow T-shirt that showed the thick muscle on his arm.

The greaser with the yellow T-shirt yelled at the barkeep to get them two doubles of I. W. Harper and the other one pounded the bar once with his fist, smiling at the barkeep. He went to get the double shots for them and one of them reached into his pocket and pulled out three or four crumpled ones and laid them on the counter. When the barkeep finished pouring out their shots he took two of the bills and came down to where we were at the other end of the bar.

"Couple more for you boys?" he said.

"Yeah," said Gus.

"Here's for the others," I said and handed him a five.

. The barkeep got us two Coors and wiped up the bar in front of us before he put them down.

"If them greasers make too much noise just let me know," he said looking at Gus like it was a secret they had.

"Damn lot o' trouble, those greasers," said Gus. "They oughta keep 'em to hell back where they belong in Mexico 'stead o' lettin' 'em take all the field labor jobs so nobody else can get one. They'll work for dirt."

The barkeep looked down at the two Mexicans to see if they were listening and then turned back to Gus. "You gotta keep 'em in their place all right, else they'd be tearin' up all the towns and rapin' the women all over the place. You gotta keep 'em in their place. Gang of 'em got a couple of our boys down by the freight yards the other night but they'll get theirs. We don't take much o' that from them."

"Rolled 'em?" said Gus.

"Rolled 'em, cut 'em up, took all their clothes, damn near killed 'em. They'll get it back though. Our boys don't take much o' that sort o' stuff."

"I bet they don't," said Gus.

"You can bet your last damn dollar on it. You know what they say about 'em out here?"

"What's that?"

"Deer, elk and bear season lasts two weeks, rabbits four months, and Mexicans, open season."

"That's pretty good."

"That's the way it should be."

"Damn right."

"They oughta put it on the statutes."

At the other end of the bar the Mexican in the yellow T-shirt raised his arm and showed two fingers.

"*Hola, amigo! Dos por dos,*" he said, smiling at the barkeep.

The other one turned toward us and smiled too, and the barkeep went down to the other end to get them their double shots. He took the rest of the money on the bar and the two greasers downed the shots as soon as he put them on the bar and called for two more.

"*Dinero, dinero,*" said the barkeep. "Money first, then whiskey."

The two greasers smiled like they were happy that he'd asked and reached for their wallets.

"*Mucho dinero,*" said the one in the yellow T-shirt, "plenty money. Bring the bottle, bring the whole bar. We got plenty money."

Both of them were smiling. Greasers always smile. The one in the yellow T-shirt turned toward us.

"*Ey, Americano!* You want a drink? We buy you drinks! Plenty money, plenty whiskey. Sure you want a drink, *ey Americano?*"

I started to say I wanted a drink but Gus nudged me in the ribs and shook his head at the two Mexicans.

"No thanks," said Gus, looking down at them and not smiling while they grinned at him.

"Sure you want a drink. Look! Plenty money! *Mucho dinero.* Look, *Americano!*"

"No," said Gus. He still wasn't smiling, and they were smiling at him very friendly.

After Gus said no the second time the two greasers shrugged to show they didn't care and took out their wallets. The barkeep was still standing across the bar from them waiting for the money, and they both pulled out big wads and started to count the bills. I just stood there and looked and the barkeep and Gus looked too. The one in the yellow T-shirt pulled a fifty first and then the rest were mostly tens and twenties that made better than three hundred bills from what I saw. The other one had a roll just as big.

"Holy Jesus!" said Gus into my ear, hardly moving his lips.

"Christ what a roll," I said. It was the biggest roll I'd ever seen.

"They must o' been layin' track for months to get a wad like that. Holy Jesus! Did you see it. Holy Jesus!"

The barkeep looked up toward us from where he was in front of the two Mexicans counting their bills and rolled his eyes. They put the big bills back in their wallets.

"Now we get whiskey?" said the one in the yellow T-shirt. He was still smiling. He had a pile of ones in his hand and he tossed them onto the bar. Two or three went clear across and landed on the floor by the barkeep's feet. "Whiskey now?" he said again. Then he laughed and hit the bar once with his fist looking at the barkeep. He turned toward us again.

"Come on, *Americano!* Drink with us!"

Gus shook his head and turned away. I didn't know what was the matter with him. I sure wanted any free whiskey anybody would give me, but I guessed he had a reason.

When the barkeep put the bottle down on the bar for them, I saw him lay his arm down across some bills on the edge and brush them off on the floor after he'd set the bottle down. It looked like a mistake and the greasers were too drunk to notice, but it wasn't a mistake because I saw him kick them under the counter with the others that had fallen. Then he counted out the money for the bottle from the rest of the ones on the bar. He winked at us after he kicked the bills under the bar to hide them and brought two beers down.

"On the house, boys."

Gus thanked him.

"If they're botherin' you, just let me know," he said and winked again at Gus. "Open season, boys." He smiled at Gus as if they had another secret.

"Those two come from around here?" Gus asked him.

"Never seen 'em before. They aren't local. I know all the locals."

"Must've laid track a long time for that money."

"Probably just off one o' the road gangs. They'll blow it all in a week. Damn greasers. Shouldn't pay 'em at all. They don't know what to do with it. Blow it all in a week, that's why they don't get nowhere. Buy all kinds o' silver knives and buckles and junk till they're broke and gotta go to work again."

"I'd know what to do with it," said Gus.

"Sure you would," said the barkeep. "But they don't."

"How about some o' them señoritas in Denver?" I said to Gus and winked.

"We'd know what to do with it sure as hell." Gus was grinning.

"You know what I said boys, open season."

"Tell 'em they gotta leave."

The barkeep didn't say anything and looked at him till Gus folded a ten and put it under a beer bottle.

"Worth more than that, ain't it?"

"The hell you say," said Gus. But he put down another ten.

"I'm the blindest guy that ever lived when it comes to greasers." The barkeep slid the two tens out from under the bottle. "Blind as a bat."

Gus smiled at him and the barkeep went down and told the Mexicans to get out.

"You think it's a good idea?" I said to Gus.

"What the hell do you mean? Sure it's a good idea."

"That barkeep might talk."

"He's got his."

"Well, they might see us or they might o' seen the license on our truck or something." I had never rolled a guy before and I didn't want to get picked up for it.

"Hell, they're blind and we'll never see this town again."

"We gotta come back through tomorrow with the tanks."

"We'll take another road."

"What if somebody in town sees us?"

"Jesus, do you want the money or not?"

"Sure, Gus. Only I just don't want to get picked up."

"Take it easy, nobody'll see us; and if they did they wouldn't say anything."

The two greasers were giving the barkeep a hard time and saying their money was as good as anybody's. They didn't want to go and they argued with the barkeep till finally they picked up the bottle and started to go out.

"Pay for that bottle before you go," said the barkeep.

"We already pay," said the one in the yellow T-shirt.

"The hell you did. Pay now."

"We already pay. Sure we pay." The greaser wasn't smiling now.

"Pay now or I'll get the sheriff."

"We already pay." He looked at Gus. "You see we pay?"

"I didn't see you," said Gus.

"I'll get the sheriff and you'll go back to Mexico. Pay now." That barkeep was smart.

The one in the yellow T-shirt looked at the other greaser and didn't say anything. Then he turned back to the barkeep.

"How much money?" he asked.

"Ten bucks." That barkeep was smart.

The greaser put it on the counter and walked out with the other one. Neither of them said anything. When they walked past the window outside, Gus and I went out too.

They walked slow down the side street where the truck was parked, stopping every little way to take a pull at the bottle they had. After they had about three pulls on the bottle, they started to talk loud in Mexican. I guess they were talking about the barkeep. He was a smart one, that barkeep.

All the way down the street I kept an eye out to see nobody was around. We kept a good distance behind them, but they weren't looking back, so it was all right. I didn't see anybody in the street.

"Think it's gonna be O.K., Gus?" I said.

"Oh, for Christ's sake, shut up!" He was tensed up, I guess.

"I just don't want to take any chances."

Gus didn't answer.

When we could see the freight yards coming up at the end of the street, Gus walked faster and we got in closer behind them, so we were about a hundred feet away. I was scared about getting too close so they'd see us but I didn't say anything. Then we came to the boardwalk that ran along in front of the stores, and there was the first track of the freight yards. The Mexicans kept on going slow ahead of us and stopped to take another pull at the bottle by a couple of empty tank cars before they turned down a track between two lines of cars.

"Where'll we get 'em?" I said to Gus.

"Come on." Gus and I turned down another track that ran beside theirs about three tracks away, only with freight cars between so they couldn't see. The rocks in the roadbed rattled when I walked and I was scared they'd hear us. It was dark as a coal pit except for a green light way down the line and I could feel the rain starting. A couple of drops hit me in the face. They were cold.

We ran down the track about two hundred yards, then turned across and went over behind a refrigerator car that was standing in the line next to the track the two greasers were coming down. Gus stepped across the coupling and I came after him. Both of us picked up rocks.

"Step out the same time I do and shut yours up the first time you hit him," said Gus.

"O.K., Gus," I said. I was scared about hitting him too hard and killing him, or not hitting him hard enough and having him start to yell so the switchman or somebody might hear. It was no picnic for me. I'd never rolled a guy before and I wanted to be damn sure I didn't get caught at it. The rain was coming down harder and colder.

The two greasers walked by in front of us going along slow and Gus waited till they were about ten feet past us before he stepped out from the shadow where we stood between the two cars. I stepped out with him and hit mine solid on the back of the head. The rock sounded funny on his head, and he went down all sprawled out on his face. Gus got the other greaser just the same place, and he was sprawled out too with the yellow T-shirt showing light against the roadbed. Then I emptied his wallet.

"Got his money?" said Gus.

"Yeah," I said. I was counting mine.

"You take it all?"

"Yeah."

"Put five back."

"What the hell for?"

"Never mind. Put five back."

"Did you?"

"Yes. Put five back."

"All right, Gus." I put five back in the greaser's wallet and stuffed it into his pocket. They were both still out cold.

"Let's get out of here," Gus said.

We went back to the truck to split the money, and I looked around all the way to see if there was anybody around. I was still a little scared somebody might see us or the greasers would come to and begin yelling.

The rain was coming hard now and I was wet when we got to the truck. Gus started the engine and put it on the road, headed for Denver. After we got out of town I felt pretty good about it, having that money in my pocket, but I was a little scared about going over Berthoud Pass on a rainy night, our brakes the way they were.

Over There

WILL WHITE

HE SAT cross-legged on the wide top bar of the roadblock, with his carbine across his hips. It was a good strong roadblock; even a tank couldn't have crashed through it. He had supervised its construction, and it was built strictly according to regulations, even a little stronger, just to be on the safe side. The three crossbars were of heavy timbers a little bigger all around than railroad ties, and these were supported on either end between piles of the same size timbers sunk deep into the ground.

He sat cross-legged on the top bar, with his left knee projecting over the road of the other country and his right knee projecting over the road of his own country. His arms were folded in his lap, resting on the carbine, which he kept cocked to fire semiautomatically. Strictly against regulations that was, but sometimes one had to hedge a little for one's own good. He had heard too many stories about border guards who had accidentally fired their carbines (regulations insisted that carbines be carried at all times) and sprayed lead all over the place before they could release the trigger. It was so easy to catch the trigger on something when the carbine was slung over one's back and one was trying to change the tire on some bigwig's car, or when one was struggling to remove the road-block bars. At semiautomatic only one bullet would go off. One had to take some regulations with a grain of salt.

Few cars ever came down the road to the barricade, and fewer could be allowed to pass into the other country. Travelers on foot were more frequent, but the bars did not have to be removed for them, and few of them had authorization to get through, so that even if the bars were lowered for them the work would be light. As it was, the bars seldom had to be lowered more than once a week.

Actually there was no physical necessity for removing the bars at all; as far as the eye could see the terrain was flat, hard-packed earth. A car could easily drive off the road, around the barricade, and back on the road again.

He was almost facing his pillbox as he sat on the top bar, and he liked to look at it affectionately now and then. It was in the shape of a squashed-down hemisphere, and the only entrance was almost completely below ground level, reached by steps leading down from the road. Two howitzer muzzles projected from either side, commanding the road in both directions. That meant that two howitzers were forever trained on the other country's road, something that the other country would have objected to, one would think. But no one lived in it, as far as the ordinary man could tell. The whole country was, by report, the same flat, packed earth, and it was hard to conceive of any life existing in it, much less wanting to live in it. But one never admitted this out loud; it was just the sort of thing one didn't admit. It would be unpatriotic.

It would be doubting one of the precepts that the form of his government was built upon. The country on his left was his country's best ally. The relationship between the two had been one of perfect harmony for centuries. The praises of this peace-loving ally were continually being sung in the press and over the airwaves; the close, friendly interdependence of the two nations was the pride of his country's diplomatic corps. Friendly relations must be preserved at all costs, both between the nations as nations and between the individual citizens of the nations.

As a means of increasing this harmony between the citizens of the two countries, the government encouraged travel "over there," and implied that it was the patriotic duty of each citizen to make a good-will tour of the neighbor state. The government always referred to the country as "our ally" or "over there." It had started this policy right after the final peace had been settled, long ago. To call their ally by name would have been too formal; the policy for years had been to keep relations on an intimate basis. People had almost forgotten the real name. Some thought it was one name, and others thought they remembered their fathers calling it something else. But whenever conversation lagged, one could always talk about one's plans for taking a trip over there, if one could find the time or save up the money. It was as conventional a gap-filler as talking about the weather.

But the government, to insure that undesirable elements did not go over there and create friction, had set up a complicated procedure for obtaining travel permission, visas, etc. The applicant's past life was minutely examined, and it was seldom that an applicant was found with a background spotless enough to make him a desirable representative of the nation, for most of the applicants were rich. And even if an applicant received clearance papers, he had to be held at the roadblock until final clearance was received by telephone. This meant a wait of several days while the government checked through its files, and by that time the visa had usually expired, or the traveler had to return to his job. Moreover, there were no accommodations for them while they waited. It was no wonder that no traveler had ever passed through the roadblock since he had been guard. But of course the government couldn't be too careful, it couldn't take the chance of having some thoughtless tourist create bad will. So the only time he had ever removed the crossbars was for the weekly diplomatic mission.

The mission arrived in a convoy of official cars and trucks just before dark every Monday. The procedure was minutely outlined in the regulations, and had never varied, as far as he knew. Every car and truck, no matter how high the official in it, had to be completely unloaded and inspected. He had to describe the convoy over the phone in detail, and receive clearance. Then, with the help of some of the drivers, he slid the three bars back, and the convoy passed through. He would watch them drive down the road over there until they disappeared in the darkness, and then, after turning on the twenty-mile alarm system, he would go to bed. Just before daybreak the next morning, the alarm would go off, and by the time he had dressed and swallowed a cup of coffee and gone outside, the convoy would have returned, and would be waiting at the roadblock. The same procedure had to be followed before he could slide back the bars again.

Aside from turning away the infrequent travelers, and making out a daily report to phone in, this weekly passing of the mission was his only work. Most of the travelers came because the publicity given to over there had fired their imaginations; they knew nothing of the regulations. A few had their papers in order, but the telephone clearance had never yet seemed to come through in time. It had always come through, but always, so far, too late. So that a good deal of the time, except when there were travelers there waiting for clearance, he was alone. On good days he would sun himself on the top bar, and on bad he would squat in the door of his pillbox. It was a comfortable job, with just the right amount of prescribed responsibility. Although he was a comparative newcomer—he had only been border guard for six years—he felt sure he would not get tired of the life. And when he retired in another thirty-four years and returned to the populated part of his country, he would be almost as much a hero as if he had actually made a trip over there.

But his job was not the mainspring of his life. It was a task, even though a pleasant one, which entitled him to sit in the sun and watch over the bare, packed earth from his vantage point on top of the roadblock. The earth stretched flat all around to the horizon, and he and his pillbox and his roadblock were the center. As such his life was in constant fulfillment. He did not think great thoughts, or revel in a sense of power; he was just there, the center, and his contentment was in being. Time was not a dead weight, nor was it nonexistent; his sense of being came from watching time. He watched it in many ways. There was the majestic arch of the sun, of course. But there was also the constant expansion and contraction of the horizon, and a definite sense of the land rotating about him. Time was a constant, barely perceptible unfolding all around him, but he could sense its minute and infinite variations. For time must have variations or it will jell. And today was Monday.

What did they do out there he wondered. The flat, packed earth stretched away to the horizon over there; it was impossible to conceive of any life there. Of course it was the same in the other direction, toward his home and the population of his country, but he had never seen anyone from over there. There was no roadblock or guardhouse on the other side, and no one except the returning mission had ever, as far as he knew, even approached the roadblock from over there. Before he had become border guard he had often heard on the radio of visiting diplomats from over there, and had heard them quoted, usually in reference to the good relations that existed between the two allies. But since he had become guard he had neither heard nor seen anyone from over there, because radios weren't allowed, and all he ever heard over the phone was official business in the formal language prescribed by regulations. If there were any people over there they certainly were peace loving, and to preserve that peace they kept as far as they could from their neighbors.

He had never thought to wonder much about what the mission did when they drove off into the night. He did what regulations prescribed he should do about the mission, and they probably did what other regulations prescribed they should do. They probably found their task as pleasant as he found his, and probably enjoyed driving off into the night as much as he enjoyed sitting on the top bar of the roadblock in the sun. He sometimes envied them.

If someone were to ask him what he had been thinking, he would have been able to say all this. He knew himself pretty well after living with himself for six years, and could, because of this intimate acquaintance, tell what he thought. But as he sat in the sun he was never conscious of thinking, and as old friends sometimes misjudge each other's thoughts, so might he have misjudged his own. But still, he was friends with himself, and it didn't much matter what he thought.

All he was conscious of was time and a Monday feeling. The sun was almost down, and instinctively he turned and looked down the road toward his home. And almost as he looked, the first car of the mission appeared as a hardly-moving speck on the horizon. In half an hour they would arrive.

He slid from the roadblock bar to the ground, and with practiced movement swung the carbine's sling along his arm and up on his shoulder. He walked a little stiffly, because he had been sitting in nearly the same position since lunch, over to the pillbox and down through the door into the cool interior. The phone was on the wall just inside the door, the crank kind. He propped the receiver against his ear with his shoulder and rang a long ring. There was always a wait of several minutes while operators shuttled the call around to different security officers to make sure it was really coming from the border station. As he waited, he remembered to switch the carbine to automatic fire. Finally the call reached the security information office, and he informed them that an indeterminate number of cars were approaching from inland, and requested instructions. When he had chanted this weekly ritual, the ritual instructions came faintly over the wire in a girl's voice. It was always a different girl's voice, but it was always soft, and he repeated the instructions in a friendly conversational manner, avoiding the formal language as much as might be attributable to human error. And although the formal signing off was in perfect official form, the girl's voice was, if possible, softer. Then he cleaned out the bores of the two howitzers that pointed down the road into his own country and loaded them. When this was done, and the guns trained on the approaching convoy, he watched it through the sights until he could read the password being flashed to him from the lead car. He had to read it three times, and then he walked out into the light and semaphored the countersign.

The lead car was a shiny open sedan with a flag fluttering at either fender, and it was a pleasure to be able to stand at port arms in the middle of the road and bring it to a halt. The rest of the spread-out convoy stopped one by one, close together, as if the head of a snake had stopped but the tail hadn't until the snake had shrunk to half its length. A young aide jumped out of the open sedan's front seat and came toward him, stopping several feet away.

"Weekly mission to our ally. Remove the roadblock," the aide said. Although this approach was strictly non-regulation, the guard was not disturbed. The two were about the same age, but the guard felt some of the condescension a successful older man feels for an impatient young one.

"May I see your papers, sir? Authorization, clearances, all that? Regulations, you know."

"Regulations be hanged. There's going to be a new order around here."

"Until I hear about a change there'll be no change here. I'm doing my job and I'm doing it according to the regulations I've always done it according to, and I'm not changing the way I do my job until I'm notified of new regulations. May I see your papers?"

"Damn it, man, *I'm* telling you. There are new regulations. You are to let the weekly mission through as soon as you get the password flashed to you. That's enough rigamarole." The guard didn't smile, because the aide was, after all, a representative of the government, but he did ignore the last part of the harangue and walked over to the car. The chief diplomat would go according to regulations. But the back seat was empty. Unusual, the chief diplomat had always ridden in the lead car. He walked back to the aide.

"Where's the chief diplomat?" he said.

"Chief diplomat be damned. As far as you're concerned I'm the chief diplomat and any other diplomat you can think of on this mission. Can't you get that through your regulation-bound skull?" The guard gave the aide up as hopeless. The only other thing to do was to proceed with the unloading and inspection of the vehicles and their loads, until he came to the chief diplomat's car. He walked back to the lead car and ordered the driver out. The driver at least put up no interference, and he was able to check under the seats and in the trunk before the aide followed him.

"Now look. Are you going to lower those bars or do I have to?" The guard ignored him. "I swear, you people are impossible. What would you do in a case not covered by regulations?" The guard still ignored him. With a groan of disgust the aide walked away, and the driver followed him.

The guard finished his inspection of the lead car and walked back to the second vehicle, a truck. Its occupants too dismounted without argument, and unloaded the truck while he counted and measured the packages. In the middle of the operation he glanced up and saw the aide and the lead car driver straining to slide back the top bar of the roadblock. He stepped away from the pile of packages, swung the carbine off his shoulder, and aimed it at the aide.

"Step away from that barricade or I'll fire," he shouted, then paused. "Step away, I said, or I'll drop you in your tracks." Still they ignored him, and he shouted a third warning. The two stolidly continued heaving at the crossbar. For the first time he felt sorry the regulations were so explicit, and he fired. Since the carbine was at automatic he hit both of them several times, and their bodies jerked and lurched before they finally tumbled to the road. He stopped firing and instinctively switched the carbine to semiautomatic, and in his mind the decision was forming that he would not carry the gun at automatic, ever, regulations or no regulations. The two drivers unloading the truck were frozen in horror, staring at him, one of them holding out a package and the other reaching for it. He stared back.

"I warned them," he said to them. "I warned them three

times, and then I had to shoot. That's regulations. That's my job, and I have to . . ." He stopped. "Well don't just stand there. They have to be put in the refrigerator car and taken with you; I haven't any place to put them here and the ground's too hard for burying. 'All personnel of the mission mortally stricken while at or beyond the barricade will be returned inland with the mission in the refrigerator car, with all due and so forth,' " he quoted. "I remember that one because it seemed so silly, so unlikely. No, on second thought, you two keep on unloading. I'll get the drivers of the next truck. It's all part of our jobs." He turned and faced down the line of the convoy.

Most of the drivers had jumped out when they heard the shooting, and were standing around their trucks indecisively. "All right now, you men know the regulations. Get back in the trucks until I get there." He looked over the groups to see if any looked like a chief diplomat, but they all split up into groups of two and walked back to the trucks. "All except you four," he added. "You load those two into the refrigerator truck, and do it gently. And cover them with something." He returned to the first truck and finished the counting and measuring. He continued down the line of trucks and official cars, inspecting, counting, and measuring. But none of the men in the cars identified themselves as the chief diplomat, or any of the other diplomats, for that matter. After what had happened he was in no mood to question them, either. If the diplomats on this mission wanted to trifle with the regulations that was their business, but he would do his job as best he could without them.

When he had inspected the last car he returned to the pillbox and cranked the phone. As he waited he closed his eyes, and wondered what his instructions would be. After six years . . . He couldn't understand why anyone would try to buck regulations, when they had worked like clockwork for as long as anyone he had ever talked to could remember. It didn't make sense.

"Clearance Office." The girl's voice was soft, and he felt comforted. He answered "Border Station One," and listed the

the number of cars and trucks, the number of personnel, the number and sizes of the packages, and then added "The authorization and clearance papers were not . . ." But the soft voice interrupted him.

"That is the mission. Your instructions are to remove the road block and allow the convoy to pass."

"But . . ."

"Over and out." The girl's voice was soothing.

"Over and out," he murmured, and replaced the receiver. When he returned outside he found that the alternate driver of the first truck had taken over the lead car. It was good to see that some people knew the regulations. The two bodies were gone as well. He motioned to the drivers of the first two vehicles, and with their help slid back the three bars of the roadblock. The two drivers returned to their vehicles, and the convoy stretched out to its usual length again as it passed through. The last car stopped, and the two men in it helped him slide back the bars. Because of the delay caused by the impatient aide, it was almost completely dark by the time the last car left, and he was able to watch the convoy for only a few moments before it disappeared in the darkness. He sat on the top bar of the roadblock for a while, but when the moon came up it was almost completely obscured by clouds. He felt sleepy anyway, so he went into the pillbox.

First he unloaded the howitzers, and then, after he had put some coffee on to brew, he sat down to make out his daily report. He described the incident of the aide in detail, and quoted the regulations he had acted under. He also explained that the head diplomat never identified himself, and added that the girl at the Clearance Office had not given him a chance to state this before she gave him clearance for the mission. He read the last half of the report over a couple of times, and decided to leave out the part about the girl in the Clearance Office. After all, he had acted strictly according to regulations throughout.

He phoned the report in, and although the girl's voice was reassuring, he knew he would feel uneasy for several days. It would probably take several days for such an unusual report to be approved. He drank his coffee, turned on the twenty-mile alarm, and turned in. In spite of his uneasiness, he went right to sleep.

He dreamed he was with the convoy, sitting in one of the trucks and watching the truck ahead. The tailgate chains jiggled with the motion of the truck and he could just hear their jangle over its rumbling. He wondered what it would be like when they really got over there. . . . The twenty-mile alarm was ringing. The convoy was coming back, and he felt he had hardly slept. He couldn't remember having spent such a restless night ever, and waking up feeling so logy. He washed his face in cold water and then doused his whole head. The jangling alarm didn't make him feel any wider awake either, and he turned it off. He loaded the howitzers that controlled the road over there. He fixed and ate a leisurely breakfast; a cold one, though, since he didn't feel like cooking. Then he stepped outside, and it was several minutes before he realized that the moon was just about at zenith.

The convoy was coming back awfully early. What was going on, he wondered. Everything was going different this time, and if some new system had gone into effect he should have been told about it. What was holding them now? It was more than half an hour since the alarm had gone off. He peered between the top and second bars of the roadblock, and looked down the road over there. He didn't feel like climbing up, and he might fall asleep if he sat down up there.

Suddenly his ears caught the faint sound of a motor, and then, as it grew louder, he whirled as he realized that the sound was coming from behind him. He was just in time to see an old battered coupe emerge from the darkness down the road from his own country. It pulled up in front of the pillbox, and he crouched beside the roadblock to see what the occupant, or occupants, would do. There seemed to be only one, and he sat looking about him for a moment. Then he turned off the motor and peered out both windows, as if expecting to see someone hiding under his running boards. The guard stepped out from the barricade with his carbine held loosely but ready at his hip. He hesitated a split second, then remembered he had set it for semiautomatic. Too many bullets at automatic; it was overdoing it.

"State your business," he said in a loud voice that sounded almost like a shout in the still night air. The man in the car jumped and banged his head on the window post.

"Take it easy, young man. I'm not trying to sneak through without your knowing it." The man clambered out of the car as the guard drew nearer. He was an old man, although still, apparently, far from feeble. He was rubbing his head where he had hit it. "What do you have to go jumping out at people like that for? Nobody's going to try and steal your roadblock."

"I know, but I have to do my job. And you did get me out of bed in the middle of the night. Let's get the formalities over with. What's your business?" The guard liked the old man's open manner. Most of the travelers who tried to go through were in an all-fired hurry and took out their impatience on him, like that young aide.

"Well, I thought I'd like to see what it's like over there before I got too old to travel. It sounds like quite a place. I think I'll like a people that minds its own business and not their neighbors'. Looks like it ought to be nice and peaceful out there, doesn't it?"

"So I've heard, but I'm afraid you'll have to get papers first—visas, clearances, that sort of thing."

"Oh, I've got all that. Saved up my money so I can spend a good long time there, too. Might decide to settle down there, if it's as nice as it sounds. Did you ever think of settling down over there?"

"No. May I see your papers?"

"Oh, that can wait. I think I'll take a little nap until it gets light and give you a chance to go back to bed. Sorry I got you up; didn't realize you'd have an alarm. Seems funny to have all this rigamarole between such good allies. Got an extra bed or a sofa in there for an old man to rest his weary bones?"

"Well, if you want to wait, all right, but I might warn you that it usually takes a little while for me to get final clearance over the phone. They have to check records and all that, you know."

"What's a few hours? Time I've got plenty of since I retired. How about a little hospitality? I should think you'd be glad of a visitor way out here."

"It's not so bad. And it isn't a few hours. It'll take several days. And I'm afraid no one is allowed in the pillbox except on business."

"A few days? Good Lord." The old man's voice was not quite as buoyant. "Oh well. What's time? Let's get some sleep."

"I'd like to accommodate you, but regulations are regulations. I can't let you into the pillbox except on business. Do you want me to check your papers and phone for clearance?"

"Look, suppose we go in to look over the papers—you can't read out here in the dark—and we just happen to fall asleep. You've got an alarm to warn you in case someone comes to check up. I mean, after all, you have to take some regulations with a grain of salt." The guard shrugged and led the way into the pillbox. There was a day bed in the office that he was allowed to use on bad days when he couldn't guard outside, and the old man flopped down on it.

"Let's see those papers. The sooner we start the ball rolling the sooner you'll get through," the guard said. The old man reached into his inside coat pocket and held out the papers, without opening his eyes. He was asleep before the guard had finished checking them. This he did seated at the desk, and he found himself nodding over them. The alarm was off, and it wouldn't do to have the convoy catch him asleep with an un-authorized person sleeping in the pillbox. He got up and switched the alarm back on, finished checking the papers, and then phoned in the information. He hardly noticed the girl's voice when she told him he would receive instructions as soon as everything had been checked. The convoy would be coming back soon, and he had to send the old man away. He almost had to lift the old man up and shake him before he would wake up, and then he was irritated and tried to flop back down.

"Look," he said to the old man, "you can't stay here. The weekly mission is coming back soon, and if they find you in here it might be my job. I don't like to kick you out, but I have to obey regulations."

"Don't you believe in the duty of hospitality to strangers?"

"Of course I do, but this isn't my home, and regulations are regulations. Come back in a couple of days, and maybe your clearance will have come through. There's no point in your sticking around here."

"You're going to choke on those regulations of yours if you don't watch out." But the old man's good-natured composure returned as he woke up. "Well, all right. I suppose you know the rigamarole. I'll be back day after tomorrow."

He watched the old man back the coupe around and drive back the way he had come. He rather wished he could hurry the clearance for the old man, but there was little chance for that. He had been very decent about it all. The guard watched the coupe until it disappeared, and then re-entered the pillbox. The alarm was on, and he might as well leave the howitzers loaded so he wouldn't have to reload them when the convoy approached in a couple of hours. He could turn right in, and he did.

Again he dreamed of the convoy, only this time it was parked on the flat, packed earth with nothing but darkness all around. The aide was smashing at the tailgate chain on one of the trucks, and that was silly, since it was an easy matter to unhook the chains to let the tailgate down. The chain jangled as the aide bashed it with a back and forth swing of the carbine butt. He woke up to the jangling of the alarm. He got up, switched off the alarm, and started to make his breakfast, when he remembered he'd already eaten. He ate a piece of bread and had a cup of coffee to fill in the gap until lunch, and went outside.

The moon was still well up in the sky, and it was a long while before daybreak. Soon he heard a distant throb, but couldn't tell if it was from down the road over there—the convoy returning early—or from the road into his own country— the old man returning, perhaps. But as the throbbing grew louder he suddenly realized that it wasn't on the road at all, but off to the side, and almost immediately the shape of a large truck appeared out of the darkness, running parallel to, but several hundred yards away from, the road. He stood in the door of the pillbox and watched it in utter amazement as it roared by, a barely discernible truck-shaped motion off on the other side of the road from the pillbox. It came from inside his country, crossed the border, heading over there. Soon it was out of sight, and the throbbing died away. He stood weakly, staring after the lost sound in the disbelief of discovery. It was so obvious and simple, yet totally unforeseen. It was right to go over there. What did the government have to do with it? He was charmed; it was so simple, so right, like time's almost imperceptible variations. There were no regulations to cover such a thing, and the howitzers which were meant to blast attempts at illegal crossing covered only the road and a few degrees on either side. There was just one regulation he could turn to.

He rushed back into the pillbox and cranked the phone long and hard. The girl's voice on the other end was softer than ever—sleepy.

"I want to make a report of Extraordinary Situation," he said.

"Extraordinary Situation? This is highly unusual. I'll have to . . ."

"Of course it's highly unusual. What else would it be if it's an Extraordinary Situation?"

"Just a moment, please." In a shorter time than usual he was connected with the proper office. He gave his report in as few words as possible, trying to keep the amazement out of his voice. Immediate consultation would be made, he was informed, and they would let him know what course of action would be taken in the future for such occurrences, as soon as a decision had been reached. He hung up and walked out to the barricade. No use going back to sleep now; the convoy would soon return. He walked back outside and climbed up on the top bar of the roadblock to wait for the convoy.

Twice more during the night trucks went roaring across the border on the flat, hard-packed earth. The first time, when he heard the approaching throb, he jumped down from the barricade, and when the truck materialized he aimed the carbine at it. But regulations didn't cover him, and anyway the truck passed too far away, out of the carbine's reach. So he lowered the weapon, slipped his arm through the sling, shrugged it up onto his shoulder, and watched the truck disappear over there. The second time the truck passed too far away to be seen. For the first time in six years he felt dissatisfied with his job. It had become pointless, and he realized that maybe it had always been pointless.

The next time he heard a motor it came from over there, and soon was blended with many more motors. He jumped down and stood at port arms in front of the roadblock. The lead car loomed up out of the intense darkness that precedes morning, and stopped. He waited for someone to step out and come forward, and when no one did, he decided that it must still be as it was when it left the border the previous evening, empty except for the driver. Why the deuce was the chief diplomat, and the others too, for that matter, being so reclusive? The only thing to do was to go on to the next step, and inspect the convoy. It didn't take long on the return trip, because the convoy always left its load over there without bringing anything back. He phoned in his report without mentioning that no one had come forward with the papers. After all, it was the same convoy, he could swear to that, and if they had been cleared to leave the country there was no reason they should not be cleared to re-enter. And he had reported the lack of papers in his daily report anyway. The girl promptly gave the convoy clearance and, after the first two drivers had helped him slide back the barricade bars, the convoy passed through. The three men in the last car helped him slide the bars back into position, and he wondered if any of them were diplomats. The diplomats were always fairly old, but the other personnel could be either young or old. It was doubtful if a diplomat would help slide the bars, anyway. He watched the convoy until it disappeared over the horizon, heading home. The sun had come up, and he climbed back up on the top bar and sat cross-legged, with the carbine in his lap. But the sense of being alone in the center was gone. Too much had happened in the night, and the reverberations lingered, distorting time.

Finally, and it was hard to tell how much time had really passed, the sun reached zenith, and he went into the pillbox to fix his lunch. After lunch he returned to his post, and it seemed the afternoon would pass in the same disjointed fashion. He found himself listening for the phone, too, and wondering if it would be instructions concerning his Extraordinary Situation report, or acceptance of his daily report—or would there be an investigation of the aide's death?—or would it be some board that had suddenly discovered it had authorized clearance of the convoy without papers, and was revoking the clearance order? There were so many threatening possibilities, none of them foreseen or foreseeable.

The sense of bewilderment that had lurked about him ever since the aide had summarily refused to have anything to do with regulations remained, and he couldn't shake it off for the sense of fulfillment, of being, that he had known for six years. And the feeling of depression in him grew, all the more depressing for being the first unpleasant emotion that had clung to him since he had become a guard. And the flat hard earth, the shifting horizon, the roving sun, were not what they had been, and he could not recapture their meaning, not sitting in the center and being. He saw again in his mind the truck-shaped roar loom up, pass, and disappear in the darkness, over there. It was so simple, so right.

He watched the growing speck of the car with complete indifference. There was no feeling of discovery when he first noticed it, no change of the gloom, and now it seemed as if it had always been there, coming, and had never come. As it grew larger he realized, but again without a sense of discovery, that it was the old man's coupe returning, and now it seemed as if the old man had always been there coming, but had never come. The car seemed to hesitate, then drew off to the side of the road and stopped. The driver got out and continued slowly on foot, and as he drew nearer the guard recognized him as the old man. And now, of course, it was as if there had always been a car by the side of the road, and the old man walking toward him.

It was almost sundown when the old man reached him, walking slowly and painfully, and he forgot to jump down and come to port arms and challenge the old man. The old man sank down in the shade of one of the uprights and leaned his back against it. He sat there for a long time, breathing heavily, and the guard looked down on him from his perch on the top bar. Finally, when the sun had gone down and there was just the pink light in the sky, the old man looked up at the guard and smiled wanly.

"Threw a rod," he said.

"Your clearance hasn't come through yet. Nothing's come through." The guard seemed to be talking to himself.

"I didn't expect it after what you told me last night. I just thought I'd come back and see what it was like, living out here. Thought you might like some company, and there was nothing for me to do back home." The old man got to his feet and leaned against the upright until the dizziness went away. "I'd better go in and lie down," he said. "A long walk in the sun isn't good for people my age." The old man turned and walked slowly toward the pillbox.

"No one is allowed in there except on official business," the guard heard himself calling, and was surprised at himself.

"Oh, bother you and your regulations," the old man called back without turning.

"I'm warning you. If you go down those steps I'll have to shoot you. That's regulations too. I had to shoot two men yesterday who thought they were bigger than regulations."

"You murdered two men?" This time the old man turned around.

"I shot two men." The guard's voice grew louder. "I didn't murder them. I gave them three warnings, and when they ignored them, I had to shoot."

"Because regulations said shoot, you shot. You're a murderer, just the same."

"Don't be absurd," the guard shouted. "I have to do my job. I'm here to guard this barricade and this pillbox with my life, and according to regulations." The old man shook his head sadly and walked down the steps into the pillbox. The guard jumped down from the roadblock and followed. "Look, old man, I don't want to shoot you, but if you don't get out I'll have to," he pleaded. "Don't you understand? I'm responsible for a critical post, and must shoot first and ask questions later. That's the summary on the last page of the regulations."

The old man sat on the day bed and looked at him. "You're in bad trouble, son," he said. "How did it happen?"

"How did what happen?"

"How did you come to shoot those two men?" The guard stared at the old man. The regulations, which had seemed so completely adequate for six years, became vague and confused in his mind, too explicit and yet not explicit enough. He sat on top of the desk, cross-legged with the carbine in his lap, and told the old man about the aide and the convoy.

When he had finished the account, the old man asked, "What did the aide say when you shouted to warn him?"

"He didn't say anything then."

"What did he say before?"

"Well, when I asked him for the clearance papers he said to hell with them, or something like that. And then when I asked him where the chief diplomat was, he shouted that as far as I was concerned he was the chief diplomat and all the other diplomats."

"And you never did see the chief diplomat? What if he was?"

"What if who was what?"

"What if the man you thought was an aide was the chief diplomat?"

"But he was a young man." The old man just looked at him. "And if there had been a change in procedure I would have been informed over the phone."

"The government is a little slow sometimes, isn't it, and they have been known to lose papers?"

"I suppose so."

"Well then, what if he was the chief diplomat?"

"Oh my God, do you suppose I did shoot the chief diplomat? My God . . . Oh my God, that's why I didn't get approval of my daily report. I shot the chief diplomat."

"You murdered two men."

"But I was just obeying regulations. There was nothing else I could do."

"But some day they'll change the regulations, and then you'll be guilty, won't you? You won't have any regulations behind you, then."

"But I didn't make the regulations."

"No, they're guilty too. But two wrongs don't make you right." The guard stared dejectedly at the floor. "Let's see those regulations," the old man added. The guard picked them up, a brown volume that had to remain on the desk top for easy reference, and tossed it onto the couch beside the old man. The two sat in silence while the old man leafed through them, clucking his tongue from time to time. Once he said, "You certainly stuck to the regulations, didn't you?" Then he said, "Is your carbine set at automatic?"

"No. Too dangerous," the guard answered. He stared at the ground, and then something made him look up at the old man.

They said nothing to each other then. After a while the guard went into the little kitchen and made supper for them both, and after supper they sat for a while in silence. The old man stretched out on the day bed and closed his eyes, and was soon asleep. The guard turned on the twenty-mile alarm, and then went into his room. Again he dreamed of the convoy. This time the aide had succeeded in lowering the tailgates, and swarms of people poured out of the trucks, chattering happily to each other, and spread out through the night. As they jumped from the tailgates the chains jangled, and he woke up to the jangling of the alarm. The old man was already outside when he got there, and they stood side by side and watched a truck roar over the border on the hard earth, several hundred yards from the road. The guard ran back into the pillbox and tried to turn off the alarm, but it kept on jangling. That meant that something else was coming. He went back outside and stood beside the old man, and they watched another truck appear momentarily, farther away, and listened to it drive on into the night over there. All night long the alarm jangled unceasingly, and cars and trucks loomed up and passed over the border, some so close that the two men could make out the shapes of the occupants. And some crossed over out of sight in the darkness, and they could only hear the motors drop in pitch when the car or truck passed over and moved away from them.

Once the old man said, "So it's started at last. I've always expected it, but not that way. It's not right. They should know better. They'll get over there all right, but they'll be renegades. There's only one right way, and that's the road, or else what's the road for?"

"Last night was the first time," the guard answered, more to himself. "Ever, as far as I know. It's so unheard-of, but so simple, and so right."

"No, not right. What's the road for?"

"But it's always been good and right to go over there. The government never says anything about how hard it is to get clearance to go over. If the government says it's right, why should they make it wrong?"

"There's only one right way, and that's the road. So many misguided people." The old man shook his head and went back inside. In a minute the guard went in too and picked up the phone to make another Extraordinary Situation report. He cranked the phone several times, but it seemed to be dead. He remembered that he hadn't made his daily report last night, but he could always say the phone had been dead. It hardly seemed important any more. The old man was asleep already, and he went into his room to try to catch a few hours himself, in spite of the jangle.

For the rest of the week the two lived as the guard had lived. They learned to ignore the jangling of the alarm, which never ceased. The roar and passing of the cars and trucks began to take on the slightly varying pattern of time that the flat empty plain had held for the guard before. The two men sat on the top bar of the roadblock during the day, and talked quietly from time to time. The old man never mentioned the shooting of the two men again, and the phone remained dead. The old man would talk about what he thought it would be like over there, and was disappointed that the guard, who lived nearer to the country than anyone else, knew so little about it. He told the guard everything he knew or had ever heard about over there. He told about how there had long ago been a raging war between the two countries, and how it had see-sawed back and forth for many years, neither country able to hold on to an advantage for long. But finally their country won more and more of the battles, and then the tide broke and the people over there had been completely and ruinously defeated. It was the war that had laid bare the earth all around them and packed it flat.

Then, when the war was finally over, the people of their country had realized how stupid and useless it had been, and they had done everything they could to help restore the other country. And some people said that the people over there had drawn away from all contact with other nations, and while they treated visitors with reserved hospitality, they would never come within sight of their own borders, but stayed inland. They were supposed to be a quiet and reserved people, but exceedingly peaceful and kindly. And other people said the war had annihilated everyone over there, and the people of their own country could not face the completeness of the stupidity, and had invented the myth of the kindly withdrawn people over there. The old man didn't care which story was true; in either case the country over there would be pervaded with the peace that comes with the realization of the stupidity of death. And as the week passed the guard came to understand what the old man sought over there, and the others. It was something like that which the guard had felt during the days when he sat alone in the middle of the flat, hard-packed earth, perched on top of the roadblock. And he vaguely understood why the old man thought the road was the only right way to go over there; it was the only way to understand the stupidity out of which the peace would come.

Monday came, and Monday night the convoy arrived. The lead car had three diplomats in the back seat, and an aide in the front with the driver, who came forward with the clearance papers. The inspection, counting, and measuring went smoothly and properly, and everything was as it had been before, except for the trucks and cars driving past over the plain, and the phone being dead. The guard went through the motions of trying to phone for clearance, and when he got no answer he went back out of the pillbox and opened the roadblock with the aid of the old man and the drivers of the first two vehicles. When the convoy had passed through, the last car stopped and the occupants helped slide back the bars.

There was room in the last car for the guard and the old man. The two looked at each other for only a moment, and then got in and drove away with the others, heading down the road inland, over there.

Too Big a Dream

WILL WHITE

IT WAS a pleasant night, cool; a blue-black, hollowed-out sort of night. Just the right sort of night for what he was going to do. It was a blue-black of vastness, and a million vibrant lines leaped from him in constant rebirth towards the stars. All the stars were out; their clean light spread the vastness. Just the stars; no moon to cast the ashen limiting light of the recently dead. He wanted to follow each of the vibrant lines at once with the speed of light, faster, faster, to fill the vastness with speed.

He stood motionless in the driveway. The soft coolness of the night was what he wanted; it gave him the necessary patience and condensed the yearning that it might the more be joyfully released. At three he would go, and not before. The roads were least crowded then, and he could get to know her. He had tried to go to sleep, but the night had drawn him, and he was glad he had got up. The temptation was not too much, as he had feared it might be. The night was calm and timeless.

Slow driving for the first two hundred miles, at not over thirty, and then short sprints at thirty-five, forty, and forty-five to let her learn her power and wear off the rough spots. And then longer dashes after five hundred, and power surged more confidently. Before he had quite grown used to her the break-in period had been over, and he tried a couple of drags to feel her pickup. He had been pushed hard against the back of the seat, and with the surge he felt he knew her.

Tonight they were both ready. She lay resting, and he could feel the dormant power of her in the night. Two hundred and fifty horses at five thousand revs; fantastically low, with sweeping fenders. Black, with gleaming white-walls, her gleaming grill like the jaws of a grinning tiger. Seven months ago he had known her intimately, a creation in his mind. Then she had become a blueprint, with the vagueness of precision. Then she became more and more unreal in the particular, a thing of ground and polished, chromed and minutely adjusted cylinders and cams and valves. Little infinite pieces of the whole that destroyed the vision. The agony of welding the tubular skeleton, and the painstaking hammer-taps of forming the aluminum sheets to the flow of her. And then the coat after coat of rubbed-down lacquer, and the tuning of the engine, and she was real, complete, but unknown. With driving the vision had returned, and he knew her again.

At three he would settle into the leather upholstered bucket seat and start her up. She would wake with a muffled roar, and then he would let her warm up and listen to her low throbbing purr. The temperature gauge would start to rise, and he would back her out slowly, turn, and ease her down the drive. He took a deep breath of the air, like an esoteric nature lover, and turned to look at the garage. The door was open, and he could see the beautiful blended curve of her trunk and fender.

His watch said a quarter past two, and the impatience he had feared began to make him restless. He walked out to the street and looked down it both ways. Way down to the right was the blinking red light on the main street into town. Already it was deserted; he waited several minutes for a car to pass underneath the light, but none did. Maybe he should take off now; it would be an extra half hour of driving. He stared at the blinking red light. No, three o'clock he had decided, and three it must be. Still no car passed down the main street into town, and the red light blinked uselessly.

Suddenly the headlights of a car flashed over his shoulder, and he turned with a start. It was a prowl car, and as it glided past, the heads of the two policemen in it pivoted slowly, their suspicious eyes fixed on him. It was as if their heads were connected by invisible gears, and when one's head turned the other's must turn also. His head might have been connected with theirs, for it pivoted, one hundred and eighty degrees out of phase, with theirs, as he returned their gaze. He laughed, because they were fools.

He looked down the road to the left, leading out of town, and he could just make out the trees that showed where the road curved. The prowl car had rounded that curve and thrown its headlight beams over his shoulder. What did they expect to find, following those two cones of light through the dark? It was ridiculous. He would be rounding that curve in the opposite direction in a short while, her powerful motor idling contentedly, and soon they would reach the edge of town. Then he would push down slowly, firmly, on the accelerator, and force the gas into her. She would rush forward with a growl, and the road would melt effortlessly into straightaways without the sickening lurch and lean of most cars. Her long hood would swing surely, and her lights would throw out beams to sweep the fields and trees.

He looked at his watch again. Only half-past. He rolled his head back and forth and from side to side to loosen the tight muscles. The stars beamed down unblinking, and he nodded. Yes, half an hour. It wouldn't be long. The policemen in the prowl car couldn't see the stars, not all of them at once, and even if they could, they wouldn't *see* them.

He walked back up the drive to the garage and looked at her. She couldn't be perfect, but so far she had acted as if she were. There was half an hour, and nothing he could do for her. He might try to tune the carburetors a little more perfectly, but that would be asking for trouble. They were as perfect as skill and gauges could make them. He walked into the garage and ran his hand over her fender. Smooth and cool and perfectly shaped. No nicks or scratches yet, not even dust. He wanted to run his fingers across the tiger's grin of her grill, but was afraid it would leave a smudge on the gleam. Like the grub that leaves a luminous oily path. He shuddered at the comparison. He walked around the other side and watched the dim light flicker elliptically around the wire spokes of her wheel. He slid into the driver's seat and gripped the wheel. He stared at the row of gauges, and the needles seemed to flicker like the eyelashes of a sleeping cat. Turning the wheel slightly, he could feel the resistance of rest. It would turn effortlessly when she was moving. He closed his eyes.

He opened them with a start and looked at his watch. Three. At last. He hadn't been sleeping, but he had lost twenty minutes, and he blinked the film from his eyes. Nervously he reached into his pocket, swore as he slapped his sides and chest looking for the lump that would be the key. He had left it inside. An hour wasted looking at the stars. He'd have to go in. He swore again.

Inside it was dark and dead, and he fumbled over the top of his dresser looking for the key. It fell with a soft plunk on the carpet, and he had to grope. Finally he found it and went outside again.

He slid under the wheel again, turned on the ignition, pushed the starter. The starter whined a moment longer than usual before the motor caught, and then she coughed uncomfortably several times. He listened to her soft mutter with a sinking feeling; her high-powered lope was catching spasmodically. She was missing. He tightened convulsively in unreasonable despair. He wondered if he had put too much strain on her while he was breaking her in. Well, he couldn't just sit there and listen to her unbalanced mutterings. He checked his first reaction to turn off the ignition, and scrambled out. Fumbling with the hood latch, he cut his finger; he wiped the blood spots from the paint, scolding himself for being so nervous. It was only a little thing, as he should have known. Just an ignition wire loose, shorting in blue sparks against the chromed head pan. He tightened the spark plug clamp and slipped it into place. The sputtering changed to a contented throb, and he smiled.

He forgot about the cut when he got in again, after being very careful not to get any more blood on the hood, and smeared some on the door, the seat, and the wheel. It was worse than he had thought. Oh well, he had put his life's blood into it; no reason he shouldn't get a little on it. Not it—her. He must have

built up an unconscious antagonism to her to think of her in
the neuter. She had deceived him maybe; the bared tiger-grin
grill was just for show; she bit with her hood like a bird with its
beak. He gave the dashboard top an affectionate pat with his
right hand as he sucked at the cut on his left. The gauges were
still alive, the tachometer needle hovering expectantly, the
water and oil temperatures rising. He tied his handkerchief
around the cut finger, shifted into reverse, and backed out into
the familiar night.

"I'm afraid," he thought. It was his first verbalized thought
all night; the rest had been wordless impressions, reactions. He
said it aloud, "I'm afraid." The loping throb of her power came
to him through the wheel, ominously, though she was his
dream, his creation. What right had he to know how to drive?
An entirely incongruous thought he knew, but it expressed
what he felt.

He shifted gently into first and let the clutch come back
slowly. She jumped forward eagerly, defiantly, with a little
squeal from her rear tires. He turned grimly to the left, heading
out of town, gripping the wheel tightly although he had
handled her effortlessly up to now. He felt like a man on a high-
tempered horse does when he mounts for the first time in years.

Suddenly he realized that he hadn't turned on the lights; it
was a clear night and his eyes had become accustomed to the
dark. Ordinarily if he had done that he would have thought the
hell with it. He could see all right, and it would be more fun.
The night would have seemed closer, and he more a part of it.
But tonight he switched the lights on automatically, and followed the two cones of light through the residential streets.
Then the houses thinned out and had barns beside them. The
tall shade trees became telephone poles. The twin cones pierced
across wide fields, and the long black hood swung the corners
smoothly, defiantly. He felt he was performing a task according
to some unreasonable ritual. The joy of speed, the sensation of
going everywhere, and being everywhere, the sensation that was
somehow connected to the stars; that, the essence of the dream,
was lacking. But he was hardly aware of the lack; an urgency
took hold of him, as if he must finish the task. He drove fast,

as fast as he had ever wanted to go, and the lights swept across the trees and the fields. The hood swung confidently and surely ahead around the bends, and he drove with sureness. But the effort was great; he was tense and uncertain of his sureness. And he followed the two cones of light through the dark. It was as if he had some place to go, and not any place. It was as if he wanted to go home to bed.

Point of View

SAM KEITH

"THERE'S a big one out on the ploughed ground," Buck said. "I saw him just now as I came past."

"Let's go up and get him," I said. "Dad will be tickled. Let's go up and get the old rascal."

"He's a big one. A shell on him as big around as a wash basin. I'd better bring the wheelbarrow." He walked behind the tool shed and appeared again with the high-sided barrow rumbling along in front of him. "I got no love for them babies," he said. "Damned if I'll lug one by the tail and have him bull-dog me on the leg."

"Dad will be tickled," I said. "He's coming down to pick me up at noon. My afternoon off you know. We can haul the cuss home."

We went up the road from the greenhouses and turned off into the trees. The ploughed field next to the pond showed through the leaves. The field had just been ploughed a few days ago. You could still smell the earth.

"There on the upper end." Buck pointed with his arm.

"I see him," I said. "He's a big one."

The snapping turtle's shell bouldered from the loam. A female laying her eggs. We used to see them every year the last few weeks in June lumbering across the fields in search of a nesting site. I used to leave them alone. They were too ugly and mean-tempered for me. I guess I was afraid of them. I promised Dad that I'd get him one if I saw one this year. Now I had my chance. Dad sure would be tickled.

The turtle's knotty head darted up as we approached. Eyes of chipped granite blinked and opened. Warts hung along her swollen, yellow throat; it swelled and sagged slowly. On her snout was a clump of dirt.

Ugliness molded into turtle—I winced as I looked at her; I felt that cold spasm through me that one feels when he comes suddenly upon a snake. Of all the snapping turtles I had ever seen I hated this one the most of all. To me this turtle was more than turtle; it was a glimpse of evil. The way the electric currents played through the hairs on the back of my neck, this creature could have been the devil in disguise. I knew that Buck was waiting for me to pick her up.

I stooped and reached down behind the shell into the loose earth and wrapped my fingers around the leathery, saw-toothed tail; it seemed to shrink in my grip, then bulge into rigidness. I had to pull hard to sweep the turtle up from the ground. The head hung in a hockey-stick curve, its mouth opening in a yawn to show the sharp mandibles of bone, the clammy, pinkish-white insides. My skin retched as the head darted out with jaws steel-trap snapping. I dropped her like something unclean. She reared up on her four legs, shell high off the ground, long serrated tail curving downward, pressing against the earth. Something older than man, I thought, something more than turtle.

Buck picked up a stick. "Watch this," he said. He touched the center of the shell with the stick; the head flipped up and over in a movement that made me step quickly backwards; its jaws nearly hinged on the stick. "Satan in the flesh," Buck said. "Jesus, how one will make my hair stand right on end."

I got behind her and grabbed her by the tail and swung her into the wheelbarrow.

"Hold on a minute," Buck said. He bent down and his fingers probed into the earth where the turtle had been entrenched when we had first come upon her. "No eggs yet. Funny, ain't it, the way one'll make a lot of dummy holes before she lays them?"

The snapper's claws rasped and pulled at the wood of the barrow. I strained back on the tail. "Crafty devils," I said, "they have to be. Skunks dig their eggs up and wipe out a whole nest." Good for the skunks, I thought, they ought to get medals for rooting out pockets of evil.

"I'll give this son of a whore a ride," Buck said, as he gripped the barrow handles and lifted. "I'll give her a ride." I let go of the tail. The barrow bounced over the ground; the turtle chattered against the wooden planks, then began to move, tried to clamber over the sides. Widespread claws hooked over the edge, gripping, pulling. Buck pushed forward on the handles and yanked back on them hard. The turtle toppled over with a thump. Her thick throat arched as her snout pressured against the planks. She lurched upright; she struck open-mouthed at the sides, making wicked bumping sounds, and she tried to scale the walls again.

"Back in there, you," Buck yelled, as he rocked the barrow like a chef does a frying pan just before he somersaults a hot cake. "Down, you ugly devil." Buck began to breathe harder.

"I'll spell you, Buck."

"I'll wheel him. I'll give the bastard a ride." He moved faster and slithered the barrow with rough jerks of his heavy arms. His face twisted with an almost scared look. Just like racing with the devil, I thought. That damned shelled nightmare sliding on the planking—a wheelbarrow of sin.

When we got back into the yard, Buck's chest was heaving. "Stubborn, warn't he?" He blew noisily and the hairs fringing his forehead flipped and fell back into place again. "Jesus, how I hate 'em," he wheezed. "Worse than a snake. Make me feel weak all over, those damn things do, and here I am like a fool wheeling one almost in my lap. Ought to have my head examined."

"I hate 'em, too, Buck, probably worse than you do. Dad said he wanted one. How the hell he can carve 'em up for a soup the way he does, I just can't figure out at all. Don't bother him.

Jesus, did you ever see so much ugliness in one heap in your life? Look at that thing."

Buck wheeled her to the edge of the pit. That was where he kept the blue lilies of the Nile in large wooden tubs. "I'll lug her down the steps," I said. Buck grunted. "I got a better idea," he said. He looked down at the clearing right below us. He tipped up the barrow and dumped the turtle tumbling; she dropped the ten feet and thudded with a sickening sound on her back. She turned herself over and was still. "Ugly bastard," Buck said, "you can't hurt them nohow."

I looked down into the pit. "Last rites for you this afternoon, you old fish pirate," I said.

"I s'pose it's about time we started on those azaleas and repotted a few," Buck said, glancing at his pocket watch. "Old Hawkeye will wonder what the hell we been doing all morning."

"Slave driver," I chuckled.

I broke up some old flower pots into pieces of crock. Buck always put some of them at the bottom of a pot before he fitted the plant into it. For drainage he told me. Then I mixed up the special loam on the bench while he scratched at the azalea roots with a wire claw. As I worked in leaf mold and sand and bonemeal and topsoil, I kept thinking about that damn turtle. I thought about how snappers laid in ambush at the bottom of a pond, waited there like an algae-slimed boulder. I thought about that head striking out at prey that moved in range. And I thought about that day on the river when I was in the canoe and heard the duck squawking around the bend. I remembered seeing the duck dragged down. I remembered looking over the side of the canoe and seeing the duck move off into the weeds and seeing the big shell, the legs driving like oars, the tail sliding out of sight. Ugly, ageless, indestructible—I tried to forget all about the damn thing.

Just as the whistle wailed the starting of the noon hour, Dad eased into the yard with the pickup truck. He leaned out the window. "Right on schedule," he said.

"We got a snapper out back," I said, seeing that Buck was about to blurt the news. "Still in the market for one?"

[105]

"You're damn right I am. Where is he?"

"Come on. You got to lug him out. We got him this far."

We walked to the backyard and went down into the pit. The turtle sulked in the corner, head pulled in beneath its pillbox.

"Thirty pounds if he's a pound," Dad whooped. "What a beauty! They'll be soup enough for the town. Just look at those legs. And that shell—say, ain't that something! I can clean that out and varnish it up for the den."

"The pleasure is all yours," I said.

He lifted the turtle from the ground. The head hung in an upward swoop, jaws partly agape, ready to lunge. Dad brushed among the saber-shaped leaves of the lilies and walked up the steps, leaning awkwardly to one side. "A corker," he said, peering down at the creature. He carried the turtle to the truck and swung her with a heave of shoulders into the back.

"Want me to bring you down some of the meat, Buck?" he said.

"Christ, no. I seen all I want to see of that old Satan."

"Don't know what you're missing."

"By God, I don't want to know either."

"Well, don't work too hard."

"Keep count on your fingers."

"See you, Buck."

"Take her easy, boys."

"See you in the morning, Buck," I said.

We backed out of the yard and then moved off down the drive. I looked through the back window at the turtle. She tried to lumber over the sides, but the jouncing over the ruts was too much for her. She teetered on her hind feet, then flipped over backwards; she righted herself and plodded over to try again. Hell, I thought, this is like dragging a witch to the guillotine.

Dad pulled up close to the barn. The turtle's claws scratched against the metal as he hauled her over the side and swung her down and away from him. The collie trotted up, fur shaking in soft jolts along his back. He stopped, stretched his muzzle to sniff at the crouching head, then shied back suddenly with a yip as the head thrust at him. "Look out there, Danny, he'll take a chunk right outa your hide." Dad carried the turtle in the feed room and came out, shutting the door behind him. "After dinner," he said.

We sat around the table. The kids didn't know yet that we had the turtle. Joey gulped down his milk, shoved his chair back, and bolted for the door still swallowing.

"I'm going to kill a big snapping turtle pretty soon," Dad said.

Joey spun around with his hand on the door knob. The faces of Deena and Betsy showed sudden interest. "Can I watch, Gramp? Can I?" sputtered Joey. "Can we watch, too," piped Deena.

"I don't see why not. Might just as well go out now and get the job over with. Come on." We got up from the table.

Deena hurried ahead of us down the steps. "Judy, Eddie," she shrilled towards the house across the road. "Come on quick. Gramp's going to kill a turtle. Gramp's going to kill a big turtle."

Judy and Eddie boiled out of their yard and scampered over to join us in the walk to the barn. The ducks in the pen complained in quick grunts as we passed.

"You get the axe, Tom," Dad said. "I'll bring out the turtle."

I went into the woodshed and picked up the axe; its edge was nicked and gouged in places. The kids must have been driving it into the ground again. I came back out of the shed. There was Dad in the middle of a circle of gawking, chattering kids.

"Wow, look at that mouth."

"Does he bite, Gramp?"

"Is he tougher'n Superman?"

"Is he a boy turtle or a girl turtle, Gramp?"

"Keep back out of the way now, all of you," Dad said.

"Some club this is," I said, holding up the axe so that he could see its edge.

"That'll do," he said.

We walked over to where the old stump block stood. The ground was littered with bark and wood splinters. We always split our kindling there. Dad held the turtle up so that she

[107]

rested on the block with her front legs. Jesus, but that turtle looked ugly; shivers raced through the length of me.

"You be the executioner, Dad," I said. "I probably couldn't hit the neck anyway. Here, I'll take hold of her." I didn't want to strike at that terrible head; I didn't even want to hold the tail, but I knew Dad couldn't do the job alone. I knew I had to help. The kids ringed in closer. "Get back," Dad said. I handed him the axe and grabbed on to that damn tail.

I tried to get the head to lay across the block, but the turtle kept paddling with her front feet, raking the stump with sharp claws. I held her in one position for a minute; her head moved out slowly. Dad waited with the axe. The head eased out farther. He struck. The head shot in beneath the shell and the axe chunked. "Damn," he muttered. Blood welled from one of the front legs. The kids laughed. "You missed him, Gramp," Deena said. The kids all laughed again.

"Deena, you run inside and ask your mother for some of that heavy twine," Dad said. Deena bounded off like a rabbit jumped out of a brushpile, her hard legs driving over the ground, her skirt flying as she raced up the kitchen steps. In a few minutes she was back. "Here, Gramp," she said, holding the ball up to him. Dad put the axe down and made a sliding noose in the end of the twine. Then he picked up a stout stick. "Put him down, Tom," he said. I pulled the turtle off the stump and settled her to the ground. She did not move.

"Hold this noose. Let it down in front of the snout when I get the stick up within a foot away." I held the noose ready. He moved the stick closer. I saw the snout begin to slide from beneath the shell, then I lowered the noose as the stick crept forward. The head streaked through the noose, jaws rapping, clenching. I yanked hard; the noose tightened on the throat. Still the turtle held on to the stick. The kids giggled.

"Get him back up on the stump, Tom. Let Joey and Eddie take hold of the line and pull. That'll stretch out the cuss's neck. That's the way, boys, haul away. Pull hard, hard."

Joey and Eddie pulled while I tugged on the tail. Slowly the head inched out; slowly the yellowed neck stretched out on the stump. Dad poised with the axe above his shoulder. He swung in a grunt. Then again—then a short, rapid stroking. The axe thumped as if biting into cable, jarred against the pimpled neck. Joey and Eddie pulled, faces grimacing and laughing. I strained on the tail that twisted in my hands. The hide on the neck parted; bared muscle bulged and the blood began to spill. Another flashing glint of the axe downward. Joey and Eddie lurched back with the severed head and stick flopping on the twine. The eye on the head shrunk and swelled in its socket; the jaws opened and released the stick and snapped shut again.

"You kids keep away from that head," Dad said. "Take the turtle over to the table, Tom, and I'll go inside and get some newspapers."

Blood dripped in a trail from the neck stump as I walked the short distance to the crude table beneath the hickory tree. Joey dragged the head behind him on a string. Eddie dragged the axe.

Dad spread a few layers of newspapers over the table, and I swung the turtle up and let it thump, legs sticking up in the air. Dad snapped open his knife; its edge glistened like mother of pearl. He pushed it into the flesh at the edge of the carapace and began to saw through the cartilage that bridged over to the plastron. The claws reached back and groped at the steel, spread and gouged at the air. Just like a dog kicking at fleas, I thought; Jesus, what do you have to do to kill this thing? Dad grasped the foot nearest to where his knife worked; the foot seemed to wrestle with his hand. The kids squealed. The tail showing the tile inlay beneath it lashed and squirmed. The sallow skin covering the upper legs was blotched with enamel islands and warts. Dad skinned out the feet as he came to them; soon he finished the circle around the carapace edge. Then he whittled out the plastron.

"Full of eggs," he said, as he pinched a white sphere resembling a ping-pong ball out of the filmy oviduct. "You count them, Deena, as I hand them to you." Deena counted aloud in her sing-song way, placing each one inside of a pen on the table made by Betsy's arms. The kids crowded closer. They were really having a time. Arms reached in to fondle the eggs.

[109]

"Leave 'em," snapped Deena, "I'm countin' for Gramp." The kids climbed on the bench seats, squatted like savages. Eddie put his hand on the soft entrails and pulled it away looking at it.

"Fifty-six eggs, Gramp," Deena said. "I counted two times."

"I'll tell you what you can do with them in a minute. Look at what I got here." He held the heart in the middle of his big hand. "See," he said, "it's still beating." The red flesh pumped in his palm, swelled and squeezed in a lump, swelled and squeezed in a lump. No sir, I thought, you just can't kill that damn thing at all.

"Let me see, Gramp," said Deena, "let me see." Dad put the heart into her outstretched hand. The kids clustered about her, fascinated by the breathing piece of meat. They poked at it with their fingers. The next thing I knew, I saw Deena tearing it apart with her fingers. The kids were laughing.

"The ducks will like those eggs," Dad said. "Why don't you kids carry them over and give the ducks a feast?"

The kids delved into Betsy's egg corral and lined eggs on top of their arms, stooping, holding them tight against their stomachs. They scurried over to the duck pen, eggs tumbling from them as they went. I followed them. They dropped the eggs through the wire into the noisy huddle of ducks. With excited quackings the ducks pounced upon the white balls. Eggs shot out of their bills; ducks snaked their necks as they wobbled after them, caught up to them, and chased them again. The kids screamed and rained in more eggs. The ducks could not break the tough skins to get at the yolks; the eggs were too big to bolt down whole. "Go inside the pen," I said, "and smash the eggs against the rock." They went in amongst the dust and swirling feathers and bombed the rock. The ducks greedily sucked at the yolks that ran down its sides; they gulped down the leathery skins as well. The kids were having a field day.

I walked back to the table where Dad was heaping meat in a deep platter.

"How's that for prime beef?" he said.

"You can keep it," I said. "That stuff gives me the cold shakes."

"Just your imagination. Nothing in the world makes a better soup. Damn fine meat. Wait till you taste it."

"Yeah," I said.

He walked into the house. The skinned hide, entrails, shell, and knife were still on the newspapers. Flies whirled around the table and made abrupt landings. The kids got tired watching the ducks and drifted back. With a puddle of blood in its bottom, the huge bowl-like shell rested on the table. The kids got up on the benches, leaned over and trailed their fingers in the blood. I looked at the axe on the ground, the blood that jellied its edge. I saw the turtle head twitch convulsively on the twine. Jesus, I couldn't stand much more of that turtle. I'll never mention any more of them, I thought. I reached over and took the knife away from Eddie. He had been jabbing it into the entrails on the newspaper. More flies feasted now. My skin began to itch.

"Scram, the lot of you," I said. "Get going. You're almost as bad as the flies. Go inside and get your hands washed." I wrapped up the entrails in the newspaper, shoved it in a bundle beneath my arm. I spilled the blood out of the shell and balanced it across the branches of the hickory tree near the trunk. Dad said he wanted that. I dragged the twine with the turtle head on it and walked into the woods. I found a deep crevice in the rocks and into it I dropped what I hoped was left of the turtle. Why fool myself, I thought, you've had a glimpse of it; you can't bury a thing like that. That was the way with a lot of things. People had their own way of looking at them, their own way of passing judgments. I laughed at my foolishness. The kids saw a plaything; Dad saw a meal and a varnished shell; I like a damn fool thought I saw the devil.

You'll Never Mind

ROBERT B. O'CONNELL

LT. MONTY Hanley, radar operator, didn't wait for the four-by-four assigned to take the crew of zero-zero-three to de-briefing; instead he left his crew at the hardstand, checking the B-17 for battle damage, and hitched a ride into de-briefing, dangerously balanced on the right front fender of the jeep that had been sent to bring the film to the processing lab. He wanted to make his mission report before the Colonel had a chance to adjust to the strike photos, and this was the sure way of doing it.

In front of the huge Quonset hut that housed Briefing, the jeep sloughed to a near stop. He pitched off into a stumbling run to keep his balance, and splashed through puddles and mud before reaching the walk that led to the entrance. The jeep growled in acceleration, heeled over in a tight 180-degree turn, and roared off down the street. He watched it broadside around a corner, straighten, and continue its race against time.

When he swung into the main corridor, he noticed the length of the queue at the Red Cross refreshment table with regret and he gave up the idea of quickly downing several cups of coffee. Then he saw the chaplain standing near the whiskey table where two enlisted men were giving each returnee his rationed two ounces. He thought: the whiskey does more good than the chaplain—fewer chaplains and more whiskey—all whiskey and no chaplains.

tell me chaplain tell me about god and how we ought to thank him because we are winning the war tell me with your voice unctuous and with your palms outstretched to reach for the god of my childhood quiver with fervor you mealymouthed hypocrite rave about things you don't understand tell me about god and osnabrück tell me how he guided my hands the hands that guided the bombs to the target tell me about him making the flak go off course and tell me about him hiding the group from the jets and i'll tell you that the flak and the jets found the group behind us and that their ships burned and their bombs missed the target and tell me if they should thank god for that

He clomped down the dusty dry concrete floor of the corridor, his boots adding their fresh tire-tread tracks of mud and water to those that had gone before him. He stopped and shifted his parachute pack to his left hand and opened the zippers of his B-15 jacket, his flying suit, his heated suit, and his boots. But the sweat that had started to spring under his multi-layered clothing after the sprint outside now ran down his chest and back and legs in streams. His rage increased the flow. It was always too hot or too cold. All the damned controls in the world couldn't regulate the temperature to suit the individual. When he came abreast of the chaplain, the chaplain read his face and turned to say "How did it go today?" to someone else.

weren't your prayers answered or were the german chaplains prayers answered how did it go today you mean whose side was god on today and whose side will he be on tomorrow how did it go today it went piss-poor for the group behind us and no thanks to him unless the german chaplains and the flak batteries and the jet pilots are thankful but one thing is certain the people of osnabrück aren't thankful o no chaplain the people of osnabrück aren't thankful any more.

His boots clomped. Their opened leather sides flapped. The unbuckled ends of the parachute leg straps clinked and clanked just behind his knees. He opened the door to Lead Crew Interrogation and, unnoticed for a minute, he slipped into a nearby corner and began to remove his equipment. He dropped his chest pack and piled his yellow Mae West on top of it. Then he opened the chest strap of his parachute harness and added that to the pile. His helmet and dangling oxygen mask were next, the green corrugated rubber hose writhing as if it were alive in some reptilian way. Even though the mask hadn't been on his face for more than an hour, he could still feel the outline of its mucky pressure. He massaged his face with both hands until the flow of blood dispelled the sensation. When he kicked off his boots, his feet felt light and cool in shoes for the first time in thirteen hours.

A voice cut through his activities, cold and sharp, "Lt. Hanley, are you ready to give your report yet?"

Without answering, he turned to face the Colonel and the rest of the field brass. Dressed in pinks and greens, clean-shaven, with combed hair and clean faces, they stood around a table in the middle of the room. And as they stood there, stiff and still for a moment, leaving an opening in the part of the circle nearest him so that the Colonel could see him, they looked like a group of wax statues at Madame Tussaud's and not at all like persons he drank and ate with. Someone moved or he blinked and the impression went away.

Major Sam Rayburn, his immediate commanding officer, left the group at the table and came over and slapped him on the shoulder.

"How did it go today, Monty?" he asked.

There was genuine concern in Sam's voice. It was not just the concern of the responsible officer, it was the concern of a pilot with a rough tour behind him. Sam had flown the mission in his mind without the release of action. This he would obtain in the recounting. For, in a sense, Monty knew he was still at the I.P., waiting to turn for the run on the target.

"I creamed it, Sam. I creamed it. The trains won't run for a long time."

Sam whacked him on the shoulder again, and said, "Let's have the poop, Monty." And with a guiding arm on his elbow, Sam steered him into the opening of the circle.

Monty drew a breath and began to talk at high speed in a flat, unemotional voice.

"You know we couldn't bomb the visual primary. I tracked Williams in on the radar set all the way. We went right over it. He said he couldn't see a thing in the bombsight except clouds. Eight-tenths cloud cover. Target completely obscured."

The Metro officer made notes on a pad.

"We took off for the radar primary, the marshaling yards

at Osnabrück. Better weather over there, only a few scattered clouds beneath us, about two-tenths, Williams said, but he also said there was heavy ground haze. He could see straight down but he couldn't see far enough ahead to make a visual run."

The Metro officer made more notes on the pad.

"I had a lot of trouble with the set. It began to arc. Must be low pressure in the modulator. Slow leak somewhere, I'd guess."

The officer from radar maintenance made a note of the malfunction.

"I had to keep turning the damn set off and on to keep the cathode ray tube from blowing. Didn't always have time to turn down all the controls so the tube must be just about shot.

The radar officer made note of it.

"But every time I threw the set back on, the picture came in fine. And the target was right on the course hair. I read drift on the A scope three times. Three degrees left. We had a lovely head wind and our ground speed was only about 162 or 163. I got 162 from my computer. Williams got 163 from the bombsight."

The Metro officer asked the heading, altitude, and airspeed.

"We dropped on the rate Williams set up in the bombsight with the slant range angles, and used the course I set up with the pilot. The target broke up into pieces on the scope as we got close to it, but the rate in the bombsight checked out with each correction and we let it run out with confidence."

Sam grinned at the Colonel, who placed his weight on the palms of his hands on the plotting table and stared at the plotting map as if he would find the bombs already there. Then he shook his head and straightened up.

"You didn't get a visual assist from Williams, Hanley?"

"No, sir. He couldn't put in any corrections, he could only see straight down."

The Colonel shook his head again, and Monty, looking around the table at the other faces, saw them change and lose belief. Only Sam's face remained firm, firm and tinged with anger.

Monty continued after an embarrassing silence. "Smith, flying in our tail, saw Eldeer's bombs burst. We were almost in his
propwash. Smith thought the first half of his pattern was in, the
second half was short. Our bombs burst after we turned off. He
saw them, too. We should have pictures."

With a wave of his hand the Colonel stopped him. "But
Eldeer had help from his bombardier. He called in a visual
assist. I'm afraid you are overconfident on your strike. Even
when a set is working perfectly we can't count on radar drops.
You know that. And with a bad set . . . I can't send that report
to division. I don't believe it myself, Hanley."

and that is why i am so sure that the strike was perfect i know
it even without the others and their words if the set had worked
perfectly i couldn't be sure because then i'd be just another
part of it and the process and the part that was the most un-
stable and most likely to malfunction but i know i didn't break
down the set became a part of me it belonged to me it did my
bidding like a live thing that was hurt but still owed obedience
i felt it and every time i called for information the information
was there indisputable better than if it had been a good set
because there was no between there was only unity of mind and
machine better because it required the mental effort that can
only be exerted when there is the utmost need for it i knew it
with the first correction and the second and third and fourth
were the same they were the first

"I tell you, Colonel, I creamed that target." He heard his
thoughts become words in angry pitch. The Colonel was going
to get so deep into this he would never get out. Or else he would
commit himself beyond the point of no return.

But Sam saved him and the Colonel. "We don't doubt your
word, Monty. But you know we all get excited up there. Are
you sure that Williams didn't see the target in time to make a
visual displacement?"

He roared at Sam, but he meant it for those who really
doubted. "Williams says he didn't touch the control knobs
and that's good enough for me. And the run is good enough
for me without his help. I claim most of the pattern on the
target."

Before the Colonel could chew him out, Sam intervened again. "Don't get excited, Monty. Perhaps if there hadn't been a malfunction, we could take a chance and send the report to division. But we have to wait to see the pictures. The target might have started to drift off as it broke up. It happens that way, even on visual strikes."

He knew when he looked around the table that they thought it all depended on whether or not Williams had put in a visual correction.

you bloody bastards you bloody bastards once your tours are over you think that everything that can be done has been done you think i'm blowing my stack that i'm getting flak-happy you don't know williams you don't know how he lies awake at night and says please god don't make it visual tomorrow please don't make it visual please god you don't see the look on his face when metro says it is socked in up to twenty thousand and we're going to bomb on radar you weren't there the time he held up my bombs on that sleepy little german village south of munich that i picked up as a target of opportunity he said he couldn't see it he said there was a cloud over it where was the cloud in the pictures you could see the grass grow from twenty four thousand feet you didn't say where is the cloud o no it was only one ships bombs the rest of the squadron had dropped on the primary on my smoke markers while my bombs hung up it was only one ships bombs wasted on a target of opportunity but that was one of the little sleepy german villages that has been hanging guys who bailed out one ships bombs my bombs i should have shot williams for the good of the war effort he couldn't hit the ground if it weren't for gravity he's a winter bombardier he likes clouds and lousy weather and no fighters and badly aimed flak and the directors all screwed up with chaff just so long as his ass is safe he doesn't care what it means to us you have heard him whine it's the mickey operators bombs they're montys bombs i didn't see the target he wouldn't dare mess with those controls after that sleepy little german village he missed he wouldn't dare make a correction it might be the wrong one and i'd kill him he knows it i'd kill him

The Colonel's voice was sharp with anger, but still it sounded restrained. "We'll send your report into division as 'results unobserved.' We will make no ridiculous assertions. Lieutenant, you seem to have a great deal more faith in this equipment than the rest of us. When there is nothing better to use, it will have to do as a substitute. But when I flew my tour in A-20's we dropped on control points with a stop watch and we had much better results than we've had with this equipment. Only last week Johnson missed Zwickau by twelve miles. Twelve miles! And he swore he had a shack. What is that comical metaphor you keep using, Lieutenant Hanley? Oh . . . er . . . yes. You 'creamed' it. If it weren't that so much depended on this radar idea, I'd be in favor of throwing it out completely as a bombing instrument and using it only for navigation."

With a quick, almost quiet chuckle, the Colonel laughed at his own joke and scanned the circle of the table with his gaze for the approval that would turn the chuckle into a laugh.

But the usual appreciative audience didn't seem to be present. Radar Maintenance, Radar Operations, Group Bombing, Group Navigation, and even Metro, all looked perturbed. Sam's face had turned poppy red. He belted the Colonel with it one word at a time.

"Colonel, when one of my men says that he hit a target he is almost always correct. Hanley thinks there are pictures to back up his claim or he would not be making such a claim. He isn't talking to pad his record. And, Colonel, may I respectfully remind you that we are not flying on the deck in A-20's. The Colonel should know that A-20's can't even take off in some of the weather we bomb in from high altitude."

i could kiss you for that sam i could kiss you for that wait till we get the pictures a-20 man a-20 man they taxied to the target in those damn toys he should have stayed with them

"Major Rayburn," the words hung in the air in near solid form, "I admire an officer's loyalty and confidence in his men as much as any man in this Air Corps. However, if you ever expect to hold a higher position than you do now, you will have to learn that that works both ways. There is no room in

command positions for officers who exhibit dewy sentimen-
tality and wide-eyed confidence."

he's held you here for six months promising you that silver
leaf sam tell him he can cut your orders for the states tomorrow
he'll crawl sam you know he will you can jam the pictures down
his goddamn throat ask him what happened the time he took
his navigators word over his mickey operators when he hadn't
seen the ground for four hours ask him how he and that
navigator felt after they got through bombing a city with our
troops in it

But Sam didn't say a word, and the Colonel turned his back
on the silent, now hostile men at the table, and walked over
to the window. The seventeens were still dropping in, one
every minute. After a time they stopped. The group was down
without a loss. Monty, watching over the Colonel's shoulder,
saw the ground crews swarming over them like ants on a picnic
cloth.

i am not going to let you get away with this you slob you
aren't good enough to fly right seat for sam the men are
separated from the boys over here colonel and that uniform
doesn't make you one of the men even if you think it does and
those eagles don't make you a leader even if you think they do

"Colonel," he said it with just the least amount of disrespect
to let the Colonel know he wasn't crawling, "if you remember
that Zwickau raid correctly, Johnson didn't miss the target
he aimed at by twelve miles. The flux-gate compass was shot
up and off twenty degrees. He went in on the wrong heading
and hit a town that looked like the right one. He hit what he
aimed at. It just didn't happen to be the right one. He, or one
of the other boys, should have noticed something had gone
wrong, but they didn't. And the equipment can't replace the
part of man that thinks, or is supposed to think."

eat it a-20 man eat it i'll never make captain but you'll eat it
watch what you say don't lose your temper sir the pictures will
be here soon and you'll be laughed out of the division

Every officer in the room froze.

The Colonel spoke in clear ice-cold tones. "Lieutenant
Hanley. You have been irritating me for some time about this.

All this. There had better be pictures of this strike. Not the ones taken by photo reconnaissance after the mission. They won't show which damage is yours. Not a scope plot worked out by our 'master' plotter in Path Finder Forces Intelligence. He makes mistakes, optimistic mistakes. Those pictures had better come from one of our planes. And, Lieutenant Hanley, those pictures had better be perfect."

The silence that followed, with everyone's meaning and position out in the open, was broken by the ringing of a telephone. The sergeant on duty answered it and handed it to the Colonel without a word. With no show of hesitancy he took it. Perhaps his back stiffened a little when he identified himself and told the caller to go ahead. He listened. Almost unknown to him the receiver moved away from his ear. His frame rigid, every joint locked tight, he moved the receiver back. "Read that to me again, please. Never mind, Captain. Send the prints over wet."

He put the receiver back on the hook gently. For a long time he hesitated. Finally he forced a faint smile, and in a strained but jovial voice he said, "Well, gentlemen, Eldeer, in the Group Lead, put about 65 per cent of his bombs in the 2,000-foot circle. Disbrow, in the low squadron, dropped his bombs one-half mile to the right and one-half mile short. Lieutenant Hanley, in the high right squadron, did 'cream it.' He put 95 per cent of his bombs in the 2,000-foot circle, and 70 per cent of them in the 1,000-foot circle."

With a quick grimace that disappeared almost as soon as it appeared, he turned to stare out the window again. Monty looked past the squared shoulders at the field. Men were in motion everywhere. And machines. Jeeps tore around. Six-by-sixes and four-by-fours rolled back and forth. A little checkered operations jeep whipped past in a cloud of blue smoke.

Monty waited for the Colonel to turn around. When he did, he looked directly at Monty and at no one else, and he spoke in a low unmilitary voice. "You may go, Hanley. You needn't worry about formal interrogation. Leave your maps and log and reports on the table. I'll see that your pilot takes care of them for you. Drop into my office tomorrow morning before your briefing for the afternoon practice mission. I want to have a long talk with you."

Monty answered, "Yes, sir." He smiled once at Sam, who whispered congratulations. Then he started to pick up his equipment, slipping the harness and Mae West over one shoulder, putting the helmet back on his head, and putting his chest pack under his left arm. He picked up his boots with his left hand, opened the door with his right, and stepped into the hall.

The chaplain wasn't in the main corridor. Monty initialed the mission roster for his rationed two ounces. He rolled the rye around in his mouth for several seconds and let it trickle slowly down his throat. When the liquor warmed his stomach, he sighed with contentment.

One of the sergeants commented, "You look as if you could use the whole fifth."

He answered gravely, "I never needed a shot more in my life."

He hitched his Mae West and harness higher on his shoulder, and transferred his boots to his right hand. On the long trek to the locker room his feet felt light and springy. The bracing cold of the English winter air and the warm glow of the rye in his stomach balanced one another perfectly. The over-all temperature was under control.

Elaine's Hope

TED M. LEVINE

THREE days and she had done nothing. Twice she had stood in the hall before his study, and once she had put her hand on the doorknob, but she had done nothing. And the thing that had been growing inside her for so long burned deep within her.

She watched Mrs. Rockwell's pink braceleted hand wave

at her from the front door. "I tucked Alan in, Lanie," Mrs. Rockwell was saying. "He ought to be asleep by now."

Lanie moved a step forward. "Have a nice evening, ma'am, sir," she said.

"Good night, Elaine," Mr. Rockwell said crisply. He looked at Lanie while he said it. He always looked at people when he spoke to them. Once, more than a dozen years before, Brian had come home from school with some kind of a painting award. "Father, they made me a Journeyman," he had yelled from the door, his cheeks pink with winter and his triumph. And Mr. Rockwell had sat him down in the leather armchair next to the piano and made him talk quietly and look at him when he spoke. "To me, Brian, not to the rug," he had said. After a while Brian had run into his room and lay on his bed, crying as if his heart would break. When Lanie had gone to him, he had exploded.

"Why can't you leave me alone?" he had screamed. "I'm not a baby any more. I'm not! I'm not!"

Mr. Rockwell turned his head and took his wife's arm, and the door slammed.

Lanie stood still in the hall and listened to their steps on the flagstones. Then she heard the car start and move away. In the new silence she thought about Brian, and then Rod, and now Alan upstairs. "Tomorrow," she said out loud. "To-morrow."

She went into the living room and sat down on the couch. She sat in the darkness and thought hard about the things she would do before she went to bed. She would set the table for breakfast. She would make herself a lettuce and tomato sandwich to eat just before she got into bed. She would write a letter to her brother Arnold in Scranton, Pennsylvania.

"Lanie."

She decided to stay where she was for a minute. She wanted him to get a little frightened.

"Lanie." The voice was stronger.

She got up and moved slowly out of the living room. On the stairs she walked loudly, so that he could hear her footsteps.

When her eyes got used to the darkness of his room, she saw that he was sitting up in bed.

"Why didn't you come right away?" he asked, still a little afraid. "I thought you weren't home. I thought I was all alone."

"Stupid Alan, of course I'm home," she said. "Goodness."

She went over to him, and he lay back in bed, his eyes closed. She pulled the blankets up about his neck and folded back the top sheet. "I thought your mother tucked you in," she said. Why had she said it? Mrs. Rockwell had nothing to do with this.

He moved over on his side so he could be closer to her. "I like you to tuck me in," he said.

She slapped him lightly on the cheek and sat down on the edge of the bed. "Two women to tuck you in, goodness," she pursued.

He said that he liked her to tuck him in better, and she sat on his bed for a long time until he pretended he was asleep.

She stood outside his door for a moment, ashamed, wondering why she had made Alan compare her to his mother. She started down the stairs, and then she turned around and walked to Mr. Rockwell's study which was at the other end of the hall from Alan's room. She closed the door quietly and turned on the light.

In the small, empty room she stood stiffly a yard in front of the old-fashioned mahogany desk. "Mr. Rockwell, sir," she said softly. "With the February vacation coming, I thought maybe Alan and I—" she stopped. She was talking too fast, and her hands were shaking. His eyes would have moved down to her hands. "Don't talk with your hands, and look at me when you're speaking," he had once said when Rod was describing for him a football game he had seen over at the high school. She looked around the familiar room thinking how intimately it was connected with her life: the soft-gray walls and the deepset bookcase lined with gold-stamped volumes, the little couch and the aluminum reading lamp. When her eyes got back to the desk, he was behind it as he had been sixteen years before, thin and straight, his hair jet black then. "He's handsome," she had thought, standing there before him in her whitest hospital uniform, "Young and yet distinguished."

"Very rich," Miss Markley the head nurse had reported to her a few hours before. "Lanie, you've really struck it this time."

"It can't be for long," she had said gaily, smiling down at him. "You see, Mr. Rockwell, I'm going to be married soon."

He had not congratulated her. He had continued to study the typewritten sheet describing her, which they had sent over from the hospital. Then he lifted his head and looked at her for a long time: at her nurse's cap and the way her hair was fixed beneath it, at her shoulders and her breasts, and the pearl buttons on her uniform. He asked her to turn around once. Then he stood up, and they shook hands. "A firm handshake." How many times had she heard him say that to Brian and later to Rod. "A firm, strong, friendly handshake."

All she had to do was cook and serve breakfast and take care of Brian, who was seven and spent most of the day in school. Other people handled dinner in the evening and there was a special nurse for Rod, who was still a baby. At night she was free to do whatever she pleased. When he had told her about her salary, she had squeezed her hands together hard. She had not thought such a sum possible.

"And I want you to have your friends here, Elai—Lanie, all of them," Mrs. Rockwell had told her that evening in the kitchen. Mrs. Rockwell loved to talk to her in the kitchen. "You're one of the family now, and I want to meet the people you care about."

So they had sat in the immense living room in the evenings, and Richard would look around him at the great black piano and the tiny Japanese water colors on the walls and the wood and chromium portable bar. The real bar was downstairs in the game room. You pushed a secret button behind the ping-pong table, and the walls opened up. "But where's the bar?" Mrs. Rockwell used to ask at her parties, and Lanie would push the button with her hand behind her back. It was one of Mrs. Rockwell's favorite jokes. Even when he was home, Mr. Rockwell never came to Mrs. Rockwell's parties.

Richard would listen to Lanie play on the piano the melodies she had learned as a child. He would look at the paintings and the bar and then at Lanie. "So maybe you don't want to leave," he'd say. "I mean with all this." And she'd stop playing the piano and sit next to him on the couch and kiss him hard. Then she'd tell him about Brian, and the scrapbook they were making out of photographs from the *National Geographic;* also about Rod and the way he was learning how to talk.

During the first week she had gone up to Mr. Rockwell's study and reminded him about her getting married. He had continued to read the printed business form that was in front of him. He had signed it and pushed it a little to one side. Then he had looked up at her—straight at her—and said he remembered perfectly what she had told him. He asked her whether she and Richard had decided on a date for the wedding, and she said they hadn't. He told her to come back when they had decided upon a date, so that he could plan on getting somebody else for Brian.

Then Mr. Rockwell went to Boston, and Mrs. Rockwell—it was 1933—became county secretary of World Peaceways. Lanie tried to explain to her about Richard, but she didn't understand. "Richard? Richard?" she would say, looking up at the ceiling and playing nervously with her hair. "Oh, yes, your fiancé. Why don't you ever ask him over to the house, Lanie? I'd like to meet him very much."

April came, and Mr. Rockwell was still away, and Richard landed the sales job he had been waiting for for five years. It was in Detroit. Richard wanted them to get married right away and go out together, but Lanie said she had to wait until Mr. Rockwell came back. They wrote each other long letters, and Brian and she finished the scrapbook and bought a set of finger-paints. Pretty soon Mrs. Rockwell was talking about their summer vacation out on the tip of Long Island. Mr. Rockwell still hadn't come home.

In June, Lanie, Brian, Mrs. Rockwell, Rod, Miss Gamble, his nurse, and Arthur, who did the cooking, were driven out in two cars to the house and dock on Peconic Bay that the Rockwells sometimes rented for the summer. They were the happiest two months of Lanie's life. She taught Brian how to swim. First he was afraid and said the water was too cold. He yelled and cried a little and told her that he hated her. Then she got him to float on his back and then the dead man's float on his stomach. He was strong and he learned terribly fast. By July he was crazy about swimming. Arthur would row them way out, and they'd swim back in together, the boat following. She'd sit on the warm beach, dead-tired and dripping wet, and he'd run around her taunting her with, "What's wrong, Lanie? You tired after a little swim like that? I wanna go swimming again. C'mon, Lanie. C'mon."

In August they got a telegram from Mr. Rockwell telling them to come home. The big house seemed sunless after the beach, and Lanie missed the hot sand under her feet. In September Brian went back to school, and Lanie started to read some of the leather-covered books in the library. Many of the pages had never been cut. She read *Paradise Lost* and *Don Quixote,* both of which she liked so well in high school. Mrs. Rockwell saw that she was reading and said that she was happy about it. For Christmas of 1933 she gave Lanie a copy of James T. Farrell's *Young Lonigan.* "It's crude, sometimes obscene, Lanie," she had warned. "But it's got a lot of truth in it." Later it turned out she had only read the little blurb on the bright cover jacket.

Richard kept writing: little angry letters asking her what she expected him to do. He told her about his job (lampshades), and said that he could offer her "security," but not "a big house with shuffleboard in the basement and a two-car garage." Lanie remembered one letter especially. "Why do you call them 'your children?'" he had asked. "They're not your children. They belong to the Rockwells. How can you be so satisfied with other people's children?"

Lanie couldn't say she would never leave the Rockwells. Maybe she didn't know it herself then. She said it was difficult to get somebody else, and that she wouldn't leave Brian in the hands of an idiot like Mrs. Rockwell, and that Mr. Rockwell was away again. Then she went on and told about Brian's drawings and the things Rod was saying. After a while Richard stopped writing. Two years before the war she got a long letter from him saying that he was still in love with her but that he was marrying a girl named Jeanne Franklin because he wanted a family of his own.

Brian's fourth-grade teacher, Miss Spottwood, suddenly got excited about a crayon sketch he had made of a walrus they had seen in the Bronx Zoo. She entered it in a children's exhibition in New York City, so one morning Lanie and Brian were driven down to Rockefeller Center. There were three walls of pictures mostly by children older than Brian. Many of them had red or blue or Honorable Mention white ribbons pinned onto them. There was no ribbon pinned onto Brian's picture. Lanie thought he'd get angry about it, but he didn't. He looked carefully at all the pictures and talked about them loudly all the way home. When they got back, he painted his biggest and best water color of a huge yellow cat they had seen the morning before.

April 3, 1937—and Lanie said she always forgot dates—Mr. Rockwell returned unexpectedly from a business trip to Milwaukee and said he wanted to see Brian in his study right away.

Brian told her about it afterward. In two weeks his father was taking him up to Boston for a few days, and he should look his best for the trip. Lanie said they better get going and buy him a new suit, but Brian shook his head. From now on, he told her, all his suits would be custom-made by his father's own tailor.

Lanie saw him off at the front door. He was in a solid-blue suit with a little gray felt hat that didn't look as silly as she thought it would. He promised he'd write her a long letter, and Lanie said she didn't care anything about letters, but he should make sketches for her of everything he saw in Boston.

When he came back, Lanie knew right away that everything had changed. She could tell by the stiff way he held his shoulders up and back under his new suit and because he shook hands with her. He had never shaken her hand before. He had made no sketches and he said the trip had been "very pleasant."

After that Brian wore only suits. His sweaters, many of which were brand-new, were given by Mrs. Rockwell to China Relief, which was just coming into its own at the time. Lanie kept his water colors and sketching crayons and new oil paint chest in the bottom two drawers of her bureau in case he should ever want them. In the beginning he went into his father's study for talks twice a week. He cried after the first two of these; but after that he never cried again. In the mornings, at breakfast, he would exchange sections of the newspaper with his father, neither of them saying a word to anybody.

It was decided that he should be an engineer. At seventeen he went away to a large northeastern university. In typewritten letters home to his parents (he alternated weekly) he asked about her with almost deadly regularity: "And don't forget to give my love to Lanie," or, "How's good old Lanie? Give her all my regards."

Rod was six when this happened; too old for his nurse, said Mr. Rockwell. So Miss Gamble went back to her mother's house in Albany, and Lanie stayed on.

Rod was no Brian. He was intelligent, but without Brian's imagination or sensitivity to form and color. He had a fine sense of humor though, and he loved to laugh. Sometimes he'd be walking with Lanie, and suddenly they'd both look at each other and burst out laughing about something that had happened to them hours before. They both knew it was the same thing and that made them laugh all the harder.

Lanie had been smarter about Rod. She herself had taught him to sit up straight at the table and look at people when he talked to them and to say, "Please" and "Thank you" about everything. If his father asked him about school (Mr. Rockwell was home more now), he was to say he liked arithmetic and geometry instead of English or music. Also, he was to talk about sports (he liked sports) as much as possible. Mr. Rockwell had once referred to Brian's sketching as "unmanly."

When Rod was seven, Alan was born. Mr. Rockwell got a white-haired New York City nurse named Miss Carton to take care of him.

Rod was eight and then he was nine and then ten, and nothing had happened. Then one morning Lanie came into the breakfast nook to clear away the dishes. Everybody, even Alan the baby, was silent, and in front of Rod on the tablecloth there was a large dull red stain and a tomato juice glass tipped over on its side. Mr. Rockwell was standing at the head of the table. "Don't put it back," he said quietly. "Leave it exactly the way it is." He went up to his study, and Rod went up after him.

It didn't change Rod as much as it had Brian. Maybe it was Lanie's earlier instruction, or perhaps it was his own glib sense of humor that cushioned the shock. A hidden streak of cruelty that Lanie had always known about came to the surface though. Once, a year later, Lanie had watched from the hall while Rod tripped Alan again and again when he tried to walk. "What's the matter? Can't you walk, Alan?" he was asking. "It looks like Alan's forgotten how to walk. Poor Alan's forgotten how to walk."

Rod wouldn't go to college like Brian. He'd finish high school and then, after a two-year training period in one of the branch offices, he'd go directly into his father's business. He was always Mr. Rockwell's favorite son.

Alan was nine now. He was the last of them. He had neither the physical strength of Brian nor the social poise of Rod. He was small for his age, with dark hair, and eyes, and skin. He had grown up during the war and postwar years, while his father was in Washington and later in Chicago. He was intensely artistic, impossibly sensitive, but without Brian's need for expression. He would listen, observe, touch things in silence, and only Lanie understood how they quivered inside him; only Lanie had watched his dark eyes and baby mouth when he read or listened to music. He could not be twisted a bit like Rod or totally changed like Brian. He would break, smash like a delicate piece of china; Lanie was sure about that. She had not taught him tricks for his father as she had Rod, because Mr. Rockwell had been away for so many years, and because he never would have learned them anyway. She had let him grow up for himself, watching him in wonder, and waiting, and hoping blindly. And now he was nine, and Mr. Rockwell had been home from Chicago for three days.

She looked at the glass desk top, at the piles of white paper in their little black wire cages, and the fat black humidor with its briar and clay and gourd pipes. Why now? she wondered. Why had it suddenly hit her so hard? After all Alan was only nine. It might be months or even a year or two, maybe not at all. Mr. Rockwell himself had said the new office needed "constant supervision." He might go back to Chicago at any moment.

She closed the door behind her and went downstairs. She turned on the lights in the living room and played *Für Elise* softly on the piano the way she had for Richard more than fifteen years before. She was surprised that she remembered it so well. She set the table for breakfast with the second-best silver and went into her own room and started to undress.

She looked at her bare head and shoulders in the small mirror above her bureau. "So how about a little marriage?" her brother Arnold would say, or, "Thirty-seven? Lanie, I protest. You're as fresh and beautiful as the day you graduated from high school."

If she was only sure there was more time, it wouldn't matter so much, she thought in bed. Then the words she had been looking for for so long floated up to her:

"Mr. Rockwell, I think Alan could do with a little winter sports this February vacation. I'd like to take him up to a place in Massachusetts I know where there's skiing and skating. It would strengthen his ankles and back and put color in his cheeks. I could buy the tickets today, sir."

And after a while Mr. Rockwell would push aside some of the papers on his desk and half smile up at her because she had put the thing so directly. "Winter sports, eh?" he would say looking straight at her. "Sounds like a good idea, Elaine. Go ahead. Go right ahead."

And then they would be at the Pine Grove Lodge, which was a mile and a half from her aunt's house, where she had spent one winter when she was fourteen. They would both be bundled up in ski suits and furry caps and mittens and red rubber boots. They could watch the professional skiers on the slope in front of the lodge, or walk in the snowy, quiet pine woods, or toast marshmallows up in their room. Every room in the Pine Grove Lodge had a big, old-fashioned Dutch brick fireplace in it. And because she hadn't been there for so many years, everybody would think that she was Alan's mother. Maybe they'd even make a game out of it and see how long it would be before anybody could find them out. When she fell asleep, they were fishing through the ice on a tiny lake she knew about a mile in back of her aunt's house.

She slept a long time. When she woke up, it was snowing softly outside her window. She looked at the big, separate, white flakes, and suddenly she knew she was going to go through with it. She dressed carefully in her best uniform and spent a long time with her hair. For breakfast she made Mr. Rockwell's favorite, which was wheat cakes, and he looked up at her over the top of his newspaper and said, "Good wheat cakes, Elaine." Mrs. Rockwell told her the play they had seen the previous evening was "gripping and important." Then she asked Lanie whether she had ever heard of an organization called the South American Reform Council and gave her two leaflets to read.

After breakfast Lanie went out to the village, which was half a mile away. People kept appearing out of the fluffy snow and waving at her and yelling, "Hi, Lanie," and, "Hello there, Lanie," and, "Cold enough for you, Lanie?" She smiled and waved and answered back, because they were her friends, and she wanted to tell them about the deep, warm secret that was inside her now.

When she came back, nobody was downstairs. Mr. Rockwell was up in his study, and Alan was in his room reading, and Mrs. Rockwell was probably on the telephone in her bedroom. In another quarter-hour Carl, who cooked lunch and supper, would come in. She went back into the bathroom and brushed her teeth again and put a tiny white handkerchief in the breast pocket of her uniform. She stood in front of the mirror smiling at herself with her hands motionless down at her sides. She repeated slowly a few of the words she would say.

She went through the kitchen and the living room and across the front hall. Then she was climbing the stairs. When she got to the second floor she turned to the right. Then she stopped.

Alan was coming out of his father's study. He turned his face away from her, but she could tell by his shoulders that he was crying.

As I Am, You Will Be

BERNARD HARPER FRIEDMAN

ALL the years of his young life Little Boy wanders the streets, looking at the beautiful girls and wanting them; all his young life he longs for the orgy that never comes. The conventions, the mores, the pressures of his group, they bother him; they never leave him free; they are to blame. The big experience never comes. Ecstasy is a word. Romance is paper and celluloid and Ernest Hemingway. He watches the truck drivers, the bartenders, the stevedores, admiring their broad chests and narrow hips and their lives, their lives which pulse in the night. There is something about a strange face, a double shot of whiskey gulped down without a cough, tattooed arms.

Little Boy wanders, hating his clothes—the uniform of his class—and envious of the men who don't wear ties.

The war comes—silently and secretly, like a worm eating an apple. At first he and his clique aren't bruised by the falling cards. But eighteen comes fast, fast enough so that Little Boy doesn't miss the big war. He may go marching off to camp with men, using all the strong words, hearing all about the big strong nights.

And Little Boy may get tattooed. Do you know what it is to walk into a tattooing parlor? Can you imagine choosing one label out of thousands as yours for life? Does the eagle seem to scream? Is the battleship too large? Is "The Sailor's Grave" too common? Is the seaman carrying the swab too cute? Would MOTHER, in capital letters, be flattered when she saw his arm? His eye finally lights upon a skull and cross bones with the motto: "As you are, I once was. As I am, you will be."

Little Boy rolls up his sleeve. Swede dry-shaves his arm and swabs it with alcohol. The stencil is applied and smeared with a black charcoal compound. Swede picks up the electric needle, dips it into heavy black ink, and follows the outline.

The boy holds fast on the left arm of the chair. Damp dead sweat trickles from under his arms. The needle works in and out on its course leaving blood in its wake, and the boy grips the chair more tightly, thinking of the sea, and breaking with the parental yoke, and the blood and the needle, and in and out and in and out, and forever, which is a long time.

The needle looks caked and dirty. What about infection? What if some sailor before him had a disease? "Ya ain't a man till you've had a dose." "Blued, screwed, and tattooed." "Darling, don't forget your rubbers." Oh Boats, Oh Mate, Oh Mother, Oh God.

Swede finishes shading the central portion of the tattoo with a thicker needle which doesn't penetrate or hurt as much. He wipes the surface again with alcohol, but this time it bites and stings. Cool, soothing vaseline and a gauze bandage.

"That'll stay on there good. Don't pick it if it starts scabbing up on ya."

"Thanks a lot."

The boy gives him the three bucks and leaves.

For about two weeks the tattoo doesn't look just right. It is scabbed in spots and indistinct in others. And then it emerges—clean and sharp and part of you. You belong to a vast fraternity, encompassing all oceans and all ports, all roads and all jobs. When you walk into a bar in Shanghai, with your sleeves rolled up, you acquire a dozen friends. And a dozen men want to know you as you swim off the beach at Manila. The world is yours, the blood, the pulse, the ecstasy, the godhead you envisaged in a thousand strange thighs. No longer the prep-school frustration. You're a man of and among men. Forever, "As you are, I once was. As I am, you will be."

II

But the worm dies. It is the summer after the war. Seduction must replace rape and purchase. "Intercourse," "sleeping with," "going to bed with," "oh shoot," all must be forced back into the vocabulary. And oh the polite cocktail parties and bridge games.

Forget that weekend in Frisco, when the water was running cold in the bathtub on a case of beer and four-fifths of rye. Three sailors with their jumpers off played cut-throat pinochle for fourteen hours (and a carton of Lucky Strikes)—waiting for the knock on the door the pimply elevator boy had promised them. He made a four-hundred hand and waiting, waiting, waiting—till finally the knock. She'd take them all on for ten bucks. They cut, and his king was high. Christ, what a run of cards.

But now Susan bids four no-trump, and he knows she's using Blackwood, asking for aces, but he wants to ask the boys to beat a full house.

"Five hearts."

"Five no."

"Six diamonds."

"Six spades."

"Pass."

"Pass."

"Pass."

He's dummy. He gets up and looks at his partner's hand. If the finesse doesn't work she'll go down—one trick—one dollar in Panama.

She makes her contract and tells him he bid it nicely. Now they all want to go swimming, and the last one in is a monkey's uncle. So long ago he had drawn king high.

His tattoo is so-ooo cute, but really how could you? Were you drunk? God you must have been really pickled. Cold sober? Early in the morning? In Norfolk? O priceless, priceless. Well, it really isn't so bad—I guess.

The cute little blonde, six years old, with her curls bouncing on her shoulders, runs up to him:

"What's that, what's that?"

"It's a tattoo."

"What's a taboo?"

"Tattoo, tattoo. They make an indelible picture by pricking coloring matter into the skin."

"What's indelible? Does it hurt? Does it hurt much?"

"Indelible means it never washes off. It didn't hurt much."

The president of his father's club sits down next to him in the "hot room":

"You're Mike's son, aren't you?"

"Yes, sir."

"How'd you ever happen to get that?"

"I guess I was trying . . . I wasn't thinking very clearly . . . I was drunk."

He is in the shower room with his fraters for the first time:

"Haha. You salty dog. Why the hell did you ever get that thing? I almost got one; I'm damn glad I didn't though. A buddy of mine back home got tattooed, and his parents made him have it taken off. Has Susan seen it yet?"

He had dreamed of his return home and strutting across beaches and tiled floors flaunting his tattoo, but he found himself deliberately draping towels over his arm and buying long-sleeve sport shirts. Now, in the shower, he spread the lather thickly on his arm.

The needle goes in and out, pricking beneath the skin. Superficially, at least, he had always belonged to his group. He had all the right labels from the Roman numeral three after his name to the Hunt Club and Beach Club. What had happened? It would be different if he were a nigger, a wop, or a Jew, but having a tattoo—that's such an unimportant thing.

Going to sleep at night, he would make a tacit pact with God that if the tattoo were gone in the morning he would always believe in Him. A thousand times he looked expecting it to be gone. Finally, he made an appointment with a dermatologist.

III

Dr. Turner looks at the slip the nurse hands him and smiles.

"I assume since you are here you have made up your mind to have the tattoo removed. It would be useless for me to try to dissuade you?"

"Yes, I've thought a lot about it, become self-conscious; I'd like it off."

"Well, let's take a look at it. Roll up your sleeve."

The doctor looks at it, pinching and stretching the skin, and remarking that the pattern is not really offensive. He calls for the nurse, and they lead the boy to the back room. Once again the surface is cleansed. The doctor keeps up a running commentary throughout the inquisition. He will try electrolysis, acid, and injections on various parts of the tattoo. When the boy returns in two weeks, whichever method has shown the best results will be used to remove the entire thing. The various treatments hurt about as much as the original tattooing, but in the sparks of the electrolysis needle he sees regained ease, and physical pain is of only secondary importance. The little sore spots are covered with a bandage.

"Goodbye, doctor, see you in two weeks."

"Righto, goodbye."

The two weeks go by surprisingly fast. A few times he catches himself wondering which parts of the thing will be the first to go. He pictures it minus a bone or an eye, a word or a phrase. Twice he peeks under the bandage. He sees three ugly little scabs.

He is early for his appointment when the time comes. The doctor removes the bandage and scrapes away the scabs with a scalpel. He shakes his head.

"I'm afraid it's in too deep, too deep. The only way to get it off is a rather painful plastic operation."

Charlie, the lifeguard, has a cruiser anchored on his chest. Joe, the locker boy at the gym, has five or six small tattoos all over his arms. What would they think of him? And what would his ex-mates think? Just before the end of the war, he used to talk a lot about what design he would get for the other arm.

"Would you make arrangements with the surgeon, please?"

The waiting room of the plastic surgeon is extremely crowded. Women with their noses bandaged and black eyes sit looking at the words in fashion magazines and National Geographics. At last a big nurse with a little voice calls out the boy's name and he is ushered into the back office.

"Dr. Turner spoke to me about you. I've arranged for an operating room at the hospital two o'clock tomorrow. Will that be all right?"

"Fine."

"Good. Now let me see your arm."

The boy removes his coat and rolls up his sleeve.

"Not bad. Not bad. I was under the impression it was much larger. That will come off nicely. We'll be able to use a local anesthetic. You can watch the whole thing. Don't eat a heavy lunch, and turn in at the incoming patients' desk about half past one."

He signs his name at the desk and is turned over to an intern who dresses him in a clean white nightgown and prepares his arm for the operation. A sickening smell of ether pervades the place, and "NO SMOKING" signs make the minutes pass more slowly. Promptly at two, the intern leads him into the operating room, where the surgeon waits all in white except for the horrible pink-tan practicality of his hands, hands that represent the ultimate in social aesthetics. Those hands and a scalpel will make him feel comfortable on the beach and in the shower room. They will deliver a scrap of flesh, a scrap of understanding and sensitivity, to the hospital sewage system, to the river, to its mother ocean. For a few days on beaches and in shower rooms laden with talcum powder he has known inferiority, but the pink-tan hands will cut this away. The left hand is smug and the right is complacent. The surgeon offers both, stretches them towards the boy.

The day before, the girl in the doctor's office with her new nose looked so relaxed, so completely untroubled and peaceful, almost animal. A bloodless operation. Black eyes and a swollen face for a few weeks. And then that wonderful freedom we all crave—freedom from feeling. The knife, cat-gut, anesthesia offer this.

Cyrano, Cyrano. What a nose, what a man.

If the bullfrog had wings, he wouldn't bump his ass on the ground. If he were stronger . . . If the war . . . If society . . . If . . .

"Ready, nurse, the novocain."

The Last Year

DOROTHY BARRIE MULHOFFER

PA AND the boys and I live alone now. Pa and Lee work the farm and Jess and Al and I go to school. Chris went off to college—he's going to be an engineer—and Thiel works on a ship out of New York. But it wasn't always this way. Things used to be different. We were all together then and Ma lived with us—and the baby.

"I guess it all really started 'way back before I was born, even. Pa was the oldest of Granther's seven sons and they were gypsies. They lived in the vans and traveled all over the country—north in the summer and south in the winter—living on what they could pick up here and there and on what they could sell. The women told fortunes and sold embroidered fancy blouses and trinkets and woven cloth goods and the men repaired pots and pans and did all odd jobs. Granther had come from Hungary with his father and nine brothers (his three sisters had married out of the tribe and stayed in Europe), and they traveled and lived as they had in the old country. When Granther's father died, although not the oldest, he made himself Chief and all his brothers and their wives followed him. Granther's first wife, Pa's mother, died in childbirth and he married again; then when she got sick on the water and died, he married his third. Some of Granther's brothers left then and took their families with them. But his own sons were growing up. Pa being oldest, Granther had hoped he'd follow in his footsteps, so to speak. But Pa was different from the rest and nothing like Granther at all. He was quiet and he didn't like the roving life. Pa always liked things different from his brothers. He liked to read and he didn't like to wrestle or dance much like all his brothers and cousins. This disappointed Granther but he never said much about it. He thought Pa was weak and just left him alone.

Then Pa married. All the other brothers married cousins but Pa was different; he never showed any interest in his dark-skinned cousins. One day, while they were camped near a farm in Pennsylvania, he met our Ma. She was German stock and slender, with golden hair and big velvet brown eyes. They fell in love then. He adored her and the thought of the life excited her so, that when Pa asked her she said yes right away. Well, when Granther laid eyes on her he didn't say much and she was married to Pa and taken into the tribe. And they say that it was then that Granther turned his eyes on her; and it was true enough he was good to her. Usually he didn't pay much heed to the women, but her he taught the dances to. And she was a born dancer; soon she could step better than any of the women. She was like wild flame or sometimes like the soft west wind when she danced. They say the women talked against her then. Anyway she soon got with child and Pa pulled out. He just told Granther he was going to be a farmer and left. Granther did a surprising thing; he lent Pa money and he and Ma bought the farm. Chris was born and then Leland and Thiel and Jesse and Alain and me.

And every year Granther and the band would stop over on their way south in the fall and often on their way north in the spring if they were in our neighborhood. They'd come for a few days or a week and camp in the meadow and then they'd go. They never announced their arrival beforehand and you never knew when they were going to leave. They'd just come and stay and then be off. Pa's brothers and cousins all had children and the band grew large. And Granther handled them all.

Then the year I was thirteen they came in the fall. I remember that year because I had got suddenly a lot taller and it was that time I met my cousin Joseph. He danced with me and I was tall and gawky, my bangs too long and getting in my eyes —and he told me I was a good dancer. He was seventeen and tall and dark, with straight white teeth. My aunts nudged one another as we walked down to the table Ma'd set out under the trees with drink and cakes on it. One of them yelled something in Romany to Joseph which I didn't understand, but I blushed and was proud to have such notice taken of me walking with him. That was a wonderful dance that year. I remember it had been a very mixed-up day too. Chris was pestering to go with them that year, but Pa was against it and finally made him quit talking about it altogether. Pa was in a temper that day, probably because Ma was not around anywhere; he seemed worried about it. She had gone berry-picking and didn't come home 'till late, all tired and disheveled but happy and excited; Pa was mad. We hadn't started dancing yet anyway, because Granther was nowhere to be found, either. It was sure a funny sort of day.

Things were changed with us somehow, after that year. Soon after they left, Ma got with child again but it didn't cheer Pa up any. He seemed glum lots of the time. That year in December, we found out later, Granther's third wife left him. She picked up and left the band and went to work for a carnival, telling fortunes. Ma's baby was born in July. She sure was a surprise to us. We were all dark and the baby was all golden, with Ma's golden hair curling in ringlets all over her head. Ma named her Angela Julie. She seemed to be all Ma's baby. Pa didn't bother with her much. He just didn't seem interested. So Ma cuddled her and spoiled her like she never had any of us.

That next fall, when the baby was about two months old, they came at the end of September.

They had come during the night—late. The boys and I were all in bed but we heard the rattling and the faint jingling. I had thought I was dreaming and it was the faery campers that lived in the big meadow in the autumn. But the next morning we were up early and looked out across the lawn and the trees,

and there they were. The vans were dusty, the bright colors
muted, the paint peeling. They were drawn up in a semicircle,
facing the house. The horses were tethered on the edge of the
wood. Smoke rose from their breakfast fires. We dressed fast
and dashed downstairs. Ma had breakfast for us and said we
had to eat it and go to school just like any other day. Ma was
always more animated and vivacious when they came and now
she glowed with excitement and her velvety dark eyes shone.
We bolted our bacon and eggs and were ready to run out but
had to wait till Ma dressed the baby; Granther hadn't seen
the baby yet and she had to be dressed in her fancy-stitched
dress to be presented to him. She cooed and clapped her hands.
She was really a lovely baby. Finally, when the baby was
ready, Ma combed out her own golden hair—it fell below her
waist—and tied a blue ribbon in it; she said Granther liked it
loose, I remember. We started for the encampment. Pa had
already gone that morning to welcome Granther before chores
and was down to the fields. Used to be, he'd spend some time
and tell Granther about the crop and the stock and the land
and all, but this time he just welcomed Granther and that was
all. He went on down to the fields and stayed there working all
day.

We came and Granther was out front of his wagon sitting on
a box and smoking. You'd have never known he was almost
sixty. He was bigger than any of his sons and stronger, 'cept
for Lize, who was the smith. Granther had thick black hair
low on his forehead and bushy black brows and long narrow
eyes that looked green. He looked up and we all paused. Chris
went up to him then and Granther shook hands with him and
then with Leland, Thiel, Jesse, and Alain in order of age. Ma
pushed me forward over in front of him and I curtsied 'till my
skirts hid my black stockings. Granther looked very stern, his
mouth straight and hard, but then he let his eyes smile. I
jumped up and stood awkwardly with the boys. Then Ma
walked toward him real slow with Angela Julie in her arms.
Granther smiled and took the baby in his lap. She laughed and
made happy noises. Granther sure liked that baby. Then he
looked at Ma and a funny look passed between them. It made

me shiver inside. It was as though Granther was happy about something and awful mad at the same time. Ma just gave that funny smile of hers so that her dimples showed. Ma was awful pretty for a woman with seven kids. And that was funny, too— I'd never really seen her smile—she laughed a lot or she didn't —but that slow smile was something new—I liked watching it. Granther rumbled something real low in his throat and Ma said, "O.K. Git, you kids," and we ran off to school, anxious to tell the kids the gypsies had come. Chris should have gone down to help Pa in the fields but he felt that day was special and went off to see the cousins. He had got out of school in June and had been after Pa again about going out with Granther and the band that year. He was nineteen and thought he was plenty old enough. Thiel was seventeen then and would be out of school soon and wanted to go too. Pa wanted them to stay home and work the farm or go to college and be some-body, or anyways, settle somewheres, like he had. It was him made us all go to school—the only ones in the whole family who had. Leland, who was eighteen, made Pa feel better; he wanted to stay home and work the farm. Ma wanted them all to go. It seemed almost like she wanted them wild.

We beat it fast to school and told our friends our exciting news. I could hardly sit still through my lessons I was so anxious for class to let out. Even my teacher said something about how excited I must be. I guess people who didn't know always took us for Italians until we spoke Romany to them; even then some of them didn't know. But my teacher had read books about the gypsies and she knew some about how they love to dance and sing and keep moving, always on the go. She made me speak Romany to her sometimes and she said it was too bad I didn't know more. But Pa didn't speak it much at home any more and so I was forgetting. Finally school was over and we hurried home. We had at least forty-five cousins and it was always fun to see them.

I went in to throw my books on the table and bumped into a tall boy coming from the pantry. I recognized him and blushed; it was Joseph. He laughed and said, "Watch out."

Then he looked at me. "You are Marth—do you remember me?"

"The boys call me Muddie, now," I said, suddenly shy at the sound of my name, "and I remember you." He laughed unaccountably and sat down on the edge of the table. He sunk his white teeth into the apple he was carrying.

"Where have you all been this year?" I asked him.

"We have been in Canada," he said, "Where have you been?"

"Here," I said, and he laughed again. "My brother hopes to go with you this year," I said. I couldn't see what was so funny.

"Which, Chris?" he asked.

"Uh huh," I said. He put out his hand and rumpled my bangs.

"How would you like to go—with me?" he said. I guess my face must have gone blank—I was that surprised. I blushed hot and then he laughed again.

"Come on out," he said. He didn't tease me none the rest of the afternoon. We went out of the house and wandered down toward the vans. We passed some of the women beginning to prepare the food for the evening's feast. They greeted us and Tante Sobrikka said to Maria Nevvra,

"She's getting to be a big one now, huh." I felt too tall and gawky but good, too, because Joseph was tall beside me. Then we met a bunch of cousins and I stayed with them 'till time for chores. I hadn't seen Ma all day. Soon after I'd finished the chores she came in and went upstairs, and then Pa came home from the fields and went and got into his good clothes too.

That night we built a big bonfire and all ate a lot at the feast and the neighbors came from miles about and we danced. We all danced—rounds and squares and all the gypsy dances. It was a hot night and dark and the red fires flickered on the trees and you could smell perfume and soap and sweat. The leaves rustled and the stars came out and there by the fire we danced in a big circle. The women wore their best fancy skirts and bodices and the men wore their bright trousers and silken sashes. Ma wore a flaring blue skirt and a silver girdle and a white blouse cut low over the shoulders. She looked like a queen. Among all the dark dancers her long golden hair shone and she stood out from them in the firelight. She danced with Pa and then with Pa's brothers and with all the young bucks. Her sons were proud to dance with her.

And then she danced with Granther—and he was like a sword flashing and she was like a flaming flower of wind—all grace and speed and silver flashing and they whirled round and round over the grass. And all the others stopped dancing and watched and Anton kept the fiddles singing and everyone was caught up in their dancing and the fiddles sang on and on and Ma and Granther danced like it would never end. And sometimes it was like they were one body and sometimes they flared apart for an instant like two flames and then they would pull back into their own swirling vortex. And on it went till we watching were hypnotized and I was dizzy. Then all of a sudden Granther and Ma closed and swirled to a deep dip—Ma's hair spreading on the ground—and Granther was holding her in a locked embrace. Pa gave a hoarse yell and ran into the circle of light. Their form broke and became two and Granther turned toward Pa. Pa plunged his fist at Granther's face and Granther broke his blow, lunging him back with a sharp crack as the bone broke. Pa fell back on the turf as the fiddles squeaked to a close. Not a sound escaped the crowd but as Granther turned away, they moved toward Pa. Granther walked out of the circle of the firelight as Chris and Lee carried Pa away. The fire burned low.

The next morning they were gone and Ma and Angela Julie with them. Pa and the boys and me stayed on till Chris and Thiel left. Now it's just us—working the farm. Pa never says much. Sometimes, I guess, I wonder about Joseph and how it might've been with him and me.

An Egg from the Sky

FINLEY C. HUNT, JR.

IF HE wasn't God or the King of England or the President of U.S. Steel (without twitching a bit his legs felt as if they were growing out of the twelve-inch ledge on which he was standing) he at least was master of the bobbing mass beneath him: the sausage links of scurrying cars, the odd-colored germ blobs, the furious idiotic roar. The wind sniffed around his legs. He could see now, fear having unsheathed his nerves, all the meaningless patterns below. People, hundreds of them, hurrying, bumping ahead and around each other on tiny errands. And around and under him were signs, big and little, portents by which the people lived: APPEARING SOON, JOAN OF ARC; TRY THE SMOKE THAT SATISFIES; FOR FIRM FOUNDA-TIONS USE NYLONO UNDERWEAR; DRINK THE DRINK THAT MILLIONS DRINK. Each punctuated by the bleat of angry horns clearing short jerky paths for their steel hulls.

Shifting the weight to his right leg, edging away from the window, he felt the terrifying surprise of momentarily losing his balance, the awful yawn of space calling him forward. (Too soon, too soon, he thought, I must have my audience.) He flushed his body against the cement, extending his arms till they found safety in crevices. Looking straight across the street at the water tank on top of the Heathcliff Building, he side-inched his way to the window cut. Carefully he turned around; the shade was down; here he could perform until the police were called. It would be a good fifteen minutes before they would come sirening to the spot, another fifteen before they would lace the nets under him. Time enough to stop the world's mad spinning, to stun a city into silent embarrassment —to drop nine stories onto cold cement.

[145]

Out of his right coat pocket he produced an egg and like a boy playing mumbly peg aimed it at the three distinct head and leg dots moving towards him. He hoped not to splatter the black hoods; they looked like nuns stiffly shuffling through traffic. All he wanted was a few minutes of their time, a few minutes to brand their memories for life.

He was fascinated by the crazy end-over-end fall of the egg, getting smaller and smaller until like a drop of milk it blended into gray.

II

Sister Bernice had just ironed her habit that morning in her study at the Sisters of St. Andrew's Convent. Her first thought, too swift to be verbalized, was that she had been killed, but after the initial wave of surprise vanished, she scowled furiously at this horrible injustice done her habit. Why should misfortune inevitably strike her? Why should she be thus humiliated by fate? Then Sister Teresa leaned back to see from what demoniacally precise bird the egg had fallen. Dabbing at the yellow spatterings on her skirt Sister Agnes was too busy to look up. Things like this happened daily in New York.

"My word," Sister Teresa rumbled, "there's a man up there."

And indeed there was, the other sisters found as, birdlike, their eyes followed Sister Teresa's raised arm up to the ninth floor. Indeed there was.

"My heavens," Sister Agnes' blue-veined hand flew to her mouth.

"Don't leap!" Sister Teresa bellowed in her man's voice, at first not realizing the impossible range it had to travel.

Sister Bernice's mouth clapped open and shut. He's the one who dropped the egg on me, she concluded, staring up at the gray figure, now waving his arms like an orchestra conductor. If he fell he would splatter just like the egg. She shuddered and crossed herself with a "Dominus vobiscum."

Like filings drawn to a magnet, men and women crowded around the three sisters, gaping up, exclaiming oh's and ah's in hushed awe. A police officer came pounding down the street waving the people back, shouting warnings and curses.

"Look out, if he jumps he'll kill someone!"

"The crazy goddamn fool," a man beside Sister Agnes said, soliciting her scornful look.

Sister Teresa, in full command and with her usual lightning insight, shouted at the police officer, a few feet away: "Call the fire department, officer. Get a net to catch the poor soul!"

"Oh, the poor, poor soul," whimpered Sister Agnes, wishing she had never walked into this horrible crosscurrent of life and possible death.

"Somebody do something; he'll fall," Sister Bernice said in a trancelike voice, the image of the splattered egg still stamped before her eyes. "Don't let him fall!"

By now a band of policemen had swiftly and silently appeared, stopping traffic, huddling the audience back out of danger. A few of them hurried into the hotel on missions of persuasion.

"Look!" a man pointed with a cigar, "what's he doing?"

"My heavens," Sister Agnes fluttered, "he seems to be doing some kind of stunt!"

"He's throwing something."

"No, he's juggling."

Sister Bernice watched the white circling blurs, knowing at once that they too must be eggs. Sharply, in a voice louder than her cheerful convent soprano, she addressed her fellow onlookers, sharing her knowledge like a woman just escaped from a burning house: "He must be insane. He's juggling eggs up there, I know. He dropped one right on my habit."

Ignoring her, Sister Teresa pulled on a policeman's sleeve.

"Why don't they get nets under him? Isn't the fire department here?"

The policeman, jetting a stream of tobacco into the gutter, turned slowly to Sister Teresa: "Sister, we're doing all we can. Even with the nets he can kill himself if he wants to. It ain't hard to hit the pavement."

"And his poor soul will go unblessed." Sister Agnes, on the verge of tears, bit the sleeve of her habit. He would go crashing through the pavement straight to hell. She knew. If only he were able to have the balm of last rites.

[147]

A man shouldered past Sister Agnes, grunting as he entered the store behind her: "It's all a phony publicity stunt. Some actor out of a job."

I'm sure he's criminally insane, thought Sister Bernice.

I'm sure this policeman would as soon have the man dead, thought Sister Teresa.

III

——onetwothree to you sweet-eyed ladies onetwothree I dedicate this onetwothree my most crystalizing clarifying act (the white juggling balls spun in their half universe straight and true from the palm of their creator) I dedicate myself and my brief talent, all this I give you, trust to your sweet minds to keep as you keep your virginity onetwothree—

Although he couldn't stare down without missing the throw-catch-throw rhythm, he knew the three hazy specks on the lower screen of sight were the three nuns. To them he was dedicated, to them he was offering this, the epiphany of his life.

He had to hurry now since any moment the police would try to snatch him to safety. The three white juggling balls sailed sharply off his right hand, dipped, plunked his left hand and were off again. Fortunately he had the wind on his side so that the allowances he had diagramed were unneeded. It was the simplest thing in the world to do. In fact it was all he knew how to do.

For a week he had sweated in his bed nights, wide-eyed, trying to prove to himself that he was real. And he couldn't do it. It was impossible, like thumping his fists against the steel doors in the bank. Ever since he had dropped the Indian club in his last performance—the Rotary Club men had laughed and jeered him back to the dressing room—the thought had haunted him and hounded him until he couldn't sleep. There was nothing he could do that would make him a man in others' eyes. He, a dull little shy silent man, had to foist off his little-boy talents on the gullibility of others. His feat of juggling was the feat of a thief and he a thief of applause. He was a parasite without beauty, without the head and shoulders of individuality. Without friends, without wife, without love.

A voice to his left nearly knocked him off balance.

"Hey, mister, what's your name?"

Still juggling he realized that the police had come, that probably a net was strung up below him to catch him like an insect. First they would try to talk him inside, not daring to grab him from behind, then, this failing, they would trap him cold, pin him against the building.

"Aren't you hungry, buddy?"

Out of the tail of his eye he could see a man's head to his left, probably a psychologist, like a siren, trying to lure him into strong steel arms.

No, he thought, not yet; although he knew his time was almost upon him, he still could captivate the nuns. Like sympathetic tuning rods, they understood, they felt the thing he was doing, they knew. It was for them. When he had first lined them out from the crowd, he knew they would understand. Like a lecturer speaking to the one face in many, he had marked them for his act. Surely they would see the picture heightened now as at this moment his life came into focus. They had to see.

Otherwise he couldn't go back.

"Listen fellow, you can't jump. There's nets all around you. Be reasonable."

He caught the last juggling ball, dropped it into his coat pocket and looked down.

But where were the three sisters?

There was a crowd, a huge caterpillar of people standing across the street, but no habits. No nuns. Carefully he scanned the spot where before they had been standing. Just grays and greens, no blacks. No nuns.

There was a brief blurring second after he leaped when he thought he might clear the net. In that second he thought he saw not nuns but angels smiling up, singing to him. Then the net swallowed him up, lifting him out of their reach back to reality. Back to the ninth floor where he was arrested on a charge of attempted suicide.

[149]

IV

In the coffee shop Sister Bernice felt much better. Sister Teresa had just overturned her cup of chocolate, staining her habit, turning her face to a wrathful red.

"Stop beaming, Bernice," Sister Teresa scolded. "It isn't proper."

"I was thinking of that egg maniac," Sister Bernice said to cover up her exposed emotion. "I hope the police have apprehended him by now."

"Those people will do anything for publicity," Sister Agnes said between sips. "To think I was almost beginning to pity him."

Siren of Hope

SAM KEITH

THEY were jumping all around him—big silver fish that lashed the water and curved into the air. He had drifted downstream in the canoe, because it had been easier than paddling up against the current. After he had passed beneath the old Grand River bridge, he had drifted right into them. Hardly any effort at all, just a dip now and then with the paddle to put the nose on course, and he had floated right into an Atlantic Salmon bonanza. Heart-jolting splashes—flashing, thrashing, teasing forms that bolted out of the blackness of the river.

He eased his small anchor over the side, felt it grab bottom, then let the rope glide through his hands until it tugged quivering at the stern thwart. He reached greedily for his fly rod. A glance into the water and he saw several large fish streak from beneath him and torpedo upstream. "Jesus," he said. His fingers trembled as he tried to tie a number four wet fly to the leader; his stomach fluttered as if it held caged grasshoppers that jumped and hit against the sides and fell back. Finally he got the fly fastened. Then the line would not shoot out, and for a long moment he did not realize that the leader knot was inside the guide at the tip. He swore. As he pushed the butt towards the bow so that he could reach the tip, the water churned and erupted less than fifteen feet away. Spray fountained; the heavy fish slapped down a ring that clapped strangely against his ears. His fingers became more clumsy. He grasped the leader; the rod tip bent and snapped upwards again as the knot passed through the bottleneck. He was jittery. He began to cast, to strip line from the grating reel, to whip line sliding through the guides along the split bamboo. His wrist rocked back and forth, the line uncoiling behind him, straightening, then bulleting forward. At the end of one of the forward motions of his rod he reared the tip back slightly. The fly dropped like a fuzzy, bright-petaled blossom and floated downstream. Fluffed and twisting slowly, it swung in an arc, then tugged, a wake forming behind it, as it used up all the slack. He lifted it into the air with a snapping back of his wrist, let the line lengthen out behind him, then pulled it forward to settle and ride the current down. The salmon rolled and played and ignored the fly. Now it was water-drenched; it sank, and as it moved along beneath the surface, he twitched his rod and made the blob of feathers jerk as if alive. He was almost afraid. It looked so easy. He was almost afraid to see the bulge of a dark back and the down lunging of his rod tip into the water. He was almost afraid to hear the harsh chatter of his reel and the hissing of tight line cleaving the current. He had read about the battlers they were, but he had yet to catch his first salmon.

The sight of the huge, glistening sides and tails, the sound of solid bodies smashing water made his heart grip and swell against his ribs. His hand clenched tight on the cork grip of the rod; he could feel his nails biting into his palm. His eyes probed at the crazy darting of the fly until they almost ached. He could almost hear his heart beating. Then after more than an hour of high tension, he was not excited any more. He switched to a dry fly and watched it drift like a wind-blown spider of down. The salmon did not touch it; they taunted with rising backs and flirted their wide tails at him. He was in the middle of a fisherman's hell. Salmon all around him and not one of them that would even nose his offering. Part of the first day already gone. A little more than two more to go now, and then it would be back home again to get up tired in the morning and go to work and come home in the evening tired and sick of it all.

A back rose like a surfacing miniature submarine and sank. He saw the big dorsal fin, its ragged edge, it was so close. The tail flipped and slashed a flurry of white water; the roil and foam drifted away downstream. "God, what a brute!" he breathed. He cast monotonously until the salmon stopped jumping. He put on a wet fly again and whipped the water for another hour. Only a dimple now and then of a small trout or a playful minnow. He was disgusted. Suddenly he felt that he had had enough of fishing for the first day. The sight of salmon had frayed his nerves; not being able to get a rise had frustrated him. Propping his rod against the thwart, he tugged on the anchor until it let go of the bottom, hauled with long pulls, hoisted, and carefully settled the weight near his feet. The canoe crept forward. The trees on the bank began to move. He backwatered hard on his paddle; he could feel the birch in his hands bend with strain. The bow pivoted slowly. He swung his paddle to the other side of the canoe, stabbed deep and out from him, then pulled with choppy, splashing strokes. He was headed upstream towards the old bridge. His head dipped forward with every flashing back of his arms that drew the broad blade straining. The water whispered and complained against the oncoming canvas. On the bridge ahead that arched low above the river he saw a tall figure leaning over the rail. The fellow looked as though he had stepped out of a story book. He wore a black suit coat and a black string tie. A closer look at the long, bony features, the protruding Adam's apple, convinced Ben that he must without a doubt be looking at none other than Ichabod Crane. The fellow looked down at him.

"How's the luck, lad?" he chirped in a twanging voice.

"Rotten. No good at all, sir. A while back they almost jumped into the canoe, but they wouldn't take the fly at all." The current was shoving him back. He saw a shallow sloping gravel bank on the shore; he pointed the bow at it and scraped into a landing. His legs were stiff from sitting down so long. It would feel good to get out and stretch cramped muscles. Maybe this scarecrow on the bridge could give him a steer. He stooped as he made his way along the midrib of the canoe bottom, then stepped out and felt land beneath his soles for the first time since early morning. He pulled the canoe halfway up the bank, bow still afloat in the water. The tall stranger approached.

"Ye'll not get a somon, lad, where ye see them jumping down-river. Ye'd best be trying the pools up in the fresh water. Somons don't rise down here to the fly where the water is still salt from the sea. Ye might take one, now, in the pools upriver. Hard to catch on the fly though, lad. Indeed they are."

"Did you ever take one on a fly?"

"Yes, oh yes. When I was a wee lad I was on the river all the day. A long time, now, it took me to catch my first somon. Indeed a long, long time. I suppose I gave up the chase fifty times, but, lad, I always found myself back on the river again with the rod in my hand. But the first one—oh, he was a handsome fish, lad—eighteen pounds and fresh run from the sea. As silver as a new coin."

"Eighteen pounds!"

"Aye, that he was, right to the ounce. And a beauty he was, lad. But what a long time to catch him. What a long, long time!"

"I'd wait a long time for a fish like that. But two days more is all I got this year. Just two more days. My camp is up the river about a mile."

"'Tis a shame, lad. 'Tis a shame ye've but two more days."

"You say the pools up the river are the best chance?"

"That they are, lad. Ye might raise one there, now. The Steeple Rock pool is a grand stretch. Ye'll see a pointed rock that near tilts across the stream. I've taken fine fish from there. 'Tis not far beyond your camp. Try it, lad. 'Tis a shame ye've but two days. 'Tis indeed a short time to catch a somon."

"Well, thank you, sir. I'd better be going. I'll be sure to try that pool at the Steeple Rock."

"Do, lad, and good luck to ye, lad. I hope ye kill a handsome fish. Don't lose your patience. Ye must keep trying."

"Thank you, sir. I'd better get in the canoe and head for camp. So long, sir."

"Goodbye, lad, and good luck to ye."

He lifted up the stern and slid the bow into the deeper water, then he shoved with his foot, jumped, and rode the back end on his knees. He stepped inside and squatted to his seat. He stirred his paddle and the canoe knifed into the current and passed beneath the bridge. The bow aimed at the middle of the river. A queer old duck, he thought, but a friendly sort. Maybe this evening he would try the pools above camp. Steeple Rock pool —the name sounded good to him. He rounded a bend and a pair of mergansers hydroplaned out of the shadows and lifted with wing tips splashing. He laughed to himself; they were getting more fish than he was. He saw the canvas of his tent peering through the spruce branches. With a twist of his paddle, he pointed the bow at the narrow beach. The bottom rubbed and grated against the sand. He was home.

He broke off some dead limbs from the spruces and made a tepee of them over some yellow birch bark curlings. Soon he had a fire snapping. Two Y-shaped sticks were butted into the ground, one on each side of the fire. Another stick formed a bridge between them by resting on the crotches. From the stream he dipped a pot pail half full of water, then lifted one end of the bridge and strung on to it the pot handle. The pot swung over the growing blaze. From his supplies he took a can of beans, stripped off the label, and lowered the can into the water. Then he opened up a package of Uneeda biscuits and nibbled on a few crackers while he waited for his dinner to warm. He should have come back earlier, he thought; it was already three o'clock in the afternoon. The water began to steam; he let it bubble awhile, then removed the pot and tipped it to spill on the ground. He took his jacket from the tree stub, wrapped its sleeve on the hot can, snapped out the opener on his knife and ran it around the edge of tin. He ate all the beans and finished up the crackers right down to the flakes left behind on the wax paper. He felt sleepy now. His eyelids felt weighted. He crawled into the tent and flopped on the sleeping bag.

It was after six o'clock in the evening when he awakened. He was ashamed of himself. "I could have slept back home," he muttered. He wouldn't have time now to fish the pools. Two more days, he rationalized, that ought to be time enough. He stayed in camp and heated up a can of spaghetti for supper.

The firelight flickered on his shirt. The embers popped and snapped. He felt the flush of the blaze against his face. His eyes lanced into the flames that waved lazily and curled around the ends of short logs. He filled his pipe without even looking at it and tucked it into the corner of his mouth. Then he held a slender stick in the coals, brought it out tipped with flame and touched it to the bowl of his pipe. Tobacco smoke drifted into the smoke of the campfire, rose up into the dark trees.

I've come a long ways, he thought. A long ways for just a week off. Too bad he didn't have more time. Two days and a night it had taken to get up here in this salmon river country of Cape Breton. It would take him that long to get back. So that left him three days to get a bellyful of the outdoors. Now one was already gone.

He had come because he was disgusted and because he had a vacation. He didn't like his job in the foundry. Who said that they freed the slaves in the Civil War, he thought. Hell, he could show a fellow plenty of slaves. He was one himself. He just worked his eight-hour sentence and got paid for it. And in the evenings when his arms and shoulders were muscle-weary from lifting heavy pigs of iron, he sat down at his desk and wrote. He wrote about all kinds of things, and he even had had a few of his stories published in some of the pulp magazines. As if that was enough! Writing was a damn discouraging business. And it seemed such an easy racket to break into! Every magazine you picked up—full of stories, full of new names. Writers that were selling their stuff. And him working all day and writing at night. As if he didn't get enough exercise! And for what? For a lousy pulp. How full of confidence he was when he slid a story with the customary self-addressed and stamped envelope into the Manila and shipped it off! He laughed. A kick in the guts when it came back a few weeks later. The same old rejection slip. He had a copy stamped upon his brain. He knew the line, word for word. "Dear Contributor: We thank you for sending us the enclosed manuscript. We are sorry that we can not find a place for it." Then there was the other short paragraph. "Although every story gets our careful attention, the volume of manuscripts received prevents us from giving individual criticisms." And then that wonderful heart-warming complimentary close. "Sincerely, The Editors." That was the part that really got him. Sincerely, The Editors. Yeah, they were sorry all right, sorry as hell. He felt so sure with every one that he sent in. It just seemed so easy! It looked as easy as salmon jumping around a canoe. But it was a tough racket; it was heart-tearing to work hard at something and have it slammed back politely in your face. Sometimes he wanted to sell that typewriter once and for all.

They gave him a week's vacation at the foundry. They really broke their hearts. They surprised him when they handed out the pay envelope. I'm taking off, he decided. I'm going to forget that long, shoe-dragging eight hours and I'm going to forget that typewriter, too. I'm going to forget them for a week. Yeah, how could a guy forget slavery in a week! The typewriter—now that was a way out, but there was a damn high fence to hurdle by that exit.

His rod slanted almost upright against a tree bole. Its windings and varnish glinted in the light; its ferrules flashed. He was suddenly reminded that his line needed to be dressed. He snipped off the leader and wound the line up on the reel. The rod sections popped as he pulled them apart. He removed his reel from its seat on the butt, then held the sections in the middle like a bunch of arrows and laid them next to the tree. His hand rummaged in his kit and came out with the line dressing. He spread a poncho on the ground and settled on it cross-legged. He wanted his line to keep clean once the dressing was on it and not collect spruce needles and grit from the earth. His fingers wiped at the white salve-like substance in the round, flat can, then pinched the line and rubbed along it. The reel clicked hoarsely as he pulled out more line. As he dressed it, the line fell sprawling on the poncho, limp and shiny. He doctored up about twenty yards, then ran his slippery fingers back over the length again. It would float well now. He turned the reel handle with one hand while the line frictioned through the fingers of his other. There was no grit on his line; it was limber and slick and clean. He thought of the Steeple Rock pool. "Maybe tomorrow," he said.

The mosquitoes began to whine around his head. The smoke from his pipe was not enough to drive them off. He let the fire burn down, then he covered the coals with ashes and heaped on some green logs. The coals should be alive when morning came. He rapped the bowl of his pipe against one of the logs. After picking up the rod sections and jointing them, he fitted the reel back on to the butt. He could see the moon coming up beyond the trees; overhead through the spruce branches there seemed to be more stars out than he had ever seen. The mosquitoes were bringing up reinforcements; he had to retreat into his tent. He fastened the cheesecloth netting shut behind him, took off his clothes and shoved himself deep into the bag. He heard an owl's call boom out in the stillness. He heard a fox squall once, twice. Then he was asleep.

He paddled up the river until he came to a shallow bar. Here he dragged the canoe out and slid it beneath the trees. He broke an alder branch and let it dangle; it would be marker enough for him. Then he pulled up his boots, strapped them to his belt and sloshed over the shoal with his rod.

He found the Steeple Rock pool. The lance-shaped rock slanted over the stream. The water was deep and dark and slow-moving. Islands of froth sailed eddying past the rock. He began to cast. He fished it upstream and he fished it down; it didn't seem to make any difference. He waded out with water pinching and squeezing at his thighs and threatening to pour into his boot tops; he roll cast into the glassy mystery that stretched on both sides of him. He fished with dry flies and wet flies and different sizes and patterns of flies. His wrist tired. He caught one small trout, but all morning long he didn't see a salmon rise. He tried other pools in the afternoon. He crouched on the bank and floated flies into water that his boots had not disturbed. He didn't even see a salmon. In the twilight he headed the canoe into his camp landing. Lonesome, hollow-sounding, a loon's quavering chuckle rained down from the sky. He saw the heavy-bodied bird disappear over the trees. "Well, there's still tomorrow," he said.

He watched the river blacken. He listened to its lisp and tinkle in the shallows. He liked the way it curled around the roots of a fallen spruce. And he knew that the salmon waited in its waters somewhere. The other day it had seemed so easy! There were so many of them jumping that morning on the other side of the bridge. He remembered all the trout he had caught, some of them big trout. He felt deflated. He thought he knew his business with the flyrod, but these big fish of the north teased him and showed him that he had a lot to learn. And now it seemed that all was lost. The salmon had disappeared.

When he stirred the next morning, he heard the rain. The big drops punched at the canvas above his head. "Damn," he said, "now wouldn't that make you want to bawl."

He went up to the pools again in the rain. They were very beautiful, but they seemed such barren places. He tried hard. He tried until he came home wet, hungry, and disgusted. He came home knowing that when the morning came, he would have to leave. "The salmon must have gone back out to sea," he muttered.

He packed his rod in its case. He loaded the canoe on the racks of his pickup truck and strapped the thwarts down fast. He ate his supper in the darkness while the fire burned low.

The mist was swirling off the river when he squatted on the bank and slopped handfuls of cold water against his face. His hands stung with numbness and his face tingled as if it was charged with electricity. He fried up a can of Spam and made some sandwiches, ate two of them for his breakfast and wrapped up the others. The tent was next. He pulled up the pegs and folded the canvas. Then he rolled up his sleeping bag and packed it with the tent snugly into the back of the truck. He

made sure he hadn't missed anything. He buried all the cans
and papers that had accumulated. He scattered the fire and
knocked down the Y-shaped sticks. The place was as he had
found it. He was ready to go, but the river, dark and smooth-
flowing, held him back.

He leaned against the big spruce trunk and gazed long and
hard at the surface that seemed to dimple with smiles and yet
brood in ugly blackness. It fascinated him. It was so damn cruel.
It was like a lot of things, almost like life itself. It taunted and
teased and reflected frustration. Double-crossing, black-hearted
river, he thought. All the way up here for one measly, under-
sized trout.

It came as a surprise, shocking and sudden. A salmon writhed
out of the water, deep-bodied, etched for one fleeting moment
against the green of trees, its side a silver, shimmering smear.
The great fish whacked resoundingly and scattered spray like
a bursting bomb. The water smiled and brooded once more.
He watched the commotion slide away downstream. His heart
beat strangely faster; it was as if the river had unveiled a
secret. "Maybe tomorrow, maybe next year," he muttered. "I
don't have the knack yet. But it'll come." He walked to the
truck. He didn't go to unpack his rod. There were no short
cuts. He swung himself into the seat behind the wheel, started
up the motor, and headed back to his typewriter. . . .

Allan Franklin

H. D. ROSSITER

ALLAN FRANKLIN worked in a basement, behind great
rolls of stiff brown paper, stacks of flat corrugated boxes, and
between moving belts and steel chutes, shiny with the polish-
ings of countless packages. Three afternoons a week, with his
books still under his arm, he would take the subway to this
shop. He would wrap packages and sweat in the tight air for

seven hours; and then, tired and sleepy, ride the subway home. And yet, despite the bad air and endless work, despite the whispers and laughter, these were the happiest days of the week, and sometimes, he thought, the happiest days of his life.

For at his side during these hours, working with him and talking to him, was Johnny Rose. Rose would bring a book along—a volume he selected with great care at a bookstall for a nickel or a dime. And Al would listen as Rose read passages aloud or, as he frequently did, recited passages from memory. Sometimes he would talk about the ideas in these books, what they meant, and how beautiful they were. If there was a lull in the work he would take up the book and plunge into a long paragraph. At times Al would not understand, but Rose seemed to sense that even before Al himself did. Then he would repeat the sentence or the paragraph, looking up after every few words, speaking very slowly and very clearly. And the idea seemed understandable just because he enunciated so clearly.

Often Rose would stand very straight with a book in one hand, following with the forefinger of his other the lines he was reading. The thought would carry him away, and his voice would become louder. He spoke in a firm tone then, as if he were a prophet, and sometimes to Allan, he seemed to be just that. Standing there with a book in his hand, a small thin old man with a pale face and a black suit. But the other packers, many of them high-school boys like Allan, would guffaw, laughing and yelling from the other side of the moving belt.

"Yea, and thus spoke Solomon," one of them would yell. "What's he preaching about now, Al? Is it going to rain tomorrow? Can he tell me if the bitch I had last night had the clap?" And their laughter would fill the warm room.

To watch Rose after these attacks was to watch the deflation of a personality who suddenly recognizes an unpardonable distention, and tries to correct it. He quickly retreated inside himself to a central gnarled shell—an impervious shield against the world. He would work feverishly, his eyes would glow, and he would mutter to himself.

Al would look at his friend's tight dark face and thinning hair and wonder what strange feelings were passing through his brain, what words his slightly moving lips were shadows of. Never succeeding, Al's skin would color. He would stand looking intently at his work and think of how he had gotten to know him.

From the very first, before he had started work, he had been warned about Rose. When Al and Marek and a few others were being taken down to the package room the first day, their guide, a red-headed pimply boy, wised them up about things. He talked about the floor walkers who were right guys, and the managers to watch out for, how to make the time clock jump, and all the other things.

"By the way, you got a queer guy working down there— Rose, Johnny Rose. Reads books all the time. You can have a lot of fun with him, but he's as queer as they come."

It did not take Al long to find out for himself what they meant. Rose worked on a bench alone while everyone else doubled up. But Rose, who was on full time, did the work of three of those who were part-time help. Everyone had fun with him. Some of the bigger guys would grab him around the waist and attempt to wrestle with him. Rose, his ordinarily pale face flushed with anger, would turn. Sometimes he scratched like a cat or a woman in a fight, leaving long red marks on faces and cheeks. That did not help. But he always apologized and was humble when it was over. For days afterwards they would call him "Killer Rose."

Al joined these escapades sometimes. He knew it was wrong, but there was something very funny about these scenes. This dark thin man, his eyes flashing, scratching his opponents like a woman.

It was many weeks before Al changed his attitude towards Rose, and it was Rose who took the first step.

Since there was no time to bring his books home, Al brought them to work with him. He left them on his bench so that he could not forget them. Coming back from supper one night, he found Rose looking at one of the books—an ancient history with a torn cover he had gotten secondhand.

Rose looked up and asked: "Do you study about Alexander?" He looked at Al closely.

"No. We haven't come to him yet."

"Well when you do, pay attention. Alexander was one of the few really great men in history."

"Why?"

And then Rose started to talk. The gnarled shell clothed itself in a mist of words. He talked of the early life of Alexander. How Olympias, Alexander's mother, hated Philip, his father. How Olympias dreamed that a thunderbolt fell on her, kindling a great fire in her womb, and that out of this union of a God and a priestess came Alexander. How he jealously regarded the victories of his father. How Aristotle came and added his wisdom to this earth-God. And he talked of his conquests.

"Think of the conquests of this one man. Three continents were in his hands. He marched across Egypt, Babylon, Assyria, the country of the Phrygians, the Armenians, the Jews, the Hyrcanians, Parthians, Bactrians. His empire extended from the Upper Nile to the Indus, from Samarkand to Babylon and beyond, from the Caspian to the Red Sea."

Al could not hold the meanings in the palm of his hand. They were too rich and fleeting for that. But they vibrated a hidden chord in him, a heavy dormant strand which needed but the right melodies to move it.

No history he had ever heard before was like this. In school they offered only the facts and dates, the names of treaties and battles—as if to disguise the chaos by making it concrete. But the human story that is poetry, when in school had they offered that?

Someone jabbed Allan in the side and he jumped. There was sudden laughter on all sides. The other packers were in a tight circle around him.

"What's he telling you, Al?"

"Has the old gal been reading a book to you, Al?"

"Giving the old prophecies?"

"What about it, Al?"

They were all laughing now, and somehow he felt ashamed. All he knew now was that he was in the center of a circle with Rose. Everyone laughed at Rose and so they laughed at Al too.

The association was simple, and Al knew it. He answered the only way he knew how.

"My friends, you have disturbed our deep and subtle conversation. Rose was revealing to me his experiences with a Union City burlesque queen—a noble woman." Everyone laughed and Al felt safe. Things were all right now.

Rose said nothing, turned, and went back to his bench.

The next night Al came back from supper early. Rose was there already, working fast as usual. Al wondered whether Rose ever went out to eat like the rest. When he went to his bench the old man came over to him.

"Here's a book for you," Rose said. He left a book on the desk and walked away.

It was an old book. The binding was torn and the price—five cents—was still on the fly leaf. It was about famous generals and their battles. Al thumbed through its thick pages. The paper was slick and there were full-page illustrations of the generals in uniform. Red jackets, patent leather belts, and shining armor.

Al was confused at this. Why should he give him a book? Why should Rose give him anything? Rose had fed his pride and attacked it too.

But it had started. Al went home and read from the book. Most of it he did not understand, but the descriptions of the battles were fine.

He was off the rest of the week but the following Tuesday he was back at work. He came in early and walked over to Rose's bench.

"I brought back your book."

"Did you like it?"

Al explained that he had time to read only part of it, and that much of it was over his head.

"That does not matter. People read books not because they already understand, but because they do *not* understand. For after all, most of us are ignorant suckling children who seek the pap of wisdom."

Again the peculiar words struck an inner chord that made Al smile with pleasure. He knew his mother or the priest in school would frown if they heard. There seemed to be a flicker of immorality about his words though Al never succeeded in discovering just where the immorality lay. "Ignorant suckling children" and "pap of wisdom" and dozens of other phrases stuck in his mind as well as his heart. Al would wake up in the middle of the night, the blankets warm and the room dark, and think about these words and how Rose had said them.

For Rose's voice made all the difference in the world. In ordinary conversation it was small and lifeless, but when he read from a book or talked about books, it would change. Then it possessed strength and roundness, and became the resonant instrument of a confident man.

In a few weeks they began to take supper together. They were given an hour. Sometimes they ate at a small delicatessen around the corner and sometimes they did not eat at all. And on those nights they walked toward the river where the big liners were, lying like children against the breast of the city. They sat on the pier and listened to the slip-slop of the water against the dock, the strange mutterings of the river. The old man's memory was sharp. He liked Boethius best of all and quoted long and beautiful passages from him:

Ah! how wretched are they whom ignorance leads astray by her crooked path! Ye seek not gold upon green trees, nor gather precious stones from vines, nor set your nets on mountain tops to catch the fishes for your feast, nor hunt the Umbrian sea in search of goats. Man knows the depths of the sea themselves, hidden though they be beneath the waves; he knows which water best yields him pearls, and which the scarlet dye. But in their blindness men are content, and know not where lies hid the good which they desire. They sink in earthly things. . . .

This was a new world for Allan, and sometimes his new world seemed to be a dream. Hours with just the sound of the water against the dock, the recurring bass of the ferries, the star points of light mirrored in the black water. And beside him, almost invisible, this dark voice.

After these supper hours, after this dream, the reality Allan had known all his life became distorted into a nightmare. His senses were too sharp. As he walked back into the long packing room the noise dug into his eardrums and the smell corroded his nostrils—the flat odor of lye and flour paste, of artificial leather and new cloth, the whip-slapping of the webbed steel belt.

The dream changed other things as well. Without the amplitude of laughter the delicate balance of tolerance is strained, and though there be no immediate movement of the scales, the reading is forever false. As long as Allan laughed, the packers could laugh with him. But when they saw that Al was no longer amused, their smiles died. Their amusement turned to resentment, and their resentment to hate. It seemed to Al at times as if they considered him a traitor who had depleted their ranks by befriending Rose, as if Al were the unwilling booty in a silent battle. And he did not like it.

Rose persuaded Al to work at his bench, and there they continued the conversations started at the river. In order to hear over the noise. Al had to lean over his work toward Rose. Once he looked up suddenly and found Marek staring at him from across the belt.

Very gradually the other packers stopped talking to him. In the halls they passed him without a word. When the packers initiated a plan for getting supplies every few days, Rose and Al were not included. They had to get the paper and twine and paste for themselves.

One evening Al and Rose returned from supper and found a sign on their desk. In black crayon on the side of a corrugated box were the words: "The Misses Al and Rose, Packing Done." Al tore the sign in pieces. His anger was so great he could say nothing. He did not talk again that evening, even to Rose.

The gnawing dislike, the silent hate of the other packers galled Al. Why couldn't they understand? There was nothing between Rose and himself. And he tried to tell himself he did not care what they thought.

But he did care and his caring changed things. The talks by the river continued but they were not the same now. Allan could no longer lose himself completely in the dream, in the voice beside him. Always, in the front of his mind, was the packing room filled with the old oppressing machine noises and the new vindictive silence of his forgotten friends. Reality then returned to vitiate his dreaming self.

Four weeks later an event occurred which decided Allan. After it he knew what he had to do.

Going home one night, he was beaten up. In the darkened street it was hard to recognize anyone, but he knew they were the other packers. They did not speak. Someone in a lumber jacket pushed his fist into Al's face. Another rubbed his ears hard against the side of his head with clammy calloused hands. And then they left.

As he cried, his inner hurt turned to hate. There was hatred for the whole world in his tears—hatred for the packers, hatred for himself, hatred for Rose.

It was Rose who was the real cause. Rose with his books and his stupid voice. Al had sold himself for words, and for words he had gotten a beating. What did he care for words anyhow? What were words to him?

The next night he came to work late. He felt the stares of the packers and looked momentarily at Rose, standing in his dark suit by their desk, his desk. Allan walked past Rose to an empty bench, put down his books, took off his jacket, and started to work.

After a while he looked up and found Marek smiling at him.

"How'ya doin', Al?" he asked.

"I'm doin' okay," Al answered, smiling back.

When the buzzer sounded, Marek and two other boys stopped by his desk and asked him to eat with them, and Al said yes. They had hot pastrami sandwiches and Marek had some beer. As they ate they talked of women, and how they wished they could leave school, and what a bastard the manager was. Allan talked little but smiled often. They did not laugh at him now.

Nothing more happened that night. Allan worked alone. He felt Rose's eyes on him but did not look up. That was over. The dream was over. He breathed the air easily now. It no longer stuck in his throat as it did after the hours on the river. After all, here was where he belonged, not in a dream.

The following night before Al started work, Rose came over to him. The gnarled shell of a face seemed in pain.

"What's the matter? What have I done?" His voice was pleading, almost tearful in its earnestness.

"Nothing. You haven't done a damn thing."

"I don't understand. Why don't you talk to me or eat with me or . . ."

". . . or sleep with you? Get the hell out of here! What do you think I am—a God-damned fairy? Leave me alone, dammit, leave me alone!" Al turned away from him and began to wrap a package.

The man seemed on the point of tears. He placed his hand on the boy's shoulder. The boy swung around and grabbed the hand savagely, twisting it, his fingers digging deep into the flesh. He pushed the man violently to the ground.

"Leave me alone, I told you!"

The man got up. Large patches of white dust clung to his trousers. He walked out of the packing room and did not return again that night. And for Al he could never return.

And Jacob Called

STANLEY SULTAN

And Jacob called unto his sons, and said, Gather yourselves together, that I may tell you that which shall befall you in the last days.

Gather yourselves together, and hear, ye sons of Jacob; and hearken unto Israel your father.

[167]

Reuben, thou art my first-born, my might, and the beginning of my strength.—*Genesis 49:1-3.*

CLAP—clap—clap—. Allen stopped now. The moon was a warm yellow pool on an infinity of ice, the stars scratched out with a pick to surround and keep it company. Shadow was everywhere on earth.

His last footstep echoed, then only silence was with him. He liked silence—liked to have it stifle everything else and make itself felt. Allen didn't like the daytime, because it was always shouting, but the night was different, and now it was night.

Bluewhite above, blueblack below.

He stood in the dark projection of a three-story building and looked on the jagged border between moonlit street and moonless sidewalk. He walked again—clap—clap—clap, and watched his breath thin and disappear. His shoe slapped against the sidewalk and the sound expanded. He had to hurry. . . .

He had walked awhile now. The metamorphic quality of the street fascinated him, as it always did.

A man, a white coat over his body, a paper bag on his head, leaned against a wall and coughed throatily, with a husk, a rasp. From a doorway near him, the sour and chalky smell of hot rye bread. A delivery truck hit a bump in the street, and squeaked and rattled and shook its way out of Allen's hearing.

A collision with a small boy, a pain in the groin, the boy clutching his pants in two claws, trying to turn him, shouting. A big man, no coat, lumbering down the block, stick in hand, guttural curses, growls—gross, obese growls, the gross, obese face.

Allen didn't move. The man clutched his shoulder, reached for the boy. Allen wrenched loose, ran, heard some of it anyway. The boy screamed like a girl.

Allen realized now that he was late. He began to pump his legs and arms. The heavy clothing made him labor and sweat. His steps were short, heavy. His breath was quick, strained. His body hot and tired. He moved his head from side to side. Some dogs and cats were feasting at an overturned garbage can. The cornucopia was rich in the fruit of the neighborhood. Two women argued out of second-story windows, pointed at each other.

They cursed each other in Arabic and Arabic-English. The shrill female voices became fists and beat on his brain, searing it, dulling it, searing it again. A lapse of a few seconds, then— once more the fists, now many more of them, and children's fists. They did not sear, for they were friendly, but they dulled and dulled.

Allen pushed to his seat, placed his books before him, and held his head. The fists had turned to stamping feet. They were mashing his brain now; he knew it.

Then the familiar shuffle—flurried beginning, building up, and the climax, when all the seats are snapped down by anxious buttocks, and all the eyes are focused on *mar* Gybie.

Good day, class.

Thin, long, graybrown lips reluctantly release the words, defile them as they pass.

Anteby, stand thou.

Lidless and lashless eyes, translucent, spherical, reached for the boy.

Anteby, it was thee I called last night on the street?

Yeah.

In Hebrew, Anteby, and correctly.

Yes, teacher.

We shall attend to this later, Anteby, no?

Yes, teacher.

Good. Seat thyself.

Son of Jacob, stand thou.

So Allen was known by the faculty. His father was a scholar, well-liked, wise and religious, and he was the eldest son of Jacob, and for this fact, and because he had the potential also to be well-liked, wise and religious, he was treated well by *mar* Gybie, and by the other instructors in the school of Jehovah.

Son of Jacob, where did we stop yesterday?

At the beginning of the plagues, teacher.

Good. Seat thyself, Son of Jacob.

Allen's face and neck were hot. He looked at Sally, on his right. Sally glanced at *mar* Gybie, bent, and whispered.

Now he won't bother you for the rest of the night.

She was like Rachel, at the well. Rachel must have looked like that. Her hair, her eyes were black and deep. Her skin was olive, her cheeks dark red. Her lips were alive. Allen liked to compare her lips with those of the other girls. Allen had once told his friend Abe that most girls' lips are asleep, but that Sally's lips were alive. Abe had looked hard, had said only that her lips seemed nice for kissing.

Mar Gybie was calling on others now; asking questions, answering questions. Those who did not answer satisfactorily wrote their names on the blackboard, in a column. Allen looked at *mar* Gybie as he told of the Spanish Inquisition, related it to the trials of the Jews in Egypt. Allen had heard of the Inquisition. He thought he also knew what the word *inquisition* ordinarily meant. But he didn't know what the Inquisition was. And he was the smartest one in the class when it came to things like that.

To Allen, *mar* Gybie did not look as wise as he obviously was. And, though he *must* be good, he didn't look good to Allen. In fact, Allen wished, over and over again, that *mar* Gybie would look a little more like his father, or like Rabbi David, who taught the older boys.

Mar Gybie had a film over his graybrown skin. Allen had once found himself thinking that he had tiptoed to *mar* Gybie while he slept, and had scraped off the film with a knife, and touched the skin beneath. Allen considered the proposition that God had made the top layer of *mar* Gybie's skin out of oil, to protect the rest of it, rejected this, and settled the problem by deciding that it didn't matter whether his skin was oily or not. (Though he knew it mattered very much.)

But Allen was sure that he was wise and good. He was teaching God's ways, so he had to be. Maybe God tested people's faith by making their teachers look like *mar* Gybie.

Now he remembered a question he'd wanted to ask.

Teacher, was Pharaoh of the time of Moses Rameses the Second?

The Rameses was said in English.

Son of Jacob, there was no such person. There was only Pharaoh.

But I read—.

In Torah?

No, in an English book.

If a book disagrees with Torah, it tells untruths.

Perhaps Pharaoh had a name.

That had slipped out. He dropped into his seat and waited. *Mar* Gybie only smiled.

Now thou seest, Son of Jacob. The English schools cannot know as much as the teachers of Torah.

Still, Allen thought, there was a picture of his statue in that book. Allen wondered about this, even thought of how lucky he was to escape having to put his name on the board.

The question period and lesson over, Allen opened his prayer book. He always opened it now, because he didn't like to look.

Mar Gybie took up a varnished twelve-inch ruler, the thick schoolroom type, and began to tap the palm of his left hand with it. A boy got up, walked to the front of the room, hands behind his back. He offered his right. ——. He replaced the right, thrust out his left. ——. He crossed them both against his thighs, said "Thank you, teacher," crossed off the first name on the list and sat down.

He was followed by another boy, a small one, who kept his hands in his pockets, then removed them timidly, together.

Then a girl went up, crossed off her name, said "Thank you, teacher," and sat down. Girls were never hit.

Allen looked down at his book part of the time, but couldn't help noticing some of it.

The list was canceled off, and *mar* Gybie called up Anteby. He advanced, hands thrust forward.

When I called to thee last night, didst thou say I was not thy teacher out of school?

Yes, teacher.

Are we now in school?

Yes, teacher.

Good.

[171]

And he slapped him, hard, on one cheek, then on the other. He repeated this. The arms were still outstretched. Again a slap on the right cheek, then on the left. Now *mar* Gybie attacked the boy's palms. He struck them each five times, bringing the varnished ruler high for every stroke. Then he told him to sit down. Anteby walked away.

Anteby, return to me. Thou didst not thank me.

Anteby said nothing.

Now the beating really began. He had Anteby on the floor before he had succeeded in making him cry. He never kicked him, only slapped him in the face, again, and again.

Anteby, stand thou.

Anteby stood, head high.

I have finished.

His head remained high for a moment, then lowered.

Thank you, teacher.

Thou art welcome, Anteby.

The evening prayer went quickly. It was the fastest hour of the night.

They were conjugating verbs when Sally began to whisper to Allen again.

I think Anteby is a dope.

Why?

He should tell his parents.

What. That he was fresh to his teacher?

Allen smiled the smile with which the initiated patronize the naive. One should respect the teachers of Torah. Allen knew that.

Anyway, he hurt him. He's mean.

Allen began to consider this, when his name was called— his family name. He stood in the aisle.

It is wrong to beat girls. Sally Abadi was talking with thee. Thou wert listening. Thou shalt have her punishment.

Allen received one slap on each cheek, thanked *mar* Gybie, returned to his seat. Sally looked at him compassionately. He sent her an angry glance, then ignored her.

For the remainder of the class, his face dug into his book, his brow burning from the recollection, Allen wondered about the justice of *mar* Gybie's punishment. The teacher of Torah slapped one because he could not slap another. He remembered his former uncertainty. He felt sure now that *mar* Gybie was wrong. He would bring the picture and show it to *mar* Gybie. He would pin it onto the bulletin board for the whole class to see. *That* would teach *mar* Gybie.

But the picture could have been a fake. Allen immediately recognized this possibility. Still, his punishment burnt his brows.

Allen sat until the noise of the disbanding class radiated into the outside darkness with the running boys and chatting girls.

When he stepped out of the building, the night splashed in his face, cooled him, spread like a salve over his hot cheeks and ears.

It had snowed while he was in class, and though young feet had made a slush moat around the doorway, across the street and in the schoolyard and through the alleys was a whiteness, like a spread on a very large and smooth bed. Allen looked about, looked up at the hard stars and soft moon, and whistled, loud. Then he said something, also loud. As he stretched his arm out, he dropped his prayer book.

He picked it up, looked around, saw no one . . . kissed it anyway.

Second Act

MONIKA BASCH

ON THE morning that Joseph got the letter, got it and opened it, seeing the London postmark and expecting a letter from an English friend, he was sitting at the breakfast table listening impatiently to his son. It was surprising that he listened at all, for he hated talk at that hour. But it was hard not to be amused at this twelve-year-old who considered his opinion on the Republican convention of equal importance to his father's. He

[173]

was bright and quick and eager, a really American boy, Joseph thought. But he could not help wishing for a little more respect, a little more quiet in the house when he was home. Frowning as the boy talked, he directed his annoyance at his wife; it was her department. She should have brought him up better. But he saw the letter then and opened it eagerly, dropping toast crumbs and marmalade on the envelope. He saw at once that he had been mistaken; it was not what he had hoped for, and he wanted to close the letter once more, unread. But he had opened it and seen the unfamiliar signature of a half-forgotten name. He turned to his wife. "It's a letter from Stephen Roucek. He got out." Helen lifted her gray eyes from her coffee, but made no comment. "He's writing from London, says he's coming here. In fact, I guess he'll be here tomorrow."

"He'll come to see you at the office?"

"Yes."

"And his family?"

"They're all out. Walked, it seems, across the frontier, with just the clothes on their backs. No money of course." Helen sighed. "Poor man," she said. Joseph nodded. They were always poor men, men without life, only a past.

It had been said by somebody that this was justice. Roucek sat when the Germans came, sat, and listened silently, and looked cautiously around corners. As long as Joseph had known him he had always done the safe thing, but now nothing was safe. You could be quiet when the enemy was Nazi, if you were an average kind of man and didn't care much. But now Prague belonged to the Communists, and many of them had always been there. He was a lawyer. He could stay and live on a little and wait till someone knocked on his door while he was out and asked the secretary to show the files. He could have joined the party; would they have him? And if . . . . Joseph tried to imagine Roucek as a party member. So Roucek had walked across the frontier. It was his turn. But Joseph's memory had not failed him. He knew the feeling. . . .

Joseph cleared his mind of all thoughts of the actual meeting until the next morning when, as he got up from the table and started towards the door, Helen said, "Give my regards to

Roucek. Bring him home for dinner if you want." And he thought how it would be to have Roucek here for dinner, actually sitting at his table. Images chased each other through his brain; they were images from the old life before the war, when he and others sat at well-filled tables. Many met again in London, and talked, day after day, about resistance. Joseph thought how Roucek too would try to talk a way out of what was before him.

But it was time to go. Joseph picked up his hat and brief-case, closed the door, and crossed the street to the bus stop. As he did so, he turned and looked at the house, a wooden house painted white with a screened porch in front of it. (What would they say to a wooden house in the home country?) And the apple tree in his yard, a yard with no fence around it. For the first time since he had wedged his path into American life he thought with a special consciousness of the pattern that was now his. Coca-Cola and ice cream, palm beach suits, the show. The obvious things. And then there was the first time a stranger had talked to him while he waited for the bus. "Warm out, isn't it?" he had said, and Joseph had answered, surprised. He thought the man was probably a plumber or an electrician. He wondered how he could tell these things to the man he would see. He must have known of them of course, together with washing machines and canned goods, but known of them only as separate lonely entities to be imported and reported abroad, not as this new thing, the life of Joe. It would not be understood, Joseph knew, any more than seven years ago he would have understood it. But he was no longer an exile. "It is better," he said almost out loud—or at least he must have mouthed the words, because the man who now sat beside him on the bus, carrying a briefcase and hat just like his, looked at him strangely. Maybe he thinks I'm crazy, Joseph thought, but he didn't laugh. He knew that he had almost been crazy seven years ago in London, with no job and no home. He had found a job, certainly, but there were the days when he walked the gray twilight streets before blackout, trying to whistle "There'll Always Be an England" as he turned up Putney High. . . .

There were the days of the resistance, the days when the

[175]

government-in-exile was formed . . . and he was always in it. Conference tables with ministers, conference tables with the president. Money for broadcasts, confidential information. State secrets and ministry scandals. It was long ago, so very long ago, and yet there was an exile again. And what a good thing it was not to be in London this time.

Joseph reached his stop and got off. Up the elevator, eleven flights, and his secretary's voice to greet him. He started working, reading the papers before him on his desk. But he was thinking, thinking about things called history. Bitterly he knew the people he had sprung from, their story, in intervals of idealism and freedom, German invasions, now Communists and again suppression. But such thoughts were of no use. He got down to work. Then the buzzer rang and he picked up the telephone. "Mr. Roucek to see you."

Then the door opened and he came in. He looked thin and old, and he entered uncertainly. The door closed behind him and he sat down, his small eyes dodging about the room, resting on no object. At last, after both men had said brief greetings he smiled shyly. "So this is how you live in the United States. Not so bad."

"No, it's not so bad. Of course it's not like the olden days. . . ." Stephen Roucek shrugged his shoulders.

"The olden days—you should see who lives now in the house you had in the olden days. A little two-bit official who has a fat job because he turned Communist. You should see them, all those nouveaux-riches, feasting like pigs in the old houses . . ." He was standing now, talking excitedly, and his face was red. Joseph sat, hoping he looked calm.

"I know, Stephen, I know. I knew a long time ago what could happen, but no one listened then to what I said . . ." Stephen sat down again and nodded sadly. Joseph wished that somehow he could speed up the most painful part of this interview, that he could get to what must have brought Stephen. He wanted to help him tell his story simply, but he couldn't. He couldn't because Stephen didn't know it simply, because he knew only the loose strands of his previous existence where they had been chopped off and left hanging, unco-ordinated. He had come here because Joseph had formed a part, at one time, of some of those strands.

"The ocean passage was very smooth," Stephen was saying. "The kids loved the ship." And then something again reminded him and he jerked forward. "But you know they told Novak he could work in the coal mines. And God knows what they might have told me . . . it wasn't safe there for anybody." Joseph offered him a cigarette. Stephen was admiring the view now, and Joseph tried in vain to fit words to what he wanted to explain as he listened to him talk, commenting casually here and there. He took his pen from his pocket and wrote out a check. He handed it to Stephen. "That's the best I can do right now."

Stephen drew back. "But I didn't mean you should give . . . I only thought if you could help me start . . . but to tell the truth . . ." There were tears in his eyes. I should have done this by mail, Joseph thought. "I'm not used to asking . . . it comes hard . . . an old man like me, you know. But they took everything. I have no money and my wife . . . the children . . ." He looked down at the hands lying in his lap, limply. Joseph filled in where he'd left off. He had no job, no place to live, no skill. His English was poor.

Suddenly Stephen looked up, and there was brightness in his eyes. "But we'll fight them, we'll fight them!" He looked at Joseph. "We'll build a resistance again, an *odboj*, won't we? You were in it last time . . . for democracy, the democracy of Masaryk. You still believe it, don't you? We can start it and some day . . ." He stopped, seeing that Joseph was shaking his head, and the room was quiet. Stephen waited, shifting his feet uneasily, but Joseph held back, he didn't say it. He didn't ask why Stephen had not fought when the Communists came to power. He didn't tell Stephen about last time, what fine parties Richard gave with the supporters' money, how Hloupy took credit for all the work and thinking others did in his ministry. He did not say how many joined because there were no other jobs in London. Stephen would not have understood. So he simply smiled a little wryly. "Once was enough for me." Stephen stood up. He shook his fists at the air as he spoke.

[177]

"I don't understand. You . . . you were a leader . . . a good Czech. Is this what American money does to you?" His face was red with anger. A good Czech? thought Joseph, a man. . . . He had no answer. Stephen calmed down, and now looked more disturbed than angry. "I'm sorry, Joseph. We were friends. I . . . don't understand."

"I know. Nor would I have. It will come later." Stephen had risen to go. "If there's anything else . . . let me know how I can help you. And of course you must come to our house some night soon—maybe next week. Helen is looking forward to seeing you." Joseph strained for a moment anxiously, as if a thread connecting the two where they stood held his lifeblood. Stephen's hand was already on the doorknob.

"Thanks . . . thanks for everything. I'll be pretty busy for a while I guess, but I'll let you know." Awkwardly he opened the door and stepped out, and Joseph heard the elevator that took him down. He leaned out and saw him leave the building and cross the street, and he knew that today, perhaps tomorrow, his name would be crossed off the list. Pulling his head back inside the office, he closed the window.

Did He Touch You?

LIN GATTY

"AND now I'll leave him to you," his mother was saying to the Teacher. She turned to him. "And mind you pay attention, Lennie. Professor Burton is very kind to give us his time. Now you behave!" His mother swept out of the living room, and he was alone with the Teacher.

Lennie was sitting uncomfortably beside him on the little music bench, playing with a rubber ball. The Teacher was playing the piano—something hard and ugly—like five-finger exercises but with lots more notes in it. This lasted a long time, and the Teacher was hot when he finished and had to wipe his fingers and clean his glasses. Then he did some more; and this time it was prettier, with a tune to it, and it danced in little spurts up the piano. Lennie had to smile—he didn't know why; his mouth just smiled by itself. He also left off fiddling with his ball.

By now the Teacher had become aware of his small listener. Musician-wise, he had noted too the child's instinctive response to the tripping scherzo. Pausing, he peered at Lennie through his thick-lensed glasses, and before putting his fingers in place for the third piece, leaned over and patted the boy's cheek, murmuring as he did, "Let us see now—let us see."

To Lennie he said, "Listen, my little one; listen carefully to this. Here I shall give you food for the heart as well as for the head." And then he began to play music that was quite, quite different from that before—and wasn't like music any more. It whispered in the bass, and while it whispered it growled; but the treble didn't growl—it cried.

And now something funny was happening to Lennie. He began to feel as if he'd like to run away; he didn't want to listen, and his heart started to beat fast. As if he *had* run. The music seemed to be getting bigger, till it was almost too tight for his chest. He let his ball fall, and pressed his fist close to where he thought his heart must be. Something hurt him in there— he didn't like this music; he wanted to call out to it to stop. But the piano didn't care; it went on and on, and though it tried once to be different, it always came back and did the same thing over again—a dreadful thing. Something would burst in him if it didn't stop—he felt all swollen inside—yes, he was going to burst.

Then the Teacher began to make a lot of little noises that sounded just like the wind, and he threw his head back and hummed softly in a strange and beautiful way.

The ecstatic relief that surged through Lennie at these sounds was too much for him. His eyes ran over and the tears dropped swiftly down his cheeks; he couldn't help it, and he sobbed soundlessly.

His mother swept regally into the room.

"Lennie!" She started. "What on earth! Is this how you say

thank you for the pretty music?" And to herself, God, not another tantrum in front of a visitor.

"No, do not be angry. He was moved by the music." The Teacher's eyes smiled as he spoke, and then he ignored her and turned again to Lennie. His voice was soft and kind. "Will I play that for you again, little one?"

"No, no!" As rude as the Teacher was polite, Lennie gave a great gulp and bolted from the room.

"Oh dear," his mother was effusive and flustered. "He's never been quite so naughty ever before. I can't imagine what's gotten into him. I do hope you aren't offended." The Teacher calmed her in a few words, but she was still a little upset by the sudden outburst. If this is the effect music has on him, she thought, I'm not so sure I like his playing.

When Lennie came back, humiliated and not quite understanding himself, his mother and the Teacher were talking about his playing.

"—without the least difficulty," his mother was saying. "Ever since he was a tiny tot—oh, here we are, are we? Now, Professor, he shall play for you."

Something turned over in Lennie at these words. "No, I won't!"

His mother threw him a look that he knew only too well, and he reluctantly climbed to the slippery top of the bench, from which his short legs dangled ungraciously. All right, if he must play, he must. But he wouldn't look at the notes, or listen to what he did. He'd count how many flies he could see in front of him, on the wall and the ceiling. One . . . two. . . .

The piece, it was a tiresome exercise, came to an end. His mother waited for the customary panegyric.

"Hmm," said the Teacher, adding as a kind of afterthought, "Fine little fingers."

When he turned to Lennie, however, it was with a pleasant, quite different voice. "Well, and how many flies did you find?"

Lennie colored to his hair roots. "Six big flies, and fourteen little," he managed to stammer. (Now he was going to catch it!)

But the Teacher threw back his head and laughed. "Six big and fourteen little." He laughed again. "That's good—that's very good." Surely, he mused, this is a good sign, this capacity to escape. "But come here, my boy, and we'll play a little game." The relieved Lennie came closer.

"The bad little boy who counts flies when he plays the bad piece shall stand there, with his face to the wall. I strike the notes—so—and you will tell me their names. That was Mr. G. wasn't it? Listen now, if you can tell me what this is."

"Huh, that's easy! That's C."

"And this fellow?"

"A," Lennie liked this; it was fun. "E—B."

"And now how many do I strike? D, F . . . right! B, D sharp . . . good! And now these?"

"That's two together—close I mean. G and A."

"My God!" cried the Teacher. "The ear is too perfect." He took Lennie's face in his hands, and turned it up to him. For a moment he stood looking down at it, and his expression was solemn. Then, stooping, he kissed the boy on the forehead. "May God bless you, my child, and prosper His most precious gift." And this, just when Lennie (after the fly episode) had begun to like him.

Then he was free to run off and play, which he did, but later in the afternoon the Teacher asked him to go walking. Lennie remembered the flies, forgot the kiss, and went off with him. They walked into the woods, further than Lennie was allowed to go alone, and the Teacher told him about the trees, and they poked among the scrub. Lennie was having a fine time.

They sat down on a log to rest, and while they were there, the Teacher picked up Lennie's right hand, looked at it as though it were something new, turned it over to the back, and stretched out the fingers and felt the tips. When he had done this he did not let go, but kept hold of it. He put his other hand on the boy's shoulder. "And now, tell me, why did you cry when I played?"

Lennie blushed furiously. He didn't like to have his hand held either. So he only looked away and kicked his heels against the log so hard they hurt him. "I dunno."

The Teacher didn't seem to be angry, but just gave his hand a little squeeze and began to talk. He talked so long that it was like being in church, and was very dull and about things Lennie didn't know. He hardly listened. He was chiefly interested in politely wriggling his hand free.

The Teacher looked so kind, even when he'd done this, though, that he plucked up enough courage to ask something he wanted very much to know. Once before when he had tried it, his mother had laughed at him and made fun of it.

"What does the music say?"

The Teacher looked as solemn as a church again, and nodded his head. "Ah," he spoke more to himself than to the boy. "The inward apperception—it begins to stir itself." Then to the boy. "The music says what is in our hearts, my boy. Each interprets it for himself. The music I played for you came from the sufferings of an unhappy man. It came from the fears that came from the shadows of night to destroy his peace, but you needn't know of that. You'll find out too soon that knowledge and beauty come of pain. But this man was so unhappy that one day everything inside him—everything that he felt—well, it just burst out of him, and he became mad. His name was Schumann—remember that name, little one."

Lennie's legs were getting tired from sitting still. Sliding down from the log, he jumped and danced, feeling all glad inside. "I will say music, too, when I grow up."

"Perhaps you will, little one." The Teacher smiled, and they walked together back towards the house.

That night, at supper, Lennie was in a thinking mood. Several times he stopped eating to stare at the centerpiece and whisper to himself. He was so unusually quiet that his father glanced anxiously at his mother.

"What's up with Lennie? He behave today?"

"Oh, yes and no." Lennie's mother was in doubt. "He was very naughty with the Professor at first—"

"What Professor?"

"You know—the music man." She went on. "He refused to play his pretty little piece; but the Professor said he was very good when they were alone."

"This Professor fellow," there was a worried note in his voice. "I've heard some funny things about him at the club."

"What do you mean—funny things?"

Lennie's father glanced uneasily at the boy. "You know—with children. Don't know whether there's any truth to 'em, but—" he turned to the boy. His voice was fatherly and confidential. "I say, Lennie. How do you like the Professor? What did you do alone?"

Lennie was still in a thinking mood. "Oh, he's all right. We went for a walk."

"What did you talk about?"

"Oh, things."

Lennie's father was a little piqued at his evasiveness. "Come on now, son, tell us about your walk. What were you talking about?"

"He said Shooman went mad." Lennie's eyes lit up. "I busted too. Right there by the piano. I busted right here." He held his hand to his heart. "The Teacher says I can say music when I grow up—and I'll go mad too—I know I will."

"Now don't be silly, Lennie," it was his mother speaking. "I'm sure the Professor didn't say that."

"I don't like the looks of this, Mabel."

"Now let's not rush into anything, George." She turned to Lennie and gave him the old look. "Now Lennie, we don't want any of your fairy tales." She was being very stern and efficient. "Did the Professor do anything funny on your walk?"

Lennie thought for a moment. "He said there was music in the wind."

"Faugh!" His mother was angry. "Now you think, Lennie. Did he do anything—did he do anything funny? Did he touch you?" There was an awkward silence.

"Well—he kept feeling my hand." He went on with a rush. "I didn't like it—I tried to let go, but—"

"What?" It was his father. "Well, that's enough. Of all—"

"Oh my God, George, keep quiet! Go on, Lennie!" Then she remembered. "George! He was kissing him!"

"Kissing him?"

"Yes. I saw it. I didn't think—Lennie, go to your room. Your father and I have to talk. Go on. Quick's the word!"

Lennie slid slowly off his chair. All this was beginning to confuse him. But he was glad to get away from all those questions.

When they called him downstairs again half an hour had passed. His mother was studiously appearing nonchalant at her sewing, and his father expansively put his book aside and called Lennie over to the sofa.

"See here, son. I've been thinking about your scouting equipment. Santa never did bring you that tent, did he?"

"No."

"Well, I think we can do something about that. How would you like to run into town with me and see what they have in the stores?"

"Gee, Dad. That's swell."

"Not at all, my boy. I've been a little worried about you lately. No fat on your bones. Ought to get out more." There was a silence. "Well, that's all, son."

"Bedtime, dear," his mother called across the room. "Come give Mummy a kiss."

That done, Lennie walked to the stairs. He turned on the first step. "I guess I don't have to practice any more."

They both looked up sharply. His father was annoyed. He hadn't wanted to make an issue of this. "Think you need a rest for a while, son. We'll talk about it another time." He was relieved when the boy continued up the stairs.

The boy stopped again. "Dad," he called.

"What is it, Lennie?"

"Can I go to the movies tomorrow afternoon. It's Saturday. It's Laurel and Hardy. All the kids are going and—"

"Yes, son. You can go to the movies."

They waited till they heard him go into his room. Lennie's father sighed heavily. "Well, that's that," he said.

"My God," his wife replied. "Think what could have happened."

The Huntress

DAVID KAULA

THEY saw them coming the other way along Eighth Street. The man who was with her looked at them casually as though they were just any two passers-by. She, however, deliberately avoided looking at them by directing her eyes across the street. From half a block away Harvey Silverman had seen them coming. He was sure that she had seen him also. He had even thought of something to say to her, something like "Hello, Amalia, long time no see," but now she hadn't given him a chance to say anything. He was feeling a little nonplussed.

He walked a few steps further, then said: "See who that was?"

"Yeah. The ex-Miss Lomano," said Bernie.

"And the now Mrs.—what is it—Brett?"

"Yeah. Brett."

Harvey turned and looked at them going away over his shoulder. She was walking with her hands in the pockets of her jacket. There must have been at least a foot of daylight between them.

"Evidently she didn't want to say hello to us," said Harvey.

Bernie grinned.

"So do you blame her?"

"Oh, no. I'm not blaming her. I suppose she's justified in never saying hello to me again. But if you think you're spotless yourself, kiddo, you've got another guess coming."

Bernie let out a small laugh.

"All right. So I called her a nasty name once. So we both rubbed her poor sensitive soul the wrong way. But that didn't do her any harm. At least she's got her man now, as you can see."

"Yeah, and they look real happy too."

Harvey looked back once more. The two of them were out of sight by this time.

Then he asked: "So who's the guy? Ever seen him before?"

"Met him once, I think," said Bernie. "He doesn't belong to any of our crowd that I know of. I think he's a floor manager or something at Bloomingdale's."

"Ah, of course, at Bloomingdale's. But only a floor manager?"

"Only a floor manager. But, anyway, he wears pants."

"God, you're a heel," said Harvey, and Bernie laughed.

They crossed Fifth Avenue and strolled into the more crowded section of Eighth Street. Just having had supper, they took their time, looking in the store windows, watching the people going by.

Amalia Brett, Harvey was thinking. From Amalia Lomano to Amalia Brett, that was quite a change. Amalia Lomano. The name half hummed itself. And there was once a smooth, half-humming sort of quality about her too. But now, Amalia Brett. It should have been Amalia Mulinero, Patruno, Toscanini. Michaelangelo, Mussolini, anything but something like Brett. And a floor manager at Bloomingdale's. Poor Amalia.

She had worked as a copywriter in Bloomingdale's advertising department. That wasn't bad for a start. Plenty of people of her intelligence in the city were only doing half as well. It was her poise that did it for her.

He would call for her at five-thirty, entering Bloomingdale's at the street level, riding the escalator down to the basement, walking down a flight of stairs to the subbasement. The subbasement was no place for claustrophobics. He had to make his way through a maze of merchandise tables under the low, pipe-covered ceiling to a door in the rear. As usual the switchboard operator, after talking into the phone a second, sent him into her office. She was sitting behind her desk with her hat and gloves on and her handbag in front of her. She smiled as he came in and introduced him to the other people in the office. Or rather, reintroduced him for about the third time. That was why she had him come all the way down to the subbasement of Bloomingdale's, to let her fellow workers get an idea of him.

Before they left she took his arm, turned and smiled to the others, and said good night.

Across a small round table, on some other night, in a night club that was priced a little too high for him, she had leaned over and laid her fingers on his arm, the way she did when her voice went soft and insinuating, saying as she smiled at him archly:

"Now why don't you ever want to have a big romance?"

She turned her head and looked at him sideways, all in a very calculated fashion.

He could have his jest too. With her he would never try anything else.

"I have a policy of keeping clear of complications," he said, liking the alliteration. "I know, it's the old bachelor cry, but it still rings true."

"But you're not going to stay that way *all* your life."

He had to grin.

"Why shouldn't I?"

Perhaps there was something genuine in the look of mock disdain she gave him.

"Oh, you're not being serious."

At times she was excellent. At other times she could carry a jest only so far. But he knew which matters to avoid and generally they succeeded very well in being unserious. That was why he liked to go out with her, to be unserious for a change and play the sophisticate. They told all, revealed all, to each other except what they truly thought and believed. To have been ingenuous, unobtuse, just once would have been to destroy the pleasant artifice of their relationship, to destroy the reason for their wasting their time and wits on each other.

Now with her hand firmly on his arm he let himself be drawn along Fifty-seventh Street. For that matter he didn't mind being seen with her either. She was smart-looking in the typical New York fashion. A little too slender, perhaps, but that was acceptable because she used her slenderness to advantage in the way she dressed. She had dark hair, dark skin, precise dark eyes, and a nose that was just a little too prominent. Her nose started pleasantly enough in a gentle, convex curve, but ended a little too far out in front of her lips—nice as those lips were. Still, taken as a totality, she had the same sort of darkish beauty that is generally associated with a movie actress whose name everyone knows. And this was what pleased him particularly.

On Fifth Avenue she steered him a block south to Fifty-sixth Street.

"Where the devil are you taking me?" he asked.

She was surprised.

"Why, I thought you knew where we were going."

"I have absolutely no idea where you are taking me."

"If you must know, to Pierre's. I trust that's all right with you."

"Well, seeing who foots the bill, I think I should have some say in the matter. Why Pierre's? Why not Tony's? I feel like a good plate of spaghetti."

He slowed down a little. She tugged him on.

"Tony's is awful. Besides, in Pierre's you get a good, wholesome meal, which is something I think you need very badly."

"Why, do I have a lean and hungry look?"

"Yes. You neglect yourself terribly. You definitely need someone to take care of you."

In Pierre's, a not too ostentatious restaurant which nevertheless showed an array of fancy prices on its menu, she ordered the meal for him, in French. When the hors d'oeuvres came she told him what to put on his plate.

In between courses he watched her practice the ritual of the cigarette. For her the cigarette was what the fan was for ladies, and what the cane and the snuff box were for gentlemen, two centuries before—an indispensable aid in the fine art of being suave and sophisticated. At certain times she could not do without it. Her mannerisms were simply incomplete in themselves without it. They lacked the final touch that synthesized them into one singular impression, into one way of behaving that was distinctively her own. She needed that cigarette cocked up by her ear, offset by the red of her fingernails, she needed to blow the smoke out in long, languid streams, just as a conductor needs a baton, or, more crudely, a fan dancer needs her own particular accessories.

In a way it was a shame, he thought, that she needed a cigarette to be what she wanted to be. That ineptitude she revealed when she was without it—whatever minor difference it did make in her behavior—at times showed itself through her mannerisms in a much more serious way. That time they were having cocktails at Zopenski's studio, the whole crowd of them, and she had behaved just as she was behaving now, impeccably, until Mike Gormley had come in to take her out on a date. She crossed the room and kissed him, took possession of him in front of everybody. Mike was quite naturally embarrassed. No one cares for that sort of treatment in public, no matter how fond he may be of his girl friend. She had asserted her sense of possession a little too much, and in so doing had disrupted that quality of self-possession which was one of her most distinguishing characteristics. It was not often, however, that she was guilty of such misdemeanors.

Now they had nearly finished their meal, were sipping their demitasses, she having seen to it that he ate properly.

"What do you have a mind to do now?" he asked. "The Italian show's right around the corner, you know. We might see what that's about."

Then she, skeptical as usual: "Is it really worth seeing?"

"So they all say. We won't know until we see for ourselves."

"Now really, I ask you, what have the Italians done compared to the French?"

He frowned at her. Although ordinarily he didn't pretend to know much about art, it was part of his game with her to give the impression that he did. He knew a few names at least.

"What have the Italians done! Maybe they don't have any Picassos or . . . or Matisses, but, well, have you ever heard of Chirico, or Marinetti, or Modigliani?"

"Of course Modigliani. But, correct me if I'm wrong," she elaborately flicked her hand away, "didn't he spend most of his life in Paris?"

"Oh, now you're quibbling. They put him in the show, I understand. So he must be Italian. What difference does it make anyway, where an artist spends his life? Picasso is a Spaniard for that matter, not French. That doesn't make him any less great. Besides, to resort to a platitude, isn't art supposed to be universal?"

"Sure, some art, like Picasso's, but there's a lot of other art —and I wouldn't be surprised if some of it was Italian—that's just plain boringly provincial. I'm sorry, I just don't go for this folk art."

He had to smile at her.

"Frankly I don't think either of us knows what we're talking about. Maybe we better not pass judgment until we've seen for ourselves—unless you can think of something better to do."

Without much enthusiasm: "Well, all right. We'll go then."

They passed quickly through some of the galleries, lingered a while in others. Amalia, coming to an interesting painting, stepped back and looked at it a long minute, resting her elbow on one hand and holding her cigarette up by her ear. Because she was one of the initiated she didn't go up close to examine it. She wasn't one of those indiscreet ones who only wanted to "see how it was done." No, it was only the total effect of a painting she was interested in.

She pronounced the Futurists "abominable—too obsessed with theories." She studied the Modiglianis long because they showed a strong French influence. She admitted that some of the others were pleasant enough in a plaintively lyrical sort of way, but concluded that on the whole Italian art just didn't have the—what was it she said? Harvey tried to recall—*éclat,* or *savoir faire,* of the French.

Then they ran into Bernie. Harvey had seen him a few minutes before working his way around the gallery in the opposite direction. There was no escaping him, however, what with Amalia so absorbed in the paintings.

"Well, hello, Silverman. Hi, Amalia," said Bernie jovially. "Hot on the trail of cultchah, I see."

"Oh, yes," replied Harvey quietly. "Just picking up a smattering of it here and there."

Amalia apparently hadn't noticed Bernie. She was still looking at a painting.

"Yessir. Cultchah with a capital K. Get it while you can they say. The elite can't do without it. I say, how do you go for this wop art?"

"This what?"

"This stuff here." Bernie made a broad sweeping gesture. "This dago stuff."

Harvey glanced at Amalia. Still looking at the picture, she took a puff from her cigarette and shifted her stance slightly.

"Some of it's not bad," said Harvey.

"I'd say some of these dago lads can really paint."

She looked at him then.

"You know, Bernie, I am an Italian."

Harvey interrupted her: "Don't pay any attention to him, Amalia. You know he doesn't mean what he says."

"Just the same—"

"I'm sorry, Amalia," said Bernie. "My mouth is too big for its own good sometimes. Believe me, I didn't mean any of that. Will you forgive me?"

He smiled, but she didn't say anything.

"Well, let's not let this bog us down," said Harvey. "Do you want to see the rest of this I hope not?"

"No, let's go. I've seen enough," said Amalia.

They were out in the street now, the two of them, walking to the subway station on Sixth Avenue. She walked apart from him, not bothering to take the arm he offered her. Neither did she attempt to return the remarks he made about the exhibit. It was going to be like this all the way home, he thought.

He said finally: "You really didn't mind what Bernie said, did you?"

Reluctantly: "I suppose I shouldn't have minded. It just threw me a little off balance, that's all."

"Well, you know he's only a kidder. You shouldn't take anything that comes out of his mouth seriously. Just don't pay any attention to him."

"I tried not to."

But she obviously couldn't help it. She couldn't prevent whatever it was that showed itself occasionally in her behavior from destroying in an instant that poise she affected so well at other times. Harvey pitied her now, because he knew wherein her insecurity lay. He had felt it himself. At one time whenever someone said "kike" in his presence he felt, despite himself, a sudden bite of anger, a flash of hatred not only for the person who said it, but for everyone who had heard it and seemed to condone it. It was only a silly, irrational response, he told himself. And yet it took everything he had to overcome it.

The evening was spoiled. Amalia chose to suffer. He took her to Brooklyn on the subway, then went with her three blocks to her home. On the way they walked through a neighborhood of delicatessens, bars, and pool rooms, of garbage cans on the sidewalk and windows with red neon lights. Her home was just beyond, a two-family frame house with a double porch and small yard in front.

Her people were first-generation Italians. She had invited him to dinner there once—for what reason he knew not, for she acted peculiarly distant all that evening. They had all sat at a huge round table that occupied nearly all the space in the dining room. The mother, who spoke little English, stayed in the kitchen most of the time, seeing to it that the table was kept well supplied. Most of the talking was done by the father, a small, wiry, energetic man who was proud to show off his handiwork, the chairs, tables, desks, and other pieces of furniture in the house he had made. Amalia's oldest brother talked about nothing but baseball. If he couldn't be an outfielder for the Dodgers he was going to jump off the Brooklyn Bridge.

He said good night to her on the front porch. They would wake the family if they went in, she explained.

"I'm sorry I spoiled the art show for you," she said.

It was his turn to be honest.

"You didn't. I was bored with it from the start."

She said nothing, so he added:

"I'll call you up next week some time, all right?"

"All right. Good night."

He walked back to the subway station, thinking that from now on, whenever he made the remotest reference to her background, he would practically be calling her "wop" to her face. The implications of what he would say would be magnified a thousand times in her mind. She had something to hide, a sore spot to protect. She was like a sensitive plant, graceful and alluring to look at, but once touched, clamping shut and presenting an array of barbs to the world.

He didn't call her up the next week, didn't see her again in fact until the evening he and Bernie saw her with her husband on Eighth Street.

"They certainly didn't look like honeymooners," said Bernie.

They had reached Sixth Avenue. They were thinking of dropping in to see some friends.

"No, I'd say they didn't," said Harvey.

She had been walking with her husband just as she had walked with him that evening after the art show, sulkily. He wondered what had passed between them.

"Why'd you drop her like that?" asked Bernie. "You made yourself look like a real heel."

Harvey shrugged his shoulders. "Oh, I just didn't want to get too tied up with her."

"A hell of an excuse. Well, I know why *I* would have dropped her. I just don't go for that lawdy-daw stuff of hers. But you said you got a charge out of it."

"So I did for a while. So I never said I wanted a steady diet of it, did I?"

Harvey hoped that that settled the matter. He didn't feel like starting an argument as to who was and who was not a heel. For Bernie's type such arguments carried very little persuasion.

"Well," said Bernie, "at least she's got her man."

"Yeah. And now I suppose she never has to go to any Italian art shows, or restaurants, or movies, or anything that she doesn't want to."

The Good People of Milton

RICHARD H. SCHWARTZ

ALL of Milton knew it in a few hours. It was washday and Mrs. McKay was there, so they asked her to call Betty Lou. Ken Reed and she had gone steady before he left, and they wrote— Betty Lou every other night, Ken whenever he got the chance. She came over to the house, and once she got there Alice and Paul Reed didn't have a chance to think of themselves any more. When Betty Lou read the telegram, she started to cry. Not loud, just quiet sobs. And when she didn't stop, they took her up and put her in Paul's bed.

Mrs. McKay went over to get some clothes for her. And of course she told Betty Lou's mother about the telegram. On the way back she stopped to get something to make supper with, and told Harvey, the stockboy, and Mary, the cashier, and Mr. Mawson, the druggist, whom she met in the store.

And then everyone knew. Someone came in looking for Paul, and Harvey told him. He met Mr. Webster who told Mrs. Sumerset who had an appointment at the beauty shop where she told Mrs. Emerson and Mrs. Gardner. Mrs. Emerson met Mrs. Carlson in the dry goods store.

"I guess you heard about Ken Reed, Mrs. Carlson?"

"Yes, and isn't it too bad?"

Mrs. Emerson remarked that it seemed just like yesterday that she had called Alice Reed to tell her that she had found her Ken smoking cornsilk out in back of the garage.

Mrs. Carlson replied that yes, he was a mischievous boy, but everyone liked him.

Mrs. Emerson wondered if Paul and Alice would hang a gold star.

Mrs. Carlson thought that no, they would leave the silver

one in for now—gold stars are hung when they're dead. Of course, as far as she could see (and she wouldn't say this to anyone else) there wasn't much hope when they're missing.

On the streets everyone was talking about it. And they kept talking about it for the next few days. A couple of women baked pies and cookies and went over to sit with Alice in the afternoons. A few of the men came up to Paul and told him not to give up hope, that they find lots of those reported "missing," yes, even "missing in action." Others just felt embarrassed when they passed Paul or Alice on the street or on their way to church.

But after a few days there was something else to think about. That is, except for Alice and Paul and Betty Lou. Every Sunday when they went to church, they prayed harder than they had ever prayed before. And every time the doorbell rang, they jumped, thinking, hoping, and yet not hoping, that it might be another telegram.

The week after they got the telegram, Paul called Sam Overland, the Congressman from the Milton area, and asked him to see if he could find something more definite for them. Four weeks later Sam called back to say that as yet he couldn't find a thing, but that he'd keep trying. Once, three months later, Paul called again, but he was told that Sam hadn't forgotten—he just couldn't find anything.

The Honor Roll in front of the school kept growing. A boy from below the freight yards got killed, and a man painted a gold star in front of his name. Another one who had been in Ken's class was reported wounded, but his mother got a letter from him saying that he was all right.

Then one day in July, about eight months after Paul and Alice got word from the War Department, they got a letter. When she saw that it was from overseas, Alice called Paul and they opened it together. It was from Ken; well, really a nurse had written it, but Ken had dictated most of it.

He had been taken prisoner, it said, and had been in a prison camp for seven months. Now he was in a hospital, trying to get back some of the weight he had lost. There was a lot more, of course, but that was the real thing—he was alive. Betty Lou got a letter the same day—almost identical. The nurse said that Ken wanted to say a lot more, but he was embarrassed that she should hear it.

Paul and Alice went down to the store, laughing and stopping to talk to everyone.

And soon the whole town knew. Mrs. Sumerset was out in front of her house when they passed and they told her. She went in and called Mrs. Gardner who told Mrs. Carlson who told Mrs. Emerson and Mr. Mawson, the druggist. Mr. Mawson went back to the drugstore to tell his wife.

When he got there he met Mr. Webster and Mr. Mawson asked him if he had heard about Ken Reed. No? Well, he's alive and he was in a prison camp and he's now in a hospital, putting on weight. Mr. Webster wondered who would have thought that he would ever be found, and wasn't he sure lucky.

Mr. Mawson thought that it was fine, just fine, that such a swell boy would come out of a thing like that okay.

Mr. Mawson wondered if he'd get a medal, and Mr. Webster replied that yes, of course he would.

Everyone in Milton was talking about how lucky Paul and Alice were and how happy they must be.

Other things happened in the town. Two new sections were added on the Honor Roll, and five new gold stars painted on.

But to Paul and Alice and Betty Lou, things were fine. Soon the mailman began delivering letters written in Ken's own hand, and they started coming more regularly.

In September they got a letter saying that he was in a hospital in this country. The doctors wanted to look him over. Paul wrote right back, asking if he and Alice might visit him there, but Ken replied that no, they had better stay home and wait for him.

About a month later he came. No one had any idea that he was coming. One day in November he just walked into the store. Paul was standing in the back, talking to one of the customers and didn't notice him at first. When he recognized him, he dropped three cans of peaches and didn't even bother to pick them up.

Together they walked home to see his mother. She couldn't

believe it at first and was so excited she couldn't even talk straight. How was he, he looked so thin and pale, and what did the doctors say and did they treat him awfully at the prison camp and they were so glad to get that first letter and the nurse must have been very nice to write it for him and on and on until Ken laughed and made her sit down and at least give him a chance to look at his mother and dad. Oh yes, he had forgotten to tell them he had invited Betty Lou over for dinner; yes, he stopped to see her when he got off the bus.

But when dinner time finally came, it wasn't what they had expected. As soon as they were seated, everyone started talking at once. And then, they stopped. Ken had been away so long, he didn't know a lot of the people they talked about and couldn't remember others. And Alice thought that the steak was tough, although everyone tried to assure her that it was fine. All the things they wanted to say got lost somewhere in the embarrassment that they each felt. For Ken, the disappointment (although he never would have admitted it), the let-down, after those months of God-knows-what, of seeing Betty Lou as she really was, without the dreamlike quality that a man away from home conjures, and his mother and father, talking about the petty things—gas rationing (the things that people have to put up with), and Mrs. McKay's new range (although where she got it Alice just couldn't see). And for Betty Lou the bewilderment of knowing that something was wrong, without knowing what it was, wondering if Ken objected to her new haircut (although everyone said she looked just darling), or if perhaps the nurse who wrote his letters had grown to be more than a friend. For Paul and Alice, the uncertainty of what to do, how to act (they'd heard that the boys who'd come back wanted to be treated naturally, but they didn't feel natural—they wanted to ask him questions, offer him a cushion, a glass of water). And for all three of them, Paul, Alice, Betty Lou, the question of Ken's quietness while they remembered him as being gay and talkative, of his thinness, even though he had been "fattened up," of his paleness, his gray hairs, of the stutter he had developed while he was away, his slow, methodical speech, and most of all, of why he had been in the hospital so long, of what the doctors had said. Ken knew that they wondered, and he was embarrassed because they were embarrassed.

After dinner Paul and Ken went into the living room, while Alice and Betty Lou washed the dishes. Paul noticed how many cigarettes Ken smoked even though he didn't appear to enjoy them. He tried to interest him in Milton small talk—the Army-Navy "E" that the mill got with a letter from the President, the new principal in the high school, the new clerks he had in the store. Every mention of the war both cautiously evaded, and once, when Paul made a slip and tried to cover up, they were both so embarrassed they stared at their hands silently for a full five minutes. And when Betty Lou and Alice came in, it was no better.

About nine o'clock Ken asked if someone would like to take a walk. Betty Lou accepted; Paul and Alice dutifully declined. Alice was about to suggest that maybe Ken shouldn't try to do too much in one day, but she caught herself just in time. After saying good night and watching Ken and Betty Lou walk up the street, Paul and Alice stood in the hall, looking at each other, silently. Even though they hadn't gone to bed early in years, both went up to bed, without even mentioning Ken.

Outside, Betty Lou and Ken walked slowly up Ore Avenue. When they had gone three blocks and were just approaching the business district, Ken turned to the left—away from the lights and the people. Neither of them had said a word since they had left the house. And they were both embarrassed—she because she wanted him to say something and couldn't understand his silence, and he because he felt her bewilderment but couldn't force himself to say the things she wanted to hear.

They walked the quiet dark streets for what seemed to Betty Lou like hours. Finally they came to a diner which hadn't been there when Ken left.

When they got in front: "Cup of coffee?"

Without answering, she walked up to the door and waited for him to open it. They walked in and sat on the low stools. Behind the counter stood a man wearing a dirty apron, splattered with grease.

"What'll it be, folks?"

The man set in front of them two steaming cups with spoons sticking out. He looked at Ken as though he were obliged to say something. Ken kept stirring his coffee.

"Been in long?" the man asked hopefully.

Ken shrugged.

"Overseas?"

"Yeh."

"See action?"

Ken nodded.

"Pretty tough, huh?"

Ken looked up at him as though to say something; then back down to his coffee.

"Don't want to talk about it, huh?"

Nobody answered.

The man looked at Ken, then Betty Lou, then shrugged and walked indignantly to the other end of the counter.

As they sat there, Betty Lou looked at Ken's profile. The wrinkles around his eyes were new. So was the deep line around the corner of his mouth. And there was a scar that showed above the collar of his shirt.

They finished their coffee and left. Neither of them said a thing till they reached Betty Lou's house.

"Want to come in for a while?"

Ken shook his head.

"No."

She stood there, waiting.

"Betty Lou," he began laboriously, "I guess I ought to . . ." He faltered.

"Ken, you don't have to tell me anything you don't want to— not tonight. And if you don't want to, you don't have to— ever."

He looked at her, patted her on the arm, and walked home.

During the next few days, things were strained in the Reed house. Paul and Alice wanted to ask all kinds of questions, but Ken remained so reserved they couldn't get up the nerve. But with Betty Lou, it was different. Ken still didn't talk about the prison camp or about the fighting, but at least he talked more.

One night, about two weeks after he was home, he took the

car, and he and Betty Lou went out to dinner. He seemed to have something to say all through the meal, but when he began, he got flustered, and after stumbling a few times gave up. When the coffee came, he tried again. He knew, he said, that everybody wanted to know about the prison camp, but he'd rather not talk about it. Besides, it was all over now. It was the scars he wanted her to know about. Of course they were all healed, but they were odd shapes and in odd places. He didn't look too pretty. And then the time he was in the hospital. He didn't stay that long just to put on weight. Oh, he was okay physically. They gave him, well, they gave him mental treatments. He was all right now—the doctors said so—or at least as well as could possibly be expected.

He was quiet for a few minutes, and when Betty Lou saw that he had finished, she told him that it didn't matter, she was happy just to have him home.

He said he wanted to tell her before he asked her to marry him. He didn't want her to answer right away, he wanted her to be sure. And then, before she could say anything, he got up to get her coat.

They went to the movie, then to the ice cream parlor, then home. He talked and laughed more that night than he had during any other night since he came home.

The next night she said "yes."

After the first two or three days that he was home, during which he stayed in the house most of the time, Ken went downtown to say hello.

The first day he was out, he met Mrs. Gardner, who said how glad she was to see him home, and how did he feel, and he looked a little thin but (ha ha) his mother's cooking would fix that and was he really home to stay and when (ha ha) would they be hearing any news about him and Betty Lou and talk and talk and talk. Then as he walked down the street he met Mr. Mawson, the druggist, who said how fine it was that he was home and come in for a soda as soon as he got a chance. When they passed the store Ken went in to say hello. Harvey, the stockboy, left the door to the butter and milk cooler open when he saw him and Paul was about to call him back; then he

saw Ken. Smiling, he closed it himself. Harvey said it was great
to see Ken again, and where were all his ribbons and how many
Germans had he killed and what was it like in the prison camp
and did he have any medals and did he bring his gun home
with him? Then Ken met Mr. Webster who was glad to see him
and Mrs. Sumerset who was glad to see him and Mrs. Emerson
who was glad to see him and Mrs. Carlson who was glad to see
him. Then he saw his English teacher and the Principal and the
barber and the woman who ran the candy store and a boy who
was home from the Navy and a man who just loafed—all glad
to see him home again.

That afternoon Mrs. Sumerset went to the beauty parlor to
have her hair washed. Did May know that Ken Reed was home
again, after seven months in a German prison camp and more
in hospitals?

Yes, May answered, she heard from one of the women who
was in this morning, and wasn't it just wonderful?

Mrs. Sumerset said that just the other week she had told her
husband what a shame it was that such a nice boy should be
killed, for who would have thought that he was still alive after
all those months.

Yes, May agreed, he is a fine boy, honest, and all that, and
wonder what he'll do.

Well, Mrs. Sumerset thought, he'll probably marry Betty
Lou and settle down. It's about time, too, after all he's been
through.

After the first week, everybody in Milton had told Ken how
glad they were that he was home. And on the street corners,
and in the stores, everyone was telling everyone else what a
nice boy he was.

They agreed that it would be a quiet wedding. Betty Lou's
mother wanted to invite a couple hundred people, at least to
the church, but in the end only twenty were asked. All through
the preparations Ken was quiet, especially when Betty Lou's
mother or Alice or Paul or Betty Lou's aunt was there, but
afterward, when they were alone, Ken would ask that the wedding be smaller, or that it not be formal or that this or that
not be done, and Betty Lou would agree and the next day

things would be changed. And every night Ken would tell her a little bit more. He was working up to the nightmares and the pains he had but he just couldn't find the right way to say it. He knew she'd find out, and yet he hoped that they'd be gone by the wedding. The doctor had given him some pills, but cautioned him about taking them too often. At least, he thought, she knows about the scars and why I was in the hospital.

He didn't talk to his mother or father much about the wedding—or about anything, for that matter. He didn't talk much to anyone at all, except Betty Lou.

After the first few days of seeing her, the disappointment he first felt was gone. He still wasn't as free as he had been before, even when they sat alone in the dark of her living room, but at least he was kissing her now, and she could feel his passion, restrained though it was.

In the quiet of his room Ken smiled as he remembered how he used to dream of getting married. He mentioned it to his mother one afternoon. He told her it was hard to believe that at last he and Betty Lou were getting married. She smiled and told him she was glad he was happy.

After the wedding they went out of town for their honeymoon.

That first night, just before they went to bed, Ken tried to tell her about his nightmares again. But all he could manage to say was that sometimes he had dreams.

He didn't dream that night. And the next day he didn't have pains. So in the morning he told her about it—most of it. In his dreams the pain would grow so intense that he'd wake up twisting and turning and the pain would last all day. But, he told her, he hadn't dreamed that night—maybe he wouldn't dream ever again.

The second night he didn't dream either, or the third night or the fourth. The next day they came home. It was Thursday. Before the wedding they had found a little two-room apartment, and while they were gone Alice and Betty Lou's mother fixed it up as a surprise. That night Ken had a dream. Betty

Lou was terrified. They had gone to bed at twelve and about four she woke up, hearing Ken muttering under his breath. He was twisting and turning in the bed furiously, and she jumped out just in time to see him roll right where she had been lying. When she called to him, he started yelling. And when she tried to shake him, he tried to hit her and then strangle her. When she started screaming, he woke up and let go of her. The pain was so great she had to help him back into bed. Then she got him one of the pills. He took another one when he got up in the morning, and then went back to sleep.

That afternoon he got up and went downtown. When he came back at suppertime, he was drunk. She helped him into bed. He took another pill. She stayed up and tried to read. Then about twelve she went to bed. She tried to be quiet, but just when she pulled the covers up, trying not to disturb him:

"Betty Lou?"

"Yes?"

"I . . . I guess I had no business getting married . . . not . . ."

"Ken! Don't say that—please."

They were quiet.

"Does . . ." she paused, "does drinking help much?"

He didn't answer for a while, then:

"A little."

He didn't dream that night. He stayed home all next day, not because he was afraid to go out, but just to help Betty Lou unpack some of the things her mother had sent over.

That night he had a dream. This time Betty Lou was more prepared for it. She started shaking him violently. He woke up, sweating. She got him a pill.

That afternoon he went out. It was dark when he came home. She had to help him into bed. He didn't dream that night.

The people of Milton soon knew that Ken Reed was drinking. Mr. Mawson, the druggist, told Mr. Webster who told Mrs. Gardner who met Mrs. Sumerset and Mrs. Emerson coming out of the candy store. As the three of them walked home together, they talked about it.

Mrs. Sumerset said that she was just telling Mrs. Emerson that she had heard that Ken Reed had started drinking.

Mrs. Carlson said that yes, she too had heard the same thing and wasn't it a shame, he used to be such a nice boy. And after all he'd been through, too.

George Graham, the captain of the bowling team, was telling one of the men on the team about it when Paul came by. They stopped when he came within hearing distance, but he knew what they were talking about and he passed by with only a "Hi, boys."

Paul told Alice about it that night at dinner.

"You know, they say that Ken's been drinking."

"I know."

They were silent, then:

"Why, Paul? Is that what he learned? Is that what the Army did to him—turned him into a common drunkard?"

"I can't understand it, Alice; it's not right."

They ate the rest of their dinner in silence.

Ken didn't dream for the next five nights. Betty Lou said that maybe he wasn't going to dream at all any more. Ken said he hoped she was right. While they were talking about it, Betty Lou asked, did he have dreams when he first came home? Ken said yes, but lately they were getting much worse. He used to take a pill when he'd wake up, and most of the pain would go away, but two days before the wedding it was so bad he had to take two pills and even then he had to stay in his room. That's why he didn't go to bed the night before they were married— he was afraid he'd have a dream.

That night it came back. It was worse than it had ever been. She had to shake him for five minutes before he woke up. And then she had to hold the glass while he drank the water to swallow the pills.

He went out before lunch while Betty Lou was out shopping. He didn't come home for dinner. He didn't come home at all that night. The next morning Betty Lou went out to look for him. She met a man who had seen him in a bar. The man went back with her. They found him sitting at a table in the back. He looked up and saw Betty Lou as she walked in. He poured another drink from the bottle which was sitting on the table. Betty Lou went over and sat down next to him.

"Ken," she said softly. "Come home with me."

He didn't answer. He didn't look at her. He drank his drink and poured another.

"Please, Ken."

He didn't answer.

She got up and went to his chair. Putting her hands under his arms, she tried to lift him. He yelled and swung around and hit her. She fell to the floor. When he saw her lying there, he gave a little cry and tried to get up to help her. He staggered and fell back into his chair. The man helped her get him home and into bed. He took three pills.

By afternoon everyone in Milton had heard about it. Mrs. Emerson heard it from the milkman and told Mrs. Carlson over the phone who told Mr. Mawson, the druggist, who told Mr. Webster who met Mrs. Gardner and Mrs. Sumerset on the street.

Mrs. Gardner thought that it was just terrible, just terrible. Mr. Webster just couldn't understand it, a fine boy like that, with such a nice wife, going to drink for no reason at all.

Mrs. Sumerset was about to say that she had heard that he was beating her, at least there were screams coming from the apartment, but just then Betty Lou passed by on her way to see Paul.

Mr. Webster stopped her and said that he had (ah) heard that (ah) Ken's (ah) Ken's drinking and that if there was anything he could do she should let him know.

Mrs. Gardner thought that it was just terrible, just terrible.

Mrs. Sumerset said that she was a poor dear and she didn't see how she stood it this long and she wouldn't blame her a bit if she left him and for that matter, she hoped she did.

Betty Lou turned to walk away. She was crying. She turned back and told them to go to hell.

The three of them stood there looking at each other.

Well!

In a Dry Country

DAVID LYLE

BECAUSE my father pushed his chair comfortably back from
the table, stretching—a good meal, Mother—and patting his
stomach, and because then I knew what would come, I rose
from the table and tried to walk casually toward the door; but
his words stopped me before I could turn the latch.

"Like to give me a hand in the garden today, son?" I knew
without testing, though I had never tested, that there was no
question to be asked or answered concerning my desire or lack
of it. The Law.

"Sure. I'll be around back in a minute."

I pushed out the side door and went down the steps, catching
as I departed the spectacle of my father rising to rummage in
the closet for his work gloves and hat, and knowing that my
mother would come finally to his aid—you helpless males!—
brushing him aside. The Law.

The front lawn was a momentary paradise. I dawdled across
it examining the texture of its greenness, crunching an occasional snail underfoot. In contrast to the yard, the burnt
countryside shimmered off into an infinite brown of baked
earth and parched grass. The morning sun had already produced slate-gray lakes at the base of the hills, making the brown
mounds into islands. Vague memories arose in my mind of an
eastern verdure—elm trees and maples—but I had already
grown used to the fertile wastes of unwatered California, and
the memory was no more than a contrast. Life and death. Green
and brown. Water only was needed for the birth; and our yard
was only one among many browns that my father hoped to
bring to life.

A rattling water tank mounted on a wagon and drawn by
two ponderous draft horses rounded the corner, pausing by

each tree to pass a gush of water into the little basins carved in the earth at the foot of the eucalyptus saplings that lined the road. Benjy rushed yapping into the road, scampering at the heels of the horses. The horses blinked calmly, stopping by a sapling at the corner of our yard. Sam climbed slowly down from the wagon box, directed a hose at the basin and released the valve. Earth drank the water eagerly, but finally the basin filled.

"Morning, Sam," I said. I wanted to be on good terms. I would have liked to ride about town with him, mounted on the wagon box.

"Morning, boy. How's your father?"

"Well," I said. Sam mumbled something and moved on, clucking at the horses. I watched the white scum swirling on the brown water. Gradually the water sank into the earth, leaving the foam clinging to the muddy basin. The trees were Father's idea—to make the town a shady place like other, older California towns. Father was a member of the town planning commission.

Behind me I heard the squeak of the toolshed door. Father was going to work. He would hoe and chop all day—growing damp and irritable in the sun—raking and scuffing the flower beds into a state of prim formality—snipping unwary grasses that had strayed upon the walks and stepping stones. To this precise universe of his it was my duty to contribute—neat garden's a thing to be proud of, son, speaks well of a man.

I walked around the house and entered the back yard through the high, wire-mesh gate. The entire garden was fenced to keep out the numerous rabbits and other vermin that infested that part of the country. Father was working near the edge of the cactus bed. As I came up he handed me a pair of clippers and directed me to begin snipping the devil grass from the rocks that bounded the bed.

Falling to my knees, I began. The tenacious shoots clung firmly to the rocks, and each piece had to be picked loose after it was clipped.

On the other side of the bed, Father snipped patiently along until, by a large rock, I saw him draw his hand back suddenly, knocking his elbow painfuly. He stood up quickly and jumped

[207]

back from the bed, not holding his elbow though it must have hurt. Then he ran toward the shed.

"What's the matter?" I called.

He returned with a hoe and a forked knife on a long stick that was used for uprooting dandelions. He looked carefully into the cactus bed, then turned to me.

"Do you know how to kill a snake, son?"

"Sure," I said. "Just like anything else, all you got to do is hit it hard enough." I could see he paid no attention to my answer, staring in among the cactus plants.

"There are dangerous snakes in this part of the country, son. It's time you learned how to deal with them." He seemed to be talking to himself. "At least you should learn how to kill them if you're going on any more scout hikes with the rest of the boys." He was still peering into the bed. "Come here!" he beckoned.

Beside him, I followed his pointing arm into the maze of prickly plants. In at the base of a cactus with huge platter-like leaves lay a brilliant blue snake.

"Do you know what it is?" he asked.

I told him it was called a blue racer, harmless.

"Yes, watch now." He stepped into the bed gingerly, avoiding the cactus.

"You don't have to show me," I said. "He's harmless. He won't hurt anyone. I can kill a snake."

He paid no attention, intent on the form of his quarry. The snake was a beautiful thing, slim, long and the color of a summer sky.

"Aw, don't," I said.

Father turned, signing me to be quiet, and brushed against the sharp prong of a century plant, the needle stabbing into the flesh of his calf so that he recoiled spring-like, afraid of a nothing behind him. The snake started rapidly, easily, swimming across the soft sand until father turning again thrust him into the earth with the hoe, writhing and twisting, the blue mixed now with red, father stabbing down again and again now at the pinioned snake—cutting him with the forked knife—breaking the supple form in a dozen places until the movement was stopped, all but a feeble twitching of the nervous system.

My father turned, his face white and nervous. "There, you see how easy it was? Now you'll know. Throw him out, will you? Throw him over the fence."

"Let's let Benjy take him," I said, not wanting to touch the bloodied form, now inert, lying with sand mixed dirtily into the clotting blood.

"The dog will only leave him around to smell. Throw him out."

"Aw, he'll be okay there. He won't smell." I didn't think of using a stick to lift him.

"Will you get rid of him? Now?"

I hesitated, looking about.

"What's the matter, are you afraid?" The color had returned to his face. "I killed him! What's there to be afraid of? I killed him! Pick it up! No son of mine . . ."

I grasped it with two fingers, holding it away from me, and threw it over the fence.

When we went to the house for lunch, he said, "There'll be no cowards in this family, do you hear? No cowards." In the house he spoke to my mother as we sat down to dinner. "Our son's a coward. He was afraid to pick up a snake I killed."

I did not look up to my mother for the comfort I knew was there. Anger grew in my throat until I knew I would cry and I left the room without eating.

That night, as always, we knelt in the living room to pray before my father's God, the God I remembered from earliest time as a child in Ohio, the strong God to whom my father spoke as though there were no hope for us anywhere.

". . . Who alone watches over us here below, Who alone moves us, directs and commands us through His Will . . . help us now to be strong to overcome the evils set in our path in this new land, and by Thy Will make these evils unavailing against us . . . and to my son, through Thy Divine Grace, give strength against the evil within him, for today he has shown himself to be weak and heedless against the sign of Thy Will . . . slothful, afraid . . ."

Kneeling, my father's words were blotted out by tears of anger rising in me. Against what God? What God? What evil in a living thing?

There were some acres of brown grassland across the road from us my father wanted for an orange grove. "A little irrigation," he said, "and we'll have the biggest, greenest groves in the county." He had contracted to buy them from the local real-estate agent, and one Saturday afternoon my mother and I walked out with him to see the piece.

We walked back and forth across the land, while my father explained just where he would place the grading sheds, the loading platforms, and machinery sheds, how build the roads for greatest efficiency at picking time, how hire his workers to cost him least. He talked and gesticulated, pointing here and there, while my mother and I walked quietly beside. Benjy snuffed at our heels or romped off on the trail of an occasional rabbit.

At a far corner of the piece, near the highway south to San Diego, there was the ruin of an old adobe house abandoned by some pioneer—Indian, Mexican, forty-niner—years before. The roof lay tumbled in and the walls were fast disintegrating under the force of the yearly rains. The reddish earth from the crumbling hut made a sort of mound that rose above the steady level of the grass. This, being near the highway, was where father planned to locate his buildings.

As we approached the spot, Benjy ran ahead and paused yapping at the base of one of the walls. Among the fallen rubble, he appeared to be barking at a gopher hole hidden back under the shade of the wall. We watched him dart forward and back excitedly.

"Gophers are an awful nuisance," suggested my father. "Let's see if we can get him."

Benjy darted back and forth now, first to us and then back again to the shade of the wall. I ran ahead with him but stopped ten feet from the wall when, above the swishing of my feet in the grass, I heard the dry buzzing of a rattler. Standing still, I could see the form of a huge diamondback coiled in the shade.

He looked fully five feet long. Benjy jumped back and forth before him, while the snake lay motionless except for the rapid buzzing of his tail, the ugly head poised a few inches above the thick coil.

Then he struck, throwing his body outward with amazing speed toward the yapping dog. Benjy leaped back and the head landed impotently in the dust. I heard the rush of my father's feet in the grass behind me.

There was a tug at my sleeve from behind. "Keep back, keep back," he said. "Let Benjy get him." His hand shook.

The snake coiled again and struck, missing. I picked up a long board that lay fallen from the roof in the grass beside me —watched for the snake to strike again.

The coil shot forward, the head falling short of its mark into the dust while I, as it fell, raised the board above my head, and running forward, brought it down hard against the outstretched form of the snake, close to the head, crushing its thick body with the sound of a melon breaking on cement, pinning its neck and the tail lashing up across the board from behind, slapping my legs as I stepped forward on the board— one foot always on the board—to grind the ugly head into the ground with my heel, grinding down and down until I was sure the head was almost worn away and the tail had stopped its futile lashing. I bent and cut the rattle from the tail. There were ten rattles.

"Look," I held it up to my father, "a big one." My throat was dry and I almost choked in saying it. Now, afterward, my knees were weak and I felt I could not stand.

"That was brave," my mother said. I could not answer. Then I thought that I was brave. Later I knew that what I did was only necessary.

Walking home, we were silent.

"Were you afraid?" I asked my father, after a little time.

"God gave you strength," he answered.

"Here, look." I offered him the rattle.

"No, no." He turned away.

"But . . ." I started, and my mother's face said—be quiet.

Watching his face, I could see fear in it. At that moment, I thought it was for me and I felt proud, walking home beside him with the rattle in my hand. I have done a brave thing and my father was afraid for me, I said to myself.

But later, later I knew. Later I knew where lay his anger and where his fear. I saw his life and I saw his love, in the midst of a parched dry country. Duty only was from within, all else was imposed. When I came to know this, his God had no more hold upon me. Then I could laugh, then I was free.

A Matter of Vanity

FAYE RITER

HANDS in pockets, shoulders huddled as though their cramped position added to the warmth of his coat sweater, Irwin moved restlessly about the tiny periodical shop that formed a bright yellow rectangle in an otherwise dark and gloomy stone building. Although his place of business was only so wide as a extra-sized door, the sign above it read: "Every Magazine You Want and Some You Don't." It was his particular pride that he could supply magazines one ordinarily found only in a city, and he enjoyed seeing the plain pleasure sweeping the faces of out-of-towners when they caught sight of their favorites in his stock.

He went to stand in the doorway, staring moodily in the direction of Peach Hill, even though there was nothing to see but foggy lights. In the air blew lightly the bitter odor of coal smoke and mist.

"Blast this weather," he spoke aloud.

It was a late spring, and eccentric as an old maid. But after people matured they never thought the seasons were the same as remembered from childhood. Nowadays the weather always seemed freakish. He shivered in the dampness, wishing without expectation for summer days, when rain clouds were freshly swept from the sky, when the wet earth steamed under the hot sun of late morning, and the good cloying heat brought a fine sweat to the skin. Yet there was still the temperamental spring to live through before summer could come. But it would be something just to have rhododendron spread its blossoms over the mountains again, the town lose its windy, cold look, and the sun settle down on the roofs like a fat, friendly pigeon to give the bleak lines a little grace.

When the gloom of the year finally faded, and the tourists with their plump pockets arrived, he would be sure summer had arrived. The town was on the national highway that rose and wound through the highest of the wooded mountains and the national park. Nearly every summer he made one Sunday trip up there himself just to take a look and then to watch tolerantly while people fed the big black bears that the highway signs warned them not to feed. But this year, if summer ever did arrive, he would not take the time to make the trip; there seemed to be no sense to such things any more. He had seen the view a hundred times and was past caring whether a loping black bear might frighten a momentarily-bold tourist into his car and then lick at the windows, wanting more of the peanuts or cookies, or whatever the food might be.

Perhaps this winter was drawn-out and the future inert and dull because he had begun all at once to feel the weight of his years and the heavy, indigestible burden they left within him. It was a shock to reach that point. Nowadays he was even surprised when he looked into a mirror, for the reflection was not at all what he expected to appear.

Once in a long time he would come to a deliberate halt before the swinging-in-a-frame dressmaking glass his wife had in her sewing room and stare unbelievingly at what he saw—the tall, spare figure with shoulders that were rounded and stooping, the bony face with its loosening skin, high forehead, balding brow. Even his teeth were yellowed and worn. "A man's nearer a dog than he thinks," he might murmur, and then, still gazing distastefully at the mirrored man with little of the consolation the words implied, "At least my hair hasn't turned yet."

He understood exactly what Uncle Billy Wade meant when he used to say in his high, anxious voice, "Funny thing—I'm

ninety-four years old—but I don't feel it. I just don't *feel*
it."

Uneasily he moved about the cubbyhole again, returning to
teeter on the doorsill and look up and down the nearly deserted street. Blanche did not like his opening for business at
night, but it gave him something to do. "Hell, I got a living to
make," he would object loudly.

Now a couple moved briskly in his direction; they must be
northerners, judging by their lively pace. He stepped back,
and they hesitated before the outdoor display on the magazine
racks.

"Look," the woman spoke, "I haven't seen a copy of it for
months."

Irwin stepped to the front again. "Raw evening."

"Oh, after Florida this feels good," the woman chided, join-
ing him in the shop and beginning to survey the rows of
magazines.

"Late spring, though," Irwin insisted. "Fruit'll all be late."

The man, reaching for his wallet, nodded. "We saw that the
peach orchards are just beginning to blossom. They must be
quite a sight later on."

Irwin bobbed his head in agreement. "Where you folks
from?"

"Well—nowhere exactly," the man answered regretfully.
"The Middle West is as good as any other answer."

Irwin hesitated before punching the cash register, trying to
think of means to prolong the contact.

"There's something I'd like to ask you," the woman spoke
slowly, as though not sure he was the proper person to consult.
"Do you know where Charles Farragher's home is?"

"I sure do," Irwin told her. "It's on Beech Street—first one
on the other side of High." He motioned toward the center of
town. "That's our main business street—High. And about three
blocks west—four-nineteen."

"Did you hear that?" the woman asked needlessly of her husband in her excitement.

"I went to school with Charlie," Irwin continued quickly,
watching for her expression of surprise. It appeared, but it was

tempered by a measured wariness. "Have you read his books?" he asked then.

"Most of them."

"You read *The Lost Is Never Found?*"

"Yes," she nodded.

"Well, I'm in that one."

"You are?" she asked a little breathlessly.

"Do you remember near the beginning where he talks about some of the boys he spent his time with?"

"Only vaguely," the woman frowned.

"Well, he calls us right out there. My name comes first on page forty-two. Irwin Spencer."

"Well, I'll be doggoned!" the man exclaimed in his hearty tone.

"I knew Charlie all my life," Irwin went on eagerly. "I grew up with him, and we went all through school together. Only difference—I went to work after high school and his dad helped send him to college. Of course there isn't much about me, but then he put a lot of town people in his books. Most of them was mad as hornets."

"I don't suppose they're angry any more—since he became famous," the woman suggested.

"Well, no. They got over it," Irwin agreed solemnly, "but at first—" He shook his head.

"Probably they appreciate him—now that he's dead," the woman persisted.

Irwin looked at the worn, unpainted floor a moment. "Charlie was a wonderful fellow; those people in New York said he was a genius," he reflected. "Most of us here didn't know how smart he was—we used to poke fun at him for some things—but some didn't know it at all. They treated him pretty hard after that first book—they liked to run him right out of town. But now they're making it up to him. A committee's planning some sort of memorial for him here in his home town."

"That's pretty representative of humankind, isn't it?" the man commented, relighting his pipe.

They were all silent a moment.

"Thank you, Mr. Spencer," the woman spoke. "It was nice to talk with you. I'll have to reread that book now."

"I'm always glad to tell folks about Charlie," Irwin assured them. "It's the least I can do. You folks better take time in the morning and go over there. Some kinfolk lives in the house; they'll be right glad to show you around. Four-nineteen West Beech Street."

He watched them as they went up the slope toward High Street. He watched until they were mere inhuman blurs beneath the street lights, and the warmth that had burned within him faded like a forgotten fire.

"I should of written it down for them," he scolded himself suddenly. He could have jotted it on the cover of one of the magazines they bought as well as not. Irwin Spencer, page forty-two. *The Lost Is Never Found.*

He began to pace in the narrow shop. Four strides this way. Four strides back. Four the other way again.

They were friendly people, but they would forget. People were careless about names. Next day the woman might say to her husband, "What was that man's name? I've forgotten it already." And they would start guessing. "Hensley? No, that's not right. . . . Swenson, wasn't it? . . . That doesn't sound like it, either." They would even forget the name of the particular book after a while, and it wasn't likely the woman would go back to the row of books in the public library and hunt through them all until she found the right title, the right page, and the name of Irwin Spencer.

Maybe he was a fool for caring. But he did care. He wanted people to remember that he was in one of Charlie Farragher's books. He might not be remembered for another thing, but people seemed to think there was a good chance Charlie's books would stay on the library shelves for a long time to come, and there his own name would be buried.

He stopped his pacing and stared at the gaudily-glazed magazine covers with unwarned nausea. Why did he care whether or not people knew the name of Irwin Spencer was on page forty-two?

As if in answer, a cold revelation swept like a tempestuous

winter wind over him, tearing away his strength with one triumphant wrench. It was like hearing that he nourished fast-sprouting seeds of death within some organ of his body or that God Himself had just announced an end to all things.

Horror at his own insignificance hung like a shroud over his rounded shoulders. Holding out his hands, he stared at them to see if he existed even physically.

"I'm nothing," he told himself in a dry, wondering tone. "I'm just nothing at all. One creature among a billion others." And page forty-two of *The Lost Is Never Found* would not help him a bit; it was totally worthless.

All this he had been seeing indirectly in the mirror, as if his reflection bore a reflection of its own, and in the fragile echo of Uncle Billy Wade's anxious voice. ". . . ninety-four years old—but I don't feel it. I just don't *feel* it." This pure insignificance was plain on the long, dispirited face he found in the mirror, on the hunched shoulders and in the fading, emotionless eyes. He had come this far, and if he could look back he would not see one track, not even half a footprint. There was nothing there at all. He looked quickly at the floor of his shop as if expecting to find at least the imprint of his rubber heels. But nothing showed. Only a general muddiness of invisible prints on a worn, dirty floor, the prints of people coming, hesitating, and departing.

He stepped to the end of the shop and sat down upon the straight chair, feeling light-headed. A man should never have to know this—the knowledge ought to be kept up there in Heaven. Any poor joker in the world ought to be able to live through his years thinking he was of at least a little importance.

"My God," he said softly, "I never thought to feel like this."

What should he do? How could he tell anyone of it and lighten his own burden by telling? If he set out to explain to Blanche, she would like as not look at him closely and demand, "Irwin Spencer, have you been drinking?"

Maybe he could speak to the minister; he ought to know what to do with such unholy knowledge as this. But he had not spoken more than twenty words alone with Reverend Prescott. When he and Blanche went to church they shook hands with him after the service, and once in a while at Brotherhood meeting, the minister might talk to him a moment about the basketball team the boys' club had, or how the young people were going to put on a play. How could you tell someone that distant from you what had just transpired here in an absent, unclocked moment?

His thought went furtively to the secondhand revolver stowed away in a secret place in the shop some months ago after there had been a series of evening robberies in local business houses. At this moment he was ready to get it out, thrust it into his belt and walk in the darkness up on Peach Hill, overlooking the town, and turn the cold weapon on himself. How could he dawdle along day after day with this terrible revelation swelling in his brain, spreading cankerously throughout, driving him to buy stores of cheap whisky blends until he had to have first a pint, then almost a quart a day to forget it, or forcing him into some dream world like Ollie Gross, who walked about town with a wild look in his eyes as though the stroke of doom was about to sound off?

"Curse—," he spoke vehemently, but did not know what to curse. "Curse *something*," he went on. He could hardly curse Heaven even if he wanted to; that was blasphemous.

"I wonder if I'd have the nerve to do it." He listened as if the echo of his words in the air might bear an answer. "More than likely I'm a coward to boot, when it comes right down to it."

What would it matter to Blanche, after she got over the first hard shock of it? She had the house and insurance, and took a couple of roomers; there was money in the bank, and her dressmaking gave her a little income. Women were nearly all widows sooner or later, anyhow.

Lost in the boundlessness of self-pity and apprehension, he sat on. The street was still fairly deserted; now and then an automobile rolled smoothly by, leaving an echo that died reluctantly. But he was thankful for the solitude; anyone coming in might see upon his face something he wanted to keep secret.

Then came the hollow sound of footsteps along the side-street on which his periodical shop faced. It was a man approaching, treading deliberately, without haste, someone as middle-aged as himself, with a stolid, settled mind, not easily moved, not easily ruffled, a little skeptical, but still, trusting. Hoping the footsteps would continue past his door, Irwin did not look up.

But they halted. Not only that, but there was the sound of a solid body being heaved up on the doorsill.

"Irwin?" a voice posed.

He looked up and then arose so that he might avert his gaze. "How you doing, Dan?" he mumbled.

"Good enough," the bulky man answered cheerfully. "What you doing back there—knittin', or reading some of those romance magazines?" He put a weighty accent on the first syllable of romance.

"Oh—just cogitating," Irwin said quickly. But Dan had noticed nothing, and was not even looking at him.

"Say, Irwin, you got any copies of the *Black Mountain Clarion?*"

"Look down there on your left," Irwin directed. "If I got any left that's where they'll be."

The visitor found the paper, and wetting his thumb, began to look through the sheets. "Violet and her brother's wife was over there for some lodge auxiliary doings, and they got in on the opening of the new hotel," he explained as he hunted. "There was some photographers taking pictures, and they got in on that, too."

He found what he was hunting—"Here they are"—and spread the paper out so that Irwin could see the page. "Well, there they are. But don't that beat all! They don't even name them."

Irwin drew closer. There was a picture of the stone and timber hotel with a smudged view of the valley spreading out below and the next ridge, another of the dining room, and one of the lobby, where a group of women at the side looked eagerly into the camera's eye.

"That's Harold's wife right next to Violet in front there," Dan pointed with a forefinger. "Now wouldn't you think they'd

[219]

say who was who?" he went on indignantly. "They could be anybody, for all a person would know."

Irwin studied the picture. "It's a fair likeness," he said. Yet he would hardly have recognized Dan's wife if he had been looking at the paper alone. It didn't look like anyone in particular. It was no more than a rather blurred face and figure close to a lot of other faces and figures just like it. There was no individuality—just a group of women. Anybody's wife, nobody's wife. It didn't matter much. It was only a matter of pride that made Dan exclaim because there were no names.

"Well," he said, stepping back, "it was nice to get in the picture just the same."

Dan folded the paper clumsily. "The women'll feel kind of bad, though, not getting their names in, too. I'll take the other one you have left; Violet wants to send one to her brother out in Nevada."

When Dan stepped out of the shop, Irwin called, "Good night, Dan," and was surprised at the routine cheerfulness that had returned to his voice. Maybe it was being alone that put a person down in the dumps.

Standing on the doorsill, he watched Dan move on up toward High Street. It wasn't that, though; he knew it wasn't. It was the picture that had brought him back, that had accidentally pointed out what he could not see before.

"You crazy fool," he reprimanded himself, "blind as a bat."

He was not the only insignificant person in the world; everybody was in the same boat, the same boat exactly, and he had been too short-sighted for a while to see it. "Every goldarn one of us," he spoke aloud.

Dan, there—walking in the shadows beyond the street light. The out-of-towners when they became blurs as they approached High Street. The bunch of women looking into that camera that really just wanted a picture of the new hotel lobby, with the women thrown in for added interest, those unidentified women all dolled up with talcum and lip rouge and their best hats and Sunday dresses. Even Charlie Farragher, because he was dead, and what significance in the world did you have if you were dead? At least he himself had old Charlie beat there; he was still alive.

It was a matter of vanity, the kind of vanity Reverend Prescott talked about once in a while at Sunday service. How was it he put it? "Thy name is vanity"—or something like that. Human beings wanted to be more than they were; they longed to be immortal, even, to have their names remembered and their faces and deeds recalled with praise. It was why they were so eager to bear sons and name them after themselves. That was what made sons more valuable on the market than daughters, even though daughters did more for the parents.

But it took more than a child to make a man be remembered; at least he hoped it did, being without a son himself or even a daughter. "Well, I guess God meant it to be that way," Blanche had said once, as if to offer comfort for them both, after a whole string of years slid away and they were still childless.

The relief and exuberance settled back then, like dust on a summer street after an automobile has passed. It wasn't anything to crow about, the insignificance of all men or any man; it was sobering, but it did make him feel better to know he was not alone. Now it was up to a fellow to forget it, or at least keep it in the back of his mind where it belonged except when it ballooned and sailed out in plain sight at times when he was duty-bound to attend a funeral or some other kind of memorial service. Otherwise, he should work at keeping up his spirits and other people's spirits as well.

Some people prayed for that purpose, and some sang or whistled or just hummed. It could be that Charlie Farragher kept his up by writing books. He himself was not the praying kind, and Blanche had more than once told him he couldn't carry a nursery rhyme tune, even.

He began to sing, though, a little mournfully, there in the quiet shop.

> If I had a cow-w-w that'd give such milk,
> I'd dress her in-n-n the fin—est silk,
> And feed her of-f-f the choicest hay—.

But abruptly he was silent again. Tonight he was going to close up shop early. And he wouldn't gather up the money in the cash register, either, but just leave it there, and if a thief wanted to break in and get it, he was welcome to it. This night he was going out and have himself a time, Blanche or no Blanche. A man had to blow off steam regularly, and once in a while there came a time when he had to blow it off at an unplanned hour.

"I'll really load up," he said. "I'll load up good."

Turning off the overhead light, he stumbled to the entrance and stepped into the street. The old stone building was gloomier than ever now with its single eye closed. With long practice he found the lock and turned the key, shaking the knob out of habit to make sure the lock had sprung.

Then, thrusting his hands into his pockets and huddling his shoulders, he walked away into the chill wet night with long strides, as if he were still young and eager and thirsty, and headed in the direction of the Mountain Girl Bar.

Black Bile

H. D. ROSSITER

PERHAPS if my own life had been different I could have helped him, perhaps if there had been enough time or enough love. Some say there are other solutions, and at times I believed them. But there is no other way, I know that now. Science, white priests, alchemists, shamans—apostates. Yahweh has truly forsaken thee. Come, Hosea, Isaiah, Jeremiah and Ezekiel. But they are not here, there is no one. I was weak and could do nothing.

. . . cut it out! Take a scalpel and cut it out. We have found it, we have found the source of trouble. All is well. An incision, a twist of the knife, a few sutures. The gods must obey, man's flesh must obey, man's mind must obey. These are no litanies, these are incantations . . .

Sitting by my desk that first day, a pale timid boy, a Pole. I am tired. So many of them, so very many. And then the forms, two green cards and a white card; a new advisee, two green cards and a white one. But his eyes attract me. They look at me but do not see me, they are like black glass or dark mirrors which have stopped reflecting, a glassy-topped well which light did not penetrate, without bottom, so that only shades and columns of darkness appeared.

I smile and ask him his name and tell him to fill out the cards. I read them and ask him questions, and all the time I look at him, but never succeed in seeing, in penetrating. To see nothing could mean there was nothing there. For depth and shallowness are much the same. Shallowness, too, has a thin look, a simplicity that is real, an overt emptiness which seems like disguise. But it is not disguise, it is real, and all your trouble is for nothing, for dust.

I kept a list once—students, hundreds of them, from the beginning. But I stopped a long time ago. They were all the same, so I stopped keeping lists. There were so many of them. But I never stopped looking.

. . . a scalpel, a twist of the knife, a few sutures . . .

I do not see him often, but from Newhardt I learn many things. Newhardt is an advisee like Fantl, but very different. Fantl, he tells me, came here when he was twelve, with his brother. His family was sent to Auschwitz.

I see him before a map. My mother died here. See—between Rybnik and Kraków, just south of Sosnowiec. My father and two brothers. We are lucky this map has a large scale. It is a small place and not on many maps. Only the big places get on maps. Many people don't believe me so I keep it to myself. And I think to myself, what is there to say after all. When one says it often enough it becomes true. And when someone asks me about it, I shake my head and say there is nothing to talk about, and there *is* nothing to talk about after all.

. . . cut it out! A small place that isn't found on many maps.

Forget it. A slight twist and what is there left. Nothing. Forget about it. New things every day. Incant and rest easy and forget . . .

But I could not forget him. Newhardt tells me more. A refugee home. The prayers, the eternal prayers, Fantl stands there and says the words and looks around him, and no one looks back. They see him looking at heaven. Fantl looks at the tin ceiling, and prays to a tin patterned God, and can hear the hollow echo falling very faintly, metallically, in his ear.

There is more to the story and I learn it bit by bit. He leaves the home with his brother. They go to college and live in a rooming house, but they still eat at the refugee home. The refugee people take care of them, but there is not much. His clothes are neat, tight, and threadbare. There is not much.

I notice his clothes again when he sees me about his work. He wants to change, he wants now to study literature, not philosophy. I ask him why, what does he have in mind, what does he have in mind.

Fairy tales! That is what he has in mind. He wants to write fairy tales. Can one believe it? I look at him but he does not smile. What kind of fairy tales? Fairy tales with political implications! This is too much and I want to laugh. What is he getting at? What is he thinking?

Fairy tales, children's stories, myths, and they live happily ever after. Meanings, meanings. Allegory? No, children's stories about animals—for the state, and for truth. He looks down and smoothes the sleeves of his jacket. And that is all.

I invite him home and he answers my questions and looks out the window. Pat does everything she can but it is awkward. I get angry as at a clod of metal. What can one say to him? Shall we all look out the window? Shall we all weep crocodile tears? There is pleasure in beer, and heat in a fireplace, and warmth in offered friendship. But fireplace fire dies without attendance, and when all is dead ashes one can wonder certainly whether there has been a fire at all. Perhaps there have been ashes from the beginning of time. Certainly one can wonder. The question is open, the possibility is there. There is no blame surely.

[224]

But I am not angry. I am sorry really. I ask the Dean about a scholarship. There are less worthy, less needy people, getting them. His dark timid face troubles me, his clothes trouble me, his eyes which do not see and which I cannot see, those too trouble me.

. . . cut them out! Cutting is science and science is life and life is not life any more. Life is dead ashes. Remove the ashes, the dust is gone and all is clean again, and empty . . .

"Oh no! I can get along. Oh no! I can get along. I have enough. Unnecessary, unnecessary." There is no helping him, there is no helping a person who doesn't want to be helped. And the balm I receive is thin, a veil of righteousness which cannot withstand the look from his dark eyes. "What do you offer?" they seem to say to me. And I answer angrily without speaking. "This *is* what I have to offer, what is in my power." But the words are no use. His look pains me, and righteousness cannot defend itself. But who will cast the first stone?

I go to a lecture—politics, one of their endless talks. The easy phrases slip gently soothingly from the loose lips of the lecturer. "The rights of men," "inalienable rights," "natural rights," "Godgiven rights," "rights." No one talks of responsibilities— ah that is more difficult. Better not to talk about them.

He sits with Newhardt in front of me to the side. He sits leaning forward, his elbows on his knees, his head resting on his hands, engrossed. I suddenly become jealous of him. I see him as a problem, my problem, slipping uncontrollably from my hands. A dark-eyed entity impinging unasked on my life, a con-tradictory corrolary casting doubt on an entire cosmology. Who, I feel, has a better right than I?

I go often now to lectures because he is there, because my problem is there. I talk to him. I greet him in the hall. "Look," I almost say, "here is your salvation. Allow me. No one but me has anything to offer." And like Krishna I threaten, cajole: "Fix thy heart on Me, thou shalt, by My grace, overcome all obstacles, but if, through egotism thou wilt not hear Me, thou shalt perish." But he does not look at me nor, I see, does he care.

. . . Oh, cut it out! There is no problem—the manufactured

dilemma of a sick mind building an insubstantial cloud from air. All we have to do is cut it out, and nothing will remain.

At the end of the summer, on my desk a note lies. In official phrases on mimeographed paper, Fantl has left the university.

I do not see him any more but the problem exists still. It walks the streets and disquiets the thoughts. A rift, a weakness arising painfully like an ever-remembered failure, vitiating to righteousness, to poise, vitiating to life.

There is still Newhardt who meets Fantl now and then, and together we talk of him. Fantl is strange, Fantl is dark, Fantl is ungrateful, unknowable—that is not what we say, but what we mean. And the answer comes disturbingly back, breaking our train of thought. "It is you who are strange and dark. You are unknowable, you who are strange and dark."

Fantl lives by odd jobs and Newhardt tells me about them. He mops floors at night with old women, standing in soapy water, mop in hand, on white marble floors. He works in a toy factory painting wide innocent black eyes in neat depressions in plastic dolls, or fitting arms and legs that squeak to a body which gives senseless gaseous maternal calls when pressed.

And then for a few weeks he feeds the animals of a bankrupt circus in a Brooklyn warehouse. And I get angry because I feel he must be angry somehow. He drives himself down to spite, to sublimate any remnant of respect. What right has he to do this to himself, to me, to everyone? But no, this is really outside of me, external to me, unimportant.

Newhardt visits him in curiosity and tells me about it. There are jackals to be fed and Fantl stands before a trough of meat which he cuts up. The jackals' yells pierce the air, and Fantl invitingly yells back, soothing them with promises of food.

I dream about him. He stands at a trough and I call to him. He turns and smiles and holds up a jagged pound of flesh, and down from his hand red blood drips on a sawdust floor.

But dreaming is foolish and there is nothing more to dream about. There is the psychiatrist; and good and evil frightened take to their heels, and all is clean and shining and sterile like the inside of a boiled test tube, an air-conditioned laboratory, or the detergent atmosphere of an operating room. There is no dirt, no seed, no germ, only clean stainless steel.

Fantl meets a psychiatrist, a neat bespeckled man who finds him interesting. They talk on benches, on couches of patent leather design, of soothing patented angles. The psychiatrist allows him to talk, encourages his tongue, unties his thoughts. "Come, reveal yourself to me and all is well." The king in the machine of the mind. Where is the interference, where is the static, where shall we oil, what obsolete part shall we remove? An interesting object on a couch, a tantalizing enigma.

The neat bespeckled man takes away and does not give. Could I have given, was I capable of giving? Was this faculty dead in me as in everyone else? But nothing is dead in me. Half my faculties wake, the other half sleep. But sleep is not death, slumber is not extinction.

Now Newhardt tells me the end of the story. I think it is both an end and a beginning. Fantl has been taken to a state hospital. His diagnosis is simple—acute melancholia, an excess of black bile. A medieval spleen has been located, spilling poison into his system, troubling the mechanism. It rests in the frontal lobes of the brain and all one has to do is remove it.

Perhaps if my own life had been different I could have helped him, perhaps if there were enough time . . .

Cut it out!